How to Stuff UP CHRISTMAS

Rosie Blake

CORVUS

Published in paperback in Great Britain in 2015 by Corvus,
an imprint of Atlantic Books Ltd.

10 9 8 7 6 5 4 3 2

A CIP catalogue record for this book is available from the British Library.

Paperback ISBN: 9781782398608
E-book ISBN: 9781782398615

Printed in Great Britain.

Corvus
An imprint of Atlantic Books Ltd
Ormond House
26–27 Boswell Street
London
WC1N 3JZ

www.corvus-books.co.uk

Blackpool Council

BUILDING A BETTER COMMUNITY FOR ALL

Please return/renew this item
by the last date shown.
Books may also be renewed by
phone or the Internet.

Tel: 01253 478070
www.blackpool.gov.uk

R
u
(h
w
in
an
on
Sh

Rosie likes baked items, taking long walks by the river and speaking about herself in the third person. Her greatest ambition in life is to become Julia Roberts' best friend.

Also by Rosie Blake

How to Get a (Love) Life

To 'Mama Christmas' aka the legend that is Basia Martin.

You can find lovely Christmas goodies to buy at
www.countrycottagechristmas.co.uk

Chapter 1

'OH, EVE, this is very unbecoming.'

'Don't, Brenda, can't you see it's too soon?'

'You could have stayed in the car, David.'

'I needed to come to ensure you didn't kill her.'

'I'm not going to kill her.'

Sigh. 'I know, it's a turn of phrase.'

'Just look at her.'

'She's fine. She's a grown woman, Brenda.'

'She's not fine.'

'She'll *be* fine.'

'You both know I can hear you? I'm sitting right here.'

'Well, young lady, enough is enough. You need to get up right now.'

'Brenda!'

'Mum, I'm thirty-two years old. You can't tell me to get up.'

'I'm your mother, I can tell you anything, I carried you in my womb for nine months.'

'I didn't have a choice in the matter.'

'Brenda, we should go, let her get on with things.'

'Thanks, Dad.'

'Get on with things! Look at her, she's wearing pyjamas and it's 3 p.m.'

'They're good pyjamas, love.'

'Thanks, Dad.'

'They're excellent pyjamas, I've always loved her in check, but it's 3 p.m.'

'It's 7 a.m. somewhere in the world.'

'David, you are not being helpful.'

'You didn't bring me to be helpful. You brought me because you don't like driving in London in the day.'

'I don't. The roads are a nightmare now, INVADED by cyclists, do they think they own the place?'

'Mum, I'm pretty sure they have as much right to cycle as you have to dri—'

'You cannot have a sensible opinion wearing pyjamas.'

'Fine, I'll get up.'

'Good. Now I brought you bananas. You need fruit, vitamins and – is that an ashtray? Are you smoking?'

'Can I have a banana?'

'No, they're Eve's – she needs her strength.'

'Dad can have one.'

'He has plenty at home. David, you have plenty at home.'

'We're not at home, though, and I need my strength too.'

'Oh for goodness sake! Fine, take one, but woe betide you if you don't eat my dinner.'

'Christ, Brenda, it's a banana not a Michelin-starred meal.'

'Eve – where are you going?'

'I'm going to get dressed.'

'Oh that's good, I am glad. David, isn't that good?'

'It's marvellous. This is an excellent banana.'

'I'll tidy up in here while you change.'

'Don't, Mum, it's a pigsty. I'll do it later.'

'It is rather unpleasant.'

'I'm allowed to live like this, Mum. After what happened. Dad...? Dad?'

'David, stop messing around.'

'Mum, he's not, he's choking on the banana.'

'Typical of him.'

'Come on, Dad...'

'Went... went down the wrong way.'

'David, stop messing about. So, Eve, do you want to talk about what happened?'

'No, Mum, I really don't. I'm going to go and get dressed, though.'

'Don't push it, Brenda – you promised.'

'I'm not pushing anything. He was just such a lovely boy, always wrote a thank-you letter. Always.'

'I wouldn't care if he had written a thousand letters.'

'And he had trustworthy eyes. Pops always said you could tell if a man was honest by looking at his eyes and they were honest.'

'I always thought they were never quite looking in the same direction.'

'Nonsense, David. They were lovely eyes. What did she do, I wonder?'

'It wasn't her.'

'But he wouldn't have dropped her.'

'Mum, I can still hear you.'

'It's rude to eavesdrop.'

'I'm not eavesdropping, Mum, you're talking loudly, in my house.'

'She has a point, Brenda.'

'Well, I'll drop, it but I... Oh, Eve, that really washes you out.'

'Brenda.'

'What? It does. I don't know why she wears all that grey.'

'Because I like grey, Mum.'

3

'It's nice, love.'
'He didn't shag someone else because I wore grey.'
'Shag...'
'Dad? Mum, he's choking again. Mum?'

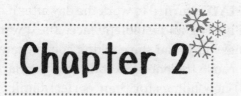

Chapter 2

Daisy's Chocolate Biscuit Cake

110g butter
110g golden syrup
200g dark chocolate

1 packet of digestive
  biscuits
200g white chocolate
1 pack of Maltesers

Method:

- Melt the butter, syrup and dark chocolate in a glass bowl on top of a saucepan of boiling water.
- When the mixture is smooth, take off the heat.
- Break up the digestive biscuits (I put them in a carrier bag and use a rolling pin to bash them with).
- Add the biscuits to the melted chocolate mixture and then put into a baking tray.
- Put in the fridge.
- When set, melt white chocolate in a bowl over saucepan of boiling water.
- Pour a layer of white chocolate over the biscuit layer and then cut Maltesers in half and scatter them over the surface.
- Put back in the fridge to set.
- Serve.

EVE HAD returned to work the day after it had happened with no ring and a blotchy face. She'd wanted to get on with things but found she couldn't concentrate on anything, couldn't rouse the energy to talk to potential buyers about beautiful new homes for their perfect family units. Where normally she'd have been gossiping with them, cooing over their excited 'we need another bedroom, my wife's expecting', now she found their happiness too much to take.

Ed, the pernickety office manager, who spent most days whining that Eve never used hole-punch protector stickers, had skirted round her in those early weeks, warned off by her permanently red-rimmed eyes and Daisy's quiet warnings. Daisy, Eve's best friend, always watchful, brought her lattes and bacon butties, and allowed her to hide at her desk updating the details of new houses and flats while Daisy went out on viewings and talked to people on the phone.

'Hey,' she called, handing Eve a slice of chocolate biscuit cake as she walked past on her return from lunch, leaning over her desk to add, 'Because I know you love it more than is normal.'

'Ooh I do, you're a goddess,' Eve said, biting into it.

Daisy pulled up at her desk and started tapping as Eve made obscene noises finishing up her biscuit cake, crumbs sticking to her chest.

'Oh hmm. You should make thish professionally, it ish soooo good,' Eve said between mouthfuls.

Daisy looked up and smiled, her freckled face creasing. 'I can give you the recipe if you like?'

Eve raised an eyebrow at her. 'Why would I make it when I can wait here for you to bring it to me? Also, I would end up burning it...'

'You can't burn it.'

'Well, melting it.'

'You can't melt it.'

'Well, I would find a way to ruin it somehow,' Eve said, staring wistfully at the empty plate.

'You wouldn't, you just need to follow the instructions, it's easy,' Daisy said, pushing a strand of ginger hair behind her ear.

'I'm nearly done with these particulars. Do you want to... you know... it's time,' Eve whispered, leaning round the desk and indicating the screen with her head.

'Okay, give me five minutes,' Daisy said.

'Yippee!' Eve clapped. 'No work, no work!'

'Ssh...' Daisy giggled as Ed looked up from his workstation, his beady eyes narrowing.

'Yes, Daisy,' Eve called out in a too-loud voice. 'Good idea, we can work on it from my computer.' Giving Daisy a discreet thumbs-up, she waited for her to finish the job she was working on. 'Take your time, woman.'

'I'm nearly done,' Daisy said, the printer churning something out behind her. 'Finished. Okay,' she said, moving her chair round the desk to sit next to Eve.

'How has Ed not worked this out yet?' Eve grinned, tapping on the familiar website. 'You'd think he'd block the website.'

'Not sure, just pretend we are looking over the details of that new house in Islington.'

'Deal... oh...' Eve said, stuffing her hand over her mouth. Daisy rolled her eyes at her, accepting one of the headphones from Eve who took the other one and popped it in her ear.

The screen popped up and the opening credits to *Deal or No Deal* appeared online, their Monday ritual. They both looked at each other gleefully as the camera scanned the studio. Eve checked on Ed who had his back to them, probably Tipp-Exing something. Ed loved to Tipp-Ex stuff.

'Love this show,' Eve breathed.

Daisy nodded in agreement.

Eve enjoyed it because she liked to complain about the contestants and bemoan the fact that some of them talked about their 'strategy'. When they did this it was her moment to squeal, to point at the screen, turn to Daisy and hiss, 'Their strategy is to open fucking boxes,' which always made her feel better. Daisy liked it because she liked Noel Edmonds; his neat, small frame, clipped beard, like a kindly uncle who'd lend you a book on the Battle of Waterloo and take you out for afternoon tea. A woman was in the chair today, showing Noel a photo of her three sons, and he was nodding at one of her holiday anecdotes in that lovely, understanding way of his.

Eve looked over at Daisy. 'Are you fantasising about Noel Edmonds again?'

'No, I'm not...' Daisy went red. This didn't mean much; Daisy always went red.

'You wuv him...' Eve laughed. 'You want him to open your box.'

'Eugh.' Daisy was red again. 'And shh!' she said as Ed looked round, frowned and returned to a phone call.

Leaving her at the screen and getting up to make them coffee, Eve felt a swell of relief that she and Daisy seemed to be back to their usual state of affairs. Although she'd been wrapped up in her own drama during the past few weeks, Eve had still been worried about her friend. She'd been chewing her lip as she waited for the kettle to boil, seeming to be on the verge of saying something and then changing her mind. If Eve didn't know Daisy better, she would think she was holding back some secret, but Daisy was the least-secretive person she knew and Eve had dismissed the thought the moment it entered her mind.

She waited for the water to boil, distracted by the corkboard in front of her, covered in adverts, messages and one cartoon she'd drawn of their small team. She'd made Ed look a lot thinner in it. She had drawn Daisy with large cartoon freckles and bunches in her hair, and made her own long, dark brown hair fall to her bottom. Touching the ends briefly, she wished it was long again. She was so engrossed that it was a few seconds before she realised that Ed had left his desk and was standing at their table, where Daisy was looking up at him, so red her cheeks clashed with her hair. Eve carried two mugs back to the table as they both turned.

'Anything wrong?' Eve asked, her eyes wide.

'I was just reminding Daisy of the office regulations about internet usage.'

'Oh, I see,' Eve said, mouth in a thin line, a quick nod. 'And I am sure Daisy will take heed of them.' Eve thought 'take heed' sounded suitably solemn.

Ed looked at her quickly. 'I have no doubt she will.'

Daisy was looking anywhere but at Eve as she set the coffee down in front of her. 'Right, Daisy, well, it is probably best if we continue to sort out those files for archiving now.'

'Good idea,' she squeaked.

Ed stayed loitering above them, his chin wobbling with unsaid words, and then turned on his heel.

'Right.' Eve grinned, flopping into her chair. 'Now, do you think she will deal?'

Daisy, determined not to be caught twice, picked up her coffee. 'We can't. Let's archive those files.'

'What files?' Eve asked, eyebrows meeting.

'The files you wanted archiving.'

'Oh, that was a made-up thing, Dais'.' Eve laughed. 'You really need to get better at lying.'

Daisy's eyes flicked left to right for a brief second. Then she laughed and picked up her coffee, taking a sip. 'Oh I see.'

'Now,' Eve said, going to press 'Play' again. 'Let's find out what she has in her box.'

Chapter 3

Pot Noodle

Method:
- Boil water.
- Pour over Pot Noodle.
- Eat Pot Noodle.

IT HAD been the photograph that set her off. A friend had uploaded photos from her wedding in the summer on the coast of Devon and Eve was trawling through them as she sat on the floor, back against the sofa.

It had been a fabulous weekend. Liam and she had left London behind in a sticky haze and stuck the *Best of the Beachboys* album on the moment they were on the M4. They'd sung along to most of the songs, sunglasses on, sunroof down. By the Slough junction Liam had been grumbling about wearing a suit in July and Eve had tried to listen, but was really far too busy admiring herself in her new red fascinator that was so over the top it bent into the ceiling of the car. 'Do you think Audrey Hepburn had a red fascinator? She did not,' she'd answered herself happily.

In this photo they'd been sitting together in one of the pews

11

of the church. Light crossed them in diagonal stripes, lighting their faces and making their eyes sparkle. Liam had his arm round her shoulders and she was smiling straight up at him, oozing happiness, her own engagement ring prominent as she clutched his arm in mirth. In the next photo they'd been sitting at the table, Eve mid-story, arms up, Liam smiling at her from his seat. In the next they were on the dance floor, Eve's fascinator abandoned, heels kicked off, slow-dancing. Her eyes were closed, her head bent as his lips brushed her forehead. They were in a world of their own and the photographer had captured it.

Marmite padded over to look at what she was doing and she stared at him miserably, reaching out a hand to ruffle his hair, before changing her mind. She had always felt he preferred Liam to her, Liam who would play with him, throw endless balls for him.

'What happened, Marmite?' she asked him.

Marmite tilted his head to one side as if he were listening. Liam always told her he was the cleverest Morkie that ever lived. Eve had disagreed after finding him eating her best bra. Now she felt he was looking at her, his eyes full of understanding. Then he made a dive for the half-empty bowl of Pot Noodles next to the laptop on the coffee table.

'Marmite, NO! Don't.' It was too late. He had already sloshed it all over the surface, splattering the keyboard and pile of magazines as he legged it away, trailing noodles from his mouth.

'Marmite.'

He sat up, swallowed, one noodle still dangling from his mouth. 'Bad dog,' she said half-heartedly. He wagged his tail.

She returned to the screen, feeling the familiar ache in her chest piercing her as she continued to click on them, staring at the photos until her eyes hurt. What *had* happened? It had all gone so wrong. They'd been great together. EVERYONE had told them so. They'd travelled to different cities in Europe doing those grinning selfies, cheeks pressed together, eyes crinkled in laughter, and uploaded them with attractive filters. They always got more than thirty likes and comments like 'Soooooo jealous right now' and 'Awwwwwww'.

And they WERE cute, irritatingly so, it hadn't all been in her head. He'd draped his DJ over her shoulders when she'd got cold at a friend's thirtieth birthday, he'd brought her breakfast in bed when she was fluey, he'd held her hand in the street and called her his 'woman'. Today was – would have been – their four-year anniversary. Four years! That was longer than a lot of things. Longer than the life of her favourite knee boots, longer than Steps were together. Long.

She couldn't do it; she wouldn't let herself think back to last Christmas. She blinked, a thin film of water blurring her eyes so that they were just a wash of green and yellow. Don't, Eve. Don't do it to yourself. She felt surprised as the first tears rolled. After a month you'd think her tear ducts would have ceased to function. No more! You've had your fill! They betrayed her now, fat droplets dripping off her chin. Pathetic. Don't think about it, Eve. He doesn't deserve it. Four years though!

Those four years seemed to play on an endless reel in her mind – hugging, laughing, arms wrapped round her, meals made, films watched, pub nights with friends, big double beds in plush hotels, listening to friends' dating stories with a detached pathos. Poor you! Gosh! Squeeze his knee under the table as friend continues. How dreadful! Half-hearted plans to set them up with mutual friends. Four years. Jokes about what they'd call their children, where they'd live, the extension they'd build, the holiday home they'd buy and then last Christmas. It all seemed to come together so beautifully.

The tears had stopped, her face was blotchy, her eyes red-rimmed, her vest-top dotted with shed tears. She looked as she felt – drained, hopeless and beaten. She knew it was pathetic. She hated that he held such power, that memories of him could leave her in this way even after two months. But she still just missed him so bloody much.

Chapter 4

WHAT IF she'd never found out? What if she'd never looked? She blamed the rain. Ridiculous to have that much rain in August.

It had been a flash flood, it had started early that morning and it had almost been romantic. Her in short dungarees, cute flecks of paint on her cheeks; she'd been wearing her hair in plaits too, like she was Pollyanna doing DIY for fuck's sake. It was destined to go tits up – no one could look that smug for that long.

Their new flat was gorgeous; airy, light rooms, huge Victorian sash windows. Their bedroom even had a window seat where she imagined herself sketching pictures or writing a journal or something as Liam cooked her favourite meal on the range cooker (it had five hobs – Eve didn't have a clue what they could all be used for, but Liam had insisted). And now she was painting the bathroom this heavenly duck-egg blue so that people would sit on her ceramic loo seat and admire her moulding.

She'd had no idea that a month later she would find herself painting over every inch of that duck-egg blue in thick, dripping stripes of magnolia, the very sight of that colour causing her fists to clench, her heart to race and her spine to tingle. No one would admire her bathroom now. It was featureless and dull.

Like she felt. She'd donated the dungarees to Oxfam, chopped her dark-brown hair into a shapeless bob which even her dad had noticed and her mum had described as 'very Puritan'.

But she had been painting and it had been raining and they'd just come back from their new sandwich shop that did the most amazing chicken and mayo baguettes and gooey brownies with walnuts, and they'd been arguing about whether brownies were better with or without walnuts (with, surely?), but arguing in that cute 'you're right, no you're right, oh okay, squeeze on the nose, we'll agree to disagree', and they'd stood in the doorway and laughed at their bedraggled, rain-soaked selves and then they'd kissed like they were that couple in *The* bloody *Notebook*. Unbelievable.

With the warmth of the flat and the memory of the kiss still on her lips, she remembered she'd been smiling as she threw the keys on the kitchen table. Then she'd heard Liam shout from the living room, holler her name, loudly, urgently, and she'd jumped, a quick patter of fear as she rushed through to him.

He was looking up in horror at the ceiling that was leaking, water running down the inside of the wall as if it were a posh feature wall in a five-star hotel. Only it wasn't a five-star hotel and they didn't have a feature wall.

'Shit, Eve – ring the builders.'

'What?'

'The water, the fucking... I knew they hadn't secured the flashing.'

'The what?'

'Phone, Eve, phone...'

She'd nodded quickly. Rushing back to the kitchen, she'd quickly grabbed his phone.

'What are they under?'

'B for Builders.'

'B,' she muttered. 'Cryptic.'

And as she was still smiling over his logical, obvious phone-log cataloguing, as she typed in his password 'ilovearsenal', it had slapped her there, right between the eyes, 'you have 1 picture message'. She wasn't sure what made her do it. She'd never felt the urge before, or maybe she didn't decide to do it, it just clicked up, but it was then, as she read the words 'Wish you were here', she realised she was staring at someone's impeccably groomed vagina.

Chapter 5

GREG HAD packed a flask of tea and was moving towards the door. Karen, vet nurse-cum-receptionist-cum-all-round-star was eyeing him with her usual curiosity, removing the badge from her sizeable chest so that Greg felt the need to look away.

'Heading home?' she asked, leaning to switch off the computer and almost toppling head first over the desk. She craned to look up at Greg's face.

'I thought I'd take a walk first,' he said, holding up his flask of tea.

'A walk.' Karen's face wrinkled as it always did when anyone mentioned exercise. Karen drove everywhere. She'd walked down the aisle to Joe at their wedding, twenty years ago, as she would tell anyone who asked, and that was the most she was planning to do, thank you very much.

'It's really mild,' Greg said, missing the point deliberately.

'Perfect for an evening in the garden with a glass of wine.' Karen nodded encouragingly.

'Or a walk.'

She shivered and shrugged on her coat, nearly knocking over the pumpkin they'd placed there in a nod to Halloween.

'I'll see you tomorrow, Karen,' he said, laughing and moving to the door.

He walked by the poster for their latest deal – half-price vaccinations for any new client, a massive St Bernard dog with his tongue out enticing the customers in – as she called goodnight.

He loved Pangbourne in the evenings, but the days were getting shorter and it was often dark when he finished work. He missed walking across the meadows at the back of the village or ambling next to the river, sunlight reflecting off the surface of the water. Mondays they closed the practice early, though, and Greg was able to take a flask of tea and a book and roam where he wanted. This afternoon he was planning to skirt the back of the village, through to the allotments and over the fields to the woods at the back.

He chuckled to himself as he walked along the high street. *Greg Burrows, you playboy, you with your tea and your book – what happened, mate?* But before he could pursue that line of thought, and take himself to a place he didn't want to be, he had pulled out his mobile and checked his messages, laughing at one from his brother and tapping a reply. Turning down an alley lined with ivy, he skirted puddles, the mud churned up, swatting at a cloud of insects. The high street disappeared the further he walked away and he felt that he was letting go of the hub and noise, the shop bells, the familiar faces, the questions: escaping to the open space outside the small cluster of buildings.

He loved the allotment even at this time of year when people were mostly clearing their patch, turning the soil. He moved down a narrow grass path, neat rectangles of soil on either side, some far more cultivated than others, boxed in with wooden planks. Early leeks and some swede were already pushing through in regimented lines, others still containing the rotting remnants of the summer, dried-out sweetpeas, wilting courgette plants. The air smelt of the soil, heightened by the rain shower that morning, and he moved through, nodding at an elderly man who was slowly raking his patch.

He knew where he was headed, a bench in the meadow next door, with the woods in the distance and a field to the left that held two brown cows who were always walking together. At this time of year the cows were inside: he missed their gentle company. Animals were so straightforward and unassuming. He sometimes missed working with farm animals, the chance to get outside, meet with farmers; working on small animals meant a lot of the work was done indoors. He usually loved the consultations, catching up with clients and their animals. Recently, though, he had craved peace, the same conversations on a loop, struggling to retain his smile. He blinked, determined not to be dragged down today, settling on the bench and opening his e-reader cover.

He loved his e-reader, mostly because he read door-stopper books that were tedious to carry around but also, if he had to admit it, so that people could assume he was busy reading some worthy classic when, in fact, he was mostly reading books about magic and other worlds and hard men with swords felling other hard men with swords. He had always loved heroic fantasy novels since he was young and his little brother had been a very willing participant in his games, often allowing him to tie him up and stick him in the attic or cellar before getting some of his friends round to try and slay the dragon (Mum) to release him from his prison. The trouble was, the dragon made really good snacks and on more than one occasion they all forgot about the lost prince in the attic and ended up eating chocolate chip cookies in the kitchen. The older his brother got, the more he'd refused to play, as young princes like chocolate chip cookies too.

He stayed for a while on the bench, lost in the story, roaming a far-off land that was in the middle of a great battle with the kingdom next door. The sun had dropped beneath the treeline in the distance and the shadows were lengthening, birds nesting in the trees above him. Behind him the train sounded, bringing commuters back to the village. He knew he couldn't stay there much longer; she would wonder where he had got to.

He walked slowly back to his car, stopping in the small supermarket to buy the dinner. He had promised he would make something that night. As he drove to the house he tried to ready himself as he always did now. He hadn't used to, used to turn the key in the front door and already be calling out questions, ready to tease, ready to sweep in and wrap her in a hug. Now he found himself nervous almost, both hands tight on the top of the steering wheel as he drove the familiar route, the radio presenters' voices buzzing in his ear.

He stopped outside the house and stared at the building. He needed to tidy up the front garden, cut back some of the branches and clear away things for compost. He'd been promising to do it for weeks, not that she ever nagged him. It was the least he could do, he thought guiltily. He saw that the light was on in the living room downstairs, the curtains already closed but a glow emanating from the edges. He pictured her sitting by the reading lamp, lost in a book or watching the television. *Go in, Greg, get out of the car.*

He unfolded himself, opening the door and stepping outside, standing in the road still staring, while the shopping bag in one hand hung by his side. He slammed the door and stepped round the car, pausing for one more moment to plaster a smile on his face, to make sure she thought everything was normal. As he turned the key in the lock, he heard her call his name and he closed his eyes and then stepped inside.

Chapter 6

'**Y**OU LOOK better, less pasty.'

Eve kissed her mum on the cheek proffered. 'Thanks. I think.'

'I'm making Yorkshire puddings so I need to get back. Oh dear, did you really have to bring him?' She'd spotted Marmite peeking out from behind her legs. 'Oh, I thought Liam might have taken him.' Her mum's face always had a wary look around Marmite.

'There was no way.'

'But you don't like him either,' Mum said, backing away.

'I do.' Eve said it in a too-loud voice. 'I love him like my own flesh and blood.'

'Well, he's not your child.'

'It's a turn of phrase, Mum.'

Dad emerged wearing a mustard tank-top and yellow cords. He looked like walking scrambled eggs. Perhaps it was that that set Marmite off, legs apart, head up, yap, yap, yap. Dad laughed and bent down to rub him behind his ears but he scampered around in a semi-circle and started yapping at his bottom. He was definitely more Yorkshire Terrier than Maltese, and Eve tugged him back.

'Marmite,' she called. He ignored her and jumped up again. 'MARMITE,' she shouted and that made him growl and spin round, almost choking himself on his own lead. She released him and he made a beeline for Mum in the kitchen.

'Hello, love,' Dad said, giving Eve a brief hug. 'Good to see you.'

'Hey.' Even his four words had made Eve glad to be home, bordering on tearful.

'So how are you holding up?' A question he'd been asking for two months now.

At that moment Marmite returned, dragging a tea towel in his mouth, Mum shouting expletives after him.

Dad grinned delightedly. 'And how's this fella, how are you?' he cooed, chasing Marmite round the room, back bent, arms swaying. Marmite went completely mental; barking and diving forward, then racing back, tail high and wagging, before barking again. The noise rose.

Mum came running back into the room. 'David, really, David.'

'Marmite, stop!' Eve called with absolutely no effect.

'DAVID!' Mum shouted.

Dad stopped mid-chase, then slowly straightened up before turning to face Mum, gaze averted, head lowered, as if he were about to be told off by the headmistress.

Mum, fortunately, was so distracted by his outfit that she failed to fully launch into a tirade. 'I told you to change that top, David, you look like a very withered sunflower.'

'Mum!'

'Eve, don't pretend he doesn't look barking.'

'He looks fine,' Eve lied. 'And Dad's colour-blind, he can't help it.'

'I thought I had changed, have I not?'

'You have not.'

'Must have put the other one on.' He chuckled, brushing

both his hands over the mustard tank-top.

Dad had this strange habit of buying two of everything that he liked. He had an underlying fear he might lose things ever since he left his favourite cashmere jumper in a student bar in the eighties.

'Well, it's lunch now, too late. I will just have to pretend you are a stranger and I never chose to marry you.'

'Fair enough.' Dad nodded, looking pleased with the outcome, or perhaps just the thought of lunch.

Eve had already left them to it, Marmite scampering at her heels as she moved through to the kitchen.

'He goes outside,' Mum called behind her. Eve felt a tiny stab of guilt as she realised she was relieved. Marmite had been playing up ever since Liam left. Yesterday he had torn the backs of her favourite sandals and she'd had a dream the week before that he had trebled in size and was planning to eat her. She had given up shouting at him as he seemed oblivious to her voice.

This morning he'd been better, panting excitedly at the bottom of her bed, lead in his mouth. They'd had a brilliant walk across Primrose Hill, looking out over London sprawled before them. As she watched him trot happily next to her, his eyes glittering with this new adventure, his tail up, she'd felt a sudden flood of affection for him: he was her link to the past. But then he'd practically savaged another woman's Shih Tzu, snarling and yapping despite Eve shouting at him to stop, and she'd trudged back despondent, wondering if he would ever do what she asked.

They'd bought Marmite together from a breeder in North London who had sent them photos of him after he was born. They cooed as they visited him after a couple of weeks, giggling as he fell around the pen, tiny yaps as he stepped on his siblings. Liam had always loved Marmite, smothering him in kisses, letting him scramble up his chest to lie there, looking at him fondly like the world's hairiest baby. He hadn't grown a great deal; his tiny body covered in grey curls, large doleful eyes allowing him to get away with murder.

Liam had sent her texts, asking her to let him have Marmite. Saying she had never really liked him. There was no bloody way she was giving up the dog. She thought back to the picture message she'd seen. Liam clearly had everything he needed; she was damn well going to have Marmite. As she looked at him racing round her ankles, snapping and growling at imaginary things in the air, she took a breath. She'd learn to love him.

On entering the kitchen she realised she wasn't the only sibling who had descended for Sunday lunch. Harriet was already ensconced, mobile held in one hand, a spoon shaped like a strawberry in the other, spooning mushed-up something into Poppy's mouth.

'I told them that would be a terrible idea, now look where we are.'

She nodded at Eve as she walked in, the brief smile on her coral lips instantly replaced by a snarl at either the person on the phone or the mush, Eve couldn't be sure. Eve's eleven-month-old niece seemed perfectly oblivious, making 'nom, nom, nom' noises every time the mush came her way. Eve mouthed a 'Hello' as she opened the back door to let Marmite outside. He ran gaily out of it, coming to a screeching halt in the middle of the garden as she closed it behind him. His little face filled with betrayal as he realised she had left him and he was alone. Then he quickly darted off to the right to dig up Mum's flowerbeds.

'Do they have ears? Are they even listening?' Harriet gave

her an apologetic wide-eyed look; Eve gave her an inadequate thumbs-up.

Mum tiptoed past, panto-style, to the cooker, always terrified around Harriet, who was more domineering than she was and whose job she didn't understand, so when Harriet talked about it she just stroked her chin and nodded.

Harriet was a legend; three years older than Eve, who had worshipped her through childhood and beyond. She wore impeccable suits, produced beautiful children and still managed to do whatever high-powered job she did. It involved shares and property and margins. She had tried to explain it to Eve a few months ago using Poppy's ABC building blocks, but they'd both got bored and drunk wine and then made a tower that spelt 'PENIS' instead, and Eve had never asked again.

Gavin appeared in the doorway, holding a beaker of water in one hand and a cloth in the other. His striped rugby shirt had already got a wet patch on the shoulder which Eve could only assume was Poppy's doing. 'Hi, Eve,' he said, pecking her on the cheek before turning to Harriet to kiss her on the head.

'Accident?' Eve nodded at the patch as he stood back up.

'Poppy didn't like her starter so she threw it up on me,' Gavin explained. 'At least I didn't get it in my hair,' he said, patting his bald head.

'Ni—'

'That is NOT what I said!' Harriet shouted down the phone. Eve jumped and stopped talking. It didn't appear to alarm Gavin, who smiled and took the strawberry spoon from Harriet's hand.

Harriet cupped her free hand over the mobile. 'Hey, Eve, you look great, thin—' She said this in admiring tones. 'NO! Tell him NO.'

The switch was terrifying. Eve's mouth was left suspended in a response, not sure who or what she should tell no.

'Ignore her, Eve,' Gavin said, sitting down and taking over, trying to get Poppy to eat something. 'She's doing some deal or firing someone or stopping someone being fired or...' He looked sideways at his wife, who poked her tongue out at him and turned her back. 'She might be doing anything.'

Mum was stirring gravy and looking worriedly over at Harriet. 'I thought she was merging something.'

Dad walked in, a purple knotted scarf at his throat, and sat at the head of the table. Mum refused to acknowledge him, muttering something into the gravy.

'Nice, Dad.'

'Thanks,' Dad smiled, adjusting the knot.

Gavin coughed and returned his attention to Eve. 'You look well,' he commented, sipping from Poppy's beaker, which made her hold out two chubby hands for it immediately.

'Too pale,' Mum commented.

'Thanks, Mum.'

Harriet put her hand over the receiver again, 'She looks thin, Mum, good thin.' Returning to the call, 'Tell him if he thinks THAT, he can think again.'

'Where's Scarlet?'

'She's not allowed home until she takes it out,' Mum called over her shoulder from the oven.

Eve frowned. 'Takes what out?'

Dad grimaced at Eve. 'She'd got another piercing. This one's in her eyebrow. Your mother thinks it makes her look—'

'Like a lesbian. Like an aggressive lesbian.'

Gavin was looking at his lap, flicking something imaginary off his jeans. Harriet cupped her hand over the mouthpiece. 'Ridiculous.'

'She's twenty-five, Mum. Can you really ban her from home for that?'

'If she wants to see me again, she'll take it out,' Mum huffed.

Eve nodded, frowning now with a new thought. 'What does an aggressive lesbian look like compared to a normal lesbian?'

Dad shrugged.

'And is she a lesbian now?' Eve asked, curious. Her ethereal sister Scarlet could well be anything, floating around Newcastle in various ill-fitting pieces of cotton and loads of really meaningful tattoos scrawled in foreign languages. She was doing a photography course and most of her Instagram pictures were arty shots of food/her eye/the sky.

Dad shrugged.

'She was sleeping with some bloke on her course, massive...' said Harriet leaning across the table and cupping the phone again. '... beard. Er... do I have to be any clearer? I said no, he can't have five per cent, it's not bloody Christmas.'

Gavin looked at his wife with a raised eyebrow. 'Swear jar.'

'Blinkin' Christmas, blinkin',' Harriet muttered, rolling her eyes at Eve who stifled a giggle.

Poppy seemed oblivious, bashing her beaker on the table of her high-chair, shouting, 'Nom, nom, nom, nom!'

Dad poured Eve some water from the blue jug with the big fish on it. Mum was standing at his shoulder.

'Sleeping with who?' she asked, pointing the gravy spoon at Harriet. 'Oh, and, Eve,' she turned to focus on her, 'Christmas reminds me, you'll be coming here, won't you?'

Eve shifted in her seat, wondering why she was taking time to reply. She wanted to agree immediately; she wanted to say, 'Of course I will.' But, as she looked around the crowded room – the mush-spattered floor, Gavin playing peek-a-boo with a tea towel on his head, her dad fiddling with the knot of his purple neck-tie, her mum holding a spoon up to the light, tutting and polishing it on her apron, Harriet still with mobile clamped to her ear – she realised with panic it would be like this, it would be like it was every year. And he wouldn't be there with her.

'Harriet and Gavin are here for three days, so I was thinking Scarlet and you could share a room rather than put Scarlet back on the sofa...'

Their voices, the chatter, clutter and noise made Eve's head swim, made her body heat up, her brain whirring as she tried to filter it all. Christmas. Christmas at home. She wanted to turn to Liam, to grip his hand, lean into his body, know that afterwards they would drive back, giggling over the lunch, her dad's outfit, Mum's outrage at Scarlet's new piercing, to marvel at Harriet's juggling prowess. But there was no one there to turn to, no one's hand to grip. Then she thought back to last Christmas and what had happened and she found herself looking back at her mum, hearing her own voice as it came from her mouth. 'Actually, I think I need to spend this Christmas alone.'

The room fell silent.

Harriet dropped the phone.

Eve wondered what she had done.

Chapter 7

> ## Baked Beans on Toast
>
> 1 tin of baked beans
> 1 slice of bread
>
> **Method:**
> • Boil baked beans until hot.
> • Toast the bread.
> • Put the beans on the toast.
> • Serve.

LUNCH HAD been decidedly frosty, her mum refusing to spoon out her seconds until she'd promised to reconsider her Christmas plans, and forcing Eve to come up with more and more outlandish reasons why she might not be around.

Harriet had tried to placate by soothing Mum with reminders that it was only October after all and maybe Eve would change her mind, and then Scarlet had phoned to announce the eyebrow piercing was still very much intact and Mum had redirected her anger at her. Eve had left as soon as she could, Marmite trailing one of Mum's freshly planted daffodil bulbs in his mouth.

So where would Eve go? Why hadn't she just said yes immediately? She knew why. She thought back to last year, to Christmas at her parents' house, and felt the familiar lump in her throat, her eyes already stinging with the tears she was inevitably about to shed. *Gah, Eve, stop being such a cry-baby loser*. But it was too late for the pep talk; they were coming, spilling down her cheeks so that she couldn't be bothered to wipe them away. The image of him leaning down to kiss her, both hands cupping her face like they were the couple on the front cover of a romance novel, his eyes darker, reflecting all her own feelings.

She hadn't been expecting it. Sure, she had made the odd exclamation if walking past jewellery shops/churches/bridal shops. Innocent remarks, e.g. imagine when we are married and, ooh I have always fancied rose gold for a wedding band and, look, a wedding dress, are you excited about what I will look like in a wedding dress? So very subtle things really.

She imagined he might do it when they were on their own. Liam wasn't one for the big show, got alarmed if she talked too loudly in restaurants, and practically died when she had once knocked over a vase on a side table in the reception of a hotel whilst she'd been re-enacting a dance sequence from *Pitch Perfect*. She thought he would do it quietly, maybe take her to a dimly lit restaurant, hold her hand over a candle, propose in a low voice. She wondered if he would buy the ring or whether they'd shop for it together.

As it happened, it really had been a surprise. She had woken on Christmas Day and headed to the shower, leaving Liam lying on his back, mouth open, chest rising and falling. They'd drunk a lot of red wine the night before and she was groggy as she pulled at the bags of her eyes in the mirror; poking a tongue out, she had despaired at her Christmas look. Not very fresh-faced. Emerging from the shower pink and damp and twisting a towel around her hair into a turban, she wrapped herself into another one and stepped back into the bedroom.

There she found Liam, eyes wide, looking up at her as he bent to pull on his jeans.

'All right?' she said, laughing at his shocked expression. 'You look like you've just seen Father Christmas.' Liam, who rarely laughed at her jokes anyway, seemed to look more startled. 'Are you actually all right?' Eve asked, worried now that something had happened.

Then she saw it clutched in his hand, the little box, and, before she could ask, he had stumbled across the bed and thrust it at her.

'Will you marry me, Eve?'

It had been a shock and Eve had dropped her towel. Her dad, who had been listening at the door and couldn't contain himself any more, then burst in to be faced with Eve's bottom and Liam's increasingly pale face. He'd backed out, muttering, 'My mistake' over and over, and Eve had picked up her towel, forgetting that she hadn't responded yet.

'So?' Liam said, looking at her.

Eve had opened the box and felt her whole body go numb as she stared at the diamond ring glistening on its cushion. 'Yes,' she croaked. 'Yes please.'

And then all she remembered was floating down the stairs into the kitchen to her parents, with everyone chorusing 'Happy Christmas' and her just holding up her hand, a sheepish-looking Liam shuffling in behind. Her dad beetroot-red, but glossing over BottomGate, her mum chastising him for not telling her about Liam asking his permission the night before ('we're married, we should share EVERYTHING, IMMEDIATELY'), Gavin shaking Liam's hand, Scarlet with a tinsel crown smiling and clapping, and Harriet, a beat perhaps, a thought, and then her face splitting into a grin, tears springing into her eyes as she squeezed Eve tight to her chest.

They'd spent the morning drinking Bucks Fizz and asking questions that Eve didn't have any of the answers to as it slowly dawned on her that this was really happening. She stared at the ring on her hand, the diamond slipping to the side as the band was a size too big. She couldn't stop fiddling with it, holding it up to the light when she thought no one was looking.

There was no way she could go back home on her own this year. It would be torture reliving the moment. The smiles across the table as they'd pulled crackers. His too-small paper crown tilted at an angle, holding a three-week-old Poppy in his arms, looking like he was auditioning for topless guy in a perfume ad. Her womb practically combusting at the sight, making her hold one hand on her stomach as if looks could suddenly get her knocked up. She remembered at the time she'd been floored by the feeling. The Eve who had never really thought about children was now suddenly imagining her own child, gorgeous sandy hair and the same amber eyes like runny honey, nestled into the crook of his arm. They'd take photos of all three of them in bed in the morning, sleepily happy, snuggled on Egyptian cotton under a status that simply said 'My family' with a smiley emoticon.

So what could she do instead?

She fetched her dinner, baked beans on toast, and spooned it into her mouth as she thought. Clicking on the Safari icon on her iPad, she typed in 'Best Christmas Breaks'. It couldn't be that hard, could it? There were plenty of places to go that wouldn't remind her of Liam. Lapland, for instance; now that didn't hold any danger. There were lots of pictures of snow-covered trees, huskies pulling sledges, frozen sunsets, reindeers, men with massive furry hoods their faces peeking out, the sky striped with the rippling greens and purples of the Northern Lights. Then Eve noticed all the photos of laughing children, of families snuggled together in wooden chalets, websites promising reindeer rides and visits to Santa. It would be worse than going home. All those happy, excitable families having snowball fights and making angels in the deep trenches of snow.

She clicked on the next idea. That was better. That was instantly calming. She would get away from it all. It was a picture of an island in the middle of nowhere. A green blob surrounded by white sand, fringed by turquoise water and then the deep navy-blue of the ocean surrounding it all. There was one particular photo that made her take a breath. A long wooden pier leading to four huts on stilts, double bedrooms that looked out over the beautiful stretch of nothingness. The air still and calm and completely silent. No families, just her in a hammock, supping from a fruity cocktail dressed in a bikini. She could feel her body unfurl at the thought, her muscles start to relax in anticipation of the massages she would request on the beach, the gentle sound of steel drumming or some such as she wafted away into another daydream, the sun round and hot in the endless blue sky above.

It would be perfect, the absolute best alternative to her family Christmas, nowhere to be at a certain time, no one there but her. At home, everything ran to a strict timetable, laid down years before.

Step One: wake.

Step Two: wake the other sisters who aren't already awake (Harriet was always awake first so really this should read 'Harriet wake up Eve and Scarlet').

Step Three: open stockings.

Step Four: eat miniscule breakfast, complain of dreadful hunger, judge anyone who eats more than muesli as not getting into the spirit of things.

Step Five: attend morning church service for obligatory carolling.

Step Six: allowed one present if went to church (good motivator, church numbers always swelled by this promise).

Step Seven: return and 'help Mum lay table.*'

Step Eight: eat Christmas lunch.

Step Nine: eat more Christmas lunch.

Step Ten: hand round Quality Street tin and force-feed people chocolate despite the fact they have just eaten their body weight in turkey and potatoes and are loudly protesting they are in danger of throwing up.

Step Eleven: stand and greet the Queen with a salute and half-heartedly listen to her speech but really just wait to comment on all of Kate Middleton's clothes in each clip.

Step Twelve: open all the presents as if you have never seen a present before.

Step Thirteen: snuggle up to watch a Christmas movie.

Step Fourteen: throw something at the person who suggests dinner.

Step Fifteen: throw something at the person who suggests Monopoly.

Step Sixteen: drink.

Repeat Step Sixteen until Step Seventeen: bed.

Christmas is Complete.

*start drinking.

She scrolled quickly down to the room choices, searching for the double room in the hut with the sea view. She looked again at the price. She must have typed in '10' not '1' person. She scrolled up. Okay, she didn't *need* the hut overlooking the ocean. It wasn't an essential. It would have been nice, lovely really, to feel the water lapping beneath it in gentle waves, the warm wood under her feet as she stepped onto the pier in the morning. She could live without it, though. She looked for another room, in a hotel near the huts; the prices were still enormous, making her eyes water. She would have to sell something to pay for it. Something massive.

Then she saw a photo. A smiling couple in white linen running along the sand, her brown hair flying out behind her, dazzling teeth, the man chasing her. In the next shot they were in the shallows kissing. In the next image they were lying on the hammock Eve had conjured in her mind, all limbs and smiles and sand. It was the perfect honeymoon destination, the website promised. The perfect place to spend your first

Christmas together. Fine, there would be no children, no sound of their laughter, but that was because there would just be the sounds of snogging and sex noises from all the huts around her. Eve imagined it now, her peaceful ocean calm shattered by someone else's ecstatic orgasm. Oh no, no, no, she wouldn't be selling something for that. Not that she had anything to sell.

Then she looked at her finger, thinking about the ring she should be wearing. Remembering the twinkling stone reminded her how everything had been so different just over two months before. She stared back at the screen. The man's face morphing into Liam's. The laughing woman on the sand Eve. They could have gone there on holiday on their honeymoon. She closed down the website. No hut overlooking the ocean. So where would she end up?

She needed to keep busy, couldn't linger over her memories. Maybe lounging around in a hammock all day would be deadly anyway, nothing but her thoughts which mostly went: Liam, gah, vagina, hate, Liam.

She typed in 'Activity Christmas holidays', hoping for some inspiration. Up popped a grinning woman in goggles, surrounded by snowcapped mountains. Of course. Eve smiled to herself, clicking on the site, already tasting the fondue, already imagining herself whooshing down a slope. She would go skiing. Skiing was a brilliant idea.

Chapter 8

'CAN YOU ski?'

'Well, no, but it can't be that hard to learn.'

'It will be cold.'

'Well I know, but...'

'You've never really liked snow. There will be snow there,' Daisy pointed out.

'Well, I think that's sort of the point and I don't HATE snow, it just has to be in the right context.'

'Like in a ski resort.'

'Exactly!' Eve said, flinging her arms out wide and dropping her Biro in the process. 'Oh hi, Ed,' Eve said in a too-loud voice. Daisy froze at her desk, mouth half-open, about to say more on the subject of snow.

Ed had walked round and was standing at their table, a hand on his hip, his wedding ring hidden under a fold of flesh. 'Are you both working?'

'Yes, Ed,' Daisy chirruped.

'Oh yes, Ed,' Eve said, hitting her keyboard a little too hard.

'Eve, I need you to go out to a viewing later. It's the flat above the florist's, you remember.'

'I do,' Eve said, knowing she couldn't keep avoiding viewing forever, but somehow still wanting to make someone else go instead.

'And, Daisy, can I have those particulars for the house on Goldman Street?'

'Yes, Ed.'

'And, Eve,' he said, turning to her, 'after the viewing you can... Carry on.' He blustered, clearly not able to think up a job in time.

'Yes, Ed.'

'So,' Eve said the moment Ed had returned to his desk, 'what do you think?'

Daisy relaxed again. 'Do you really want to go skiing? If you have the whole month to play with, is that the best thing you can think of doing?'

Eve opened her mouth and shut it. Daisy could be so quietly unnerving at times. 'Well, I suppose the idea appeals in some ways, but in other ways, like the fact that I normally hate sports and the fact that I am not a huge fan of the cold, puts me off a bit.'

'So we need to think of something else,' Daisy pointed out, tapping her pen on her freckled nose. 'How about snowboarding?'

'Well, that's sort of the same as skiing, Dais'.'

'Good point. A month-long cruise?' she suggested.

'I'm not eighty-five.'

'A safari?'

'Too many lions.' Eve shivered.

'Well, how about something in this country?'

'Bit dull, isn't it?'

'It doesn't have to be,' Daisy said, straightening and staring at her. 'What about an extension of something you really do enjoy?' she suggested in her matter-of-fact way.

'Like what?' Eve asked, adding another doodle to the paper in front of her.

'Something that would really fit in with your interests.'

'What interests?' Eve said, realising she was starting to sound sulky and drawing a pouting face onto the sheet in front of her.

'Well, you like dancing.'

'I'm not sure clubbing in Ibiza could hold my interest for a month.'

'Not clubbing, obviously, but you could learn to dance properly, like Baby in *Dirty Dancing*?'

'I do love *Dirty Dancing*.' Eve nodded. 'But I'm not sure dancing is really me.'

'Well,' Daisy said pointedly, looking at the pictures Eve was drawing, 'you've always loved art. Why don't you do something related to that?'

Daisy had always encouraged Eve to draw more, fascinated by Eve's ability to translate what was in front of her onto the page. While Daisy stabbed desperately at a sheet of paper, the shapes and colours clashing hopelessly, Eve had always managed to make things look absolutely right. Daisy had exclaimed over hand-drawn birthday cards, the little sketches Eve produced on occasion.

Eve went to dismiss the idea with a hand but paused. Something within her was sparked.

Chapter 9

THE GROUND was rock solid and Greg ran a slow circuit in his hoodie, his breath a cloud in front of him as he skirted the pitch. In the middle of the Astro the last game was playing, the clash of hockey sticks at the other end now, the goalkeeper sliding into a dive, one enormous padded leg down on the ground to stop the ball going in. A whistle blew, the ref's arms went up, voices, another whistle, and Greg paused to watch the short corner.

Danny arrived as the teams were jogging back to the centre and Greg met him at the gate, a brief one-armed hug.

'Hey, bro,' Danny said, still wearing his overalls from the garage.

'You going to play in that? It's a bit Bob the Builder, mate,' Greg said, grinning as Danny rolled his eyes and unzipped the front, a grubby T-shirt underneath.

'I still play better than you in it.'

'Harsh.'

'True.'

Danny balled up his overalls and took his T-shirt off, his skin instantly covered in goosebumps. 'Holy shit, it's freezing,' he said before diving into his hockey shirt.

'It's November.'

A wolf-whistle from behind made them both turn round

and half the team ambled through the gate onto the pitch, nodding at them. 'Looking good, Daniel,' Andy shouted, his hair sticking up, an orange mouthguard already in.

'I need to keep in shape for your mum,' Danny called back. A lame jeer from the others.

Greg felt better already, sliding the ball across the ground with the others, talking about nothing as they warmed up. He took off his hoodie, rearranging the collar of his hockey shirt as he jogged into a huddle before their game began. Looking round at the faces of the other players, he felt his breathing calm as he listened to Andy's voice calling out the positions. They were a good team; no individuals and most of them had played together for a season already so they knew each other pretty well. As the other team trailed on in red and white striped tops, Andy tapped his hockey stick on the ground.

'Let's do it,' he said.

Greg lost himself on the hockey pitch, focusing on the ball zipping across the pitch, the ache in his legs, the burn in his lungs as he breathed in, his ears numb, his nose running with the cold. If he could put all his energy into the game he wouldn't have to think about anything else. It was the first time that week that he'd started to relax; unable to check his mobile or sit and mull over things, he felt free. Making a run up the left wing, he passed it quickly to his brother in front of goal, who swept it in; a satisfying clack on the wooden boards behind the goalkeeper. Greg jogged over, high-fiving Danny.

They were up by a goal at half-time and Andy talked them through a short corner they had practised in training. Greg held out his water bottle to Danny, who never remembered to bring his own. The other team were big lads but many of them slower, less athletic. There were a couple of skilful guys to watch in the middle but, if they stayed focused, they could win the game. Greg felt a surge as the whistle for the second half went.

He didn't know how it happened; time seemed to be running at high speed. It wasn't like it was the first time he'd been hit. His opposite number had been hustling him all game, cannoning off him to make a run, breathing down his neck when he had possession. It was a bad tackle, there was no doubt about that, but normally Greg would hop about, rub at the spot he'd been hit, nod at the player and take the free pass. When the stick went into his leg, he could feel it despite wearing shin pads and he just saw red. He didn't remember what he'd shouted, but remembered the expression on the other guy's face as he launched himself on him. Then it was just white noise in his brain and shouts from the other players.

He was pulled off him by Danny. 'Greg, hey, Greg.' It was usually the other way round, him sweeping in to fix his little brother's mistakes. Not tonight. He felt the rage soaring through his body, like he just wanted to pound the ground, the fence, anything, and roar, mouth open into the night. His breathing was thick, heavy; he stood planted to the ground, his chest rising and falling, the team scattered around the pitch staring at him, Andy, face in a frown, the other team muttering and looking put out.

'Have a time out,' Andy said, walking over, his voice not unkind as he beckoned the sub on.

Greg couldn't speak. He could still see spots in his eyes, words coming at him, slower, harder to distinguish; his knuckles were white on his hockey stick. His opposite number had backed off, straightening his shirt as he talked in a low voice to a teammate. Greg didn't even have the energy to feel

44

bad, thrown by the sudden rage that had swept over him, that still seemed to be stamping around in his head.

Danny patted him on the back, no more the cheeky cherub, his face serious. At any other time this would have been enough to make Greg laugh. Not tonight, though. He held his gaze and then turned and left the pitch, feeling the throbbing anger in his head, everything he was trying to forget crowding in, knowing the guys in his team were watching him leave, wondering what the hell had happened.

Chapter 10

Singapore Sling

1 part cherry brandy
2 parts gin
3 drops of Angostura
  bitters

1 lime
Ginger ale

Method:
- Put ice in a glass.
- Pour the cherry brandy and gin over the ice.
- Add the Angostura bitters and a generous squeeze of lime.
- Top up with ginger ale.

THEY WERE standing in a vintage clothes shop, holding various items up to the mirror as they chatted. Eve was clattering across the wooden floorboards exclaiming at every pair, trying to squeeze her size eight feet into dainty Jimmy Choo heels, pretending they fitted.

'I can see your heel hanging over the back,' Daisy pointed out. She was wearing a brown suede leather jacket that she'd shrugged on moments before.

'That really suits you,' Eve commented, noting how Daisy's hair seemed even more prominent tumbling over the jacket. 'You are like a Titian biker. It's a hot look.' Not for the first time, Eve regretted chopping off her dark-brown hair, lifting a hand to touch it absent-mindedly.

Daisy blushed and took it off, putting it back on the hanger and causing the shop assistant's shoulders to fall. 'We're meant to be after something from the eighties.'

'I know.' Eve's nose wrinkled as she selected a pink-sequinned ra-ra skirt with no less than three layers. She checked the tags. 'Ooh, size twelve, I might actually be able to get one leg through this.'

'You'll get more than one leg through it,' Daisy protested.

'How about this to go with it?' Eve held up the most monstrous yellow zipped shell-suit top.

Daisy shrugged. 'It's certainly the right decade.'

Eve giggled and popped it on, parading in front of the mirror as if she were on a catwalk, spinning round with her hands on her hips. 'I'm soooo sexy for this jacket, soooo sexy for this jacket, so sexy it hurts...'

Daisy was hiding her flaming cheeks in her hands. Eve laughed, knowing Daisy would be embarrassed at her performance. She wouldn't get Daisy dancing around with her in a shop in the middle of the day. Somehow it always made Eve behave even more appallingly, enjoying watching Daisy squirm. Then suddenly Eve stopped, aware that Daisy was looking at her in the strangest way, a sort of nostalgia on her face, tears filming her eyes.

'Hey,' she said, face full of concern, a frown forming between her eyebrows. 'You okay?' She touched her arm and Daisy brushed her off.

'Of course! Hey,' she said, by way of distraction, 'you

missed the trousers that go with that.'

Eve let herself be distracted, pushing the thought that Daisy was hiding something to the back of her head. Sighing, she turned round. 'I knew you would see them. I can't... don't make me...' she said, holding one hand to her forehead in true Drama Queen fashion.

'They *are* a set.'

That had Eve nodding solemnly. 'You are right. They need to stay together and I can totally rock this look. And look Dais'... this is perfect for you.'

She revealed a stonewashed denim dress with so many pockets and embroidered flowers Daisy didn't know where to look. 'You can wear it with these pixie boots that nearly fit me.'

Daisy took them and rolled her eyes. 'They're a size four.'

'I said nearly, didn't I?'

They left the shop with their bags, Eve linking her arms through Daisy's as they weaved back to her flat to get ready, a bottle of Prosecco chilling in the fridge. It was Rachel's hen do that night. Or Ro-Ro, as her friends called her. Aside from Eve, who once announced that if she had to call her Ro-Ro in public she would never see her in public again. She relented, of course; people always relented in the face of Ro-Ro.

The hen do was in a jungle-themed restaurant in Clerkenwell. Lots of women stood round glass-topped tables, next to enormous drooping ferns and large squishy armchairs covered in tropical birds. The room looked to be nestled on the floor of a rainforest. Eve and Daisy had known Ro-Ro since schooldays, when she had hair to her bottom and thought attaching sequins to clothing made them infinitely cooler. She'd taken a year off to 'find herself' and had quickly found herself on a fashion course in central London. There, she had suddenly chopped all her light-brown hair off into a sharp crop, lost two stone and started wearing prescriptive sunglasses everywhere. She was now pretty high up in the magazine world, attending catwalk shows and writing articles about the latest trends.

A lot of Ro-Ro's friends were so thin that they almost disappeared when turning sideways.

'One might be hiding behind a fern and we would never know,' whispered Eve to Daisy, who instantly heated up as a girl emerged from behind one of the plants.

Eve opened her eyes wide to indicate 'I told you so'. Daisy snuffled into her hand.

Eve glided over across the room to kiss Ro-Ro on both cheeks, cheerfully calling her 'Rach', which earned her a thin smile. She looked over-the-top absurd in her bright-yellow shimmering shell-suit and massive plastic hooped earrings. Daisy and she had thrown a load of blue eyeshadow onto their eyelids and their lips were streaked with the same dreadful hot pink.

'Hi, Ro-Ro,' said Daisy, kissing her on both cheeks.

Ro-Ro threw two matchstick arms round her. 'Gorgeous girl,' she said as one of the stick insects took a photo of the three of them. 'Eve, you look...' She trailed away as another stick insect arrived in a tiny leather miniskirt and wedges. Another, wearing a body over sheer black tights and leg warmers, looked like a very beautiful girl in an exercise video. She confided in Daisy that she'd spent £120 having her hair permed for the occasion. Together they looked like a fashion spread in eighties *Vogue*. Daisy tugged on her denim dress.

Eve had ordered a jug of Singapore Sling and had befriended Ro-Ro's bridesmaids at the bar. Hugo's sisters were both looking relieved to have an arm flung round their shoulders, both perspiring in matching lilac shell suits. Eve was now offering them a straw from the jug, the zip of her yellow jacket pulled down to reveal a massive photo of Jason Donovan's face across her chest. Eve had pretty big boobs so Jason looked quite wide-eyed already. 'To Ro-Ro and Hugo,' she shouted.

Ro-Ro beamed at her and jumped in for another selfie. Eve felt a flood of affection for her old friend and winked at her. She could be sharp but Daisy and Eve had known her for years. That meant something. She sometimes missed their old friendship; Rachel was always a little bit tense nowadays, the muscles in her neck on show, always looking like a greyhound straining to be released down the track. There were glimmers of the old days, though, when it was just the three of them hanging out – Eve, Daisy and Rachel on a tartan rug in Primrose Hill, listening to Nina Simone and painting their nails.

Tonight Eve felt better than she had in weeks. She was on her schoolfriend's hen do, she was dressed in something she could dance in (no matter the flammable nature of it put her at risk every time she braved a flaming Sambuca) and she finally didn't feel like her heart was full of holes. She might be a bit drunk, but she felt a warm, fuzzy feeling sneak over her. She loved her friends, and London, and dressing up and drinking. She could stay out as late as she liked and no one would tell her off for eating a kebab at 3 a.m. Standing up, she raised a glass to Rachel. 'To Ro-Ro and Hugo, may you have plentiful sex, wonderful children and... to Ro-Ro,' she said, before hiccoughing and sitting back down. Yes, maybe a teeny bit drunk.

She was probably more than a teeny bit drunk three hours

later when she was bouncing around a red padded room in a purple curly wig and comedy-sized sunglasses, singing into a microphone. Her yellow jacket had long gone and Jason Donovan looked to have developed a terrible bloody facial injury from some red wine. She had screamed at most of the hen do to get out of the private karaoke bar so that she and Daisy and Ro-Ro could 'do justice to 'A Whole New World'.' 'Some of you keep ruining Jasmin's part and it upsets me.' She had bought the whole room shots of tequila to make up for being a bitch and then proceeded to scream at them to get out again when 'I will Always Love You' came on, so she could be Whitney 'in peace'.

She and Daisy finally left arm in arm, throats hoarse and outfits in tatters, as they weaved out of the bar and into the nearest cab. The hot-pink lipstick had long since faded and patches of blue eyeshadow clung stubbornly to their lids. They sank together into the leather, propping each other up as the driver asked for instructions, one weary eye on them from his driving mirror.

'I love my friends, I love you, Daisy,' said Eve, hugging Daisy to her so that her ginger hair tickled her nose.

'I love you too, Eve,' Daisy replied, in a voice that made Eve look up at her.

They lurched through the flat door and Daisy looked around the living room, her face morphing into bemusement as she took in the splayed photos on the floor, the empty wine glasses, crumb-covered plates.

'Need to tidy,' Eve mumbled, dropping inelegantly onto the rug, legs stuck out in front of her, yellow shell-suit trousers rolled up.

She idly scooped up a pile of photos under the pretence of moving them and then felt her shoulders droop, her eyes deadening as she stared at the images, numerous: her smiling on holidays, her and Liam wrapped round each other, the Eiffel Tower behind them, them scrawling names on a padlock, them in Rome raising glasses to the camera, heads bent over the most enormous pizza. Them building a snowman in the garden of Eve's parents' house.

'So what are you going to do about Christmas?' Daisy asked, picking up another photo; both of them all flushed and excited, tumbling off a sledge.

'Christmas? Oh yeah.' Eve had vague memories of her previous dilemma over her Christmas plans. It all seemed less important right now. Then she picked up another photo of them. They were wearing matching Christmas jumpers. They thought they'd been hilarious, marching out of dressing rooms to show them off to each other, giggling as they unveiled them to the family when they appeared for lunch on Christmas Day. The jumpers and the diamond ring. This had been the first photo taken after he had proposed. Eve could see how happy she was in the crinkle of her eyes, the lightness in her smile.

She found herself reaching across to take the lighter from the coffee table, flicking it determinedly beneath the photo.

'He proposed at Christmas,' Eve said, solemnly holding the flame beneath the photo until the corner started smoking, an orange flame slowly nibbling the corner.

'I know he did,' said Daisy, who looked so sad for her that Eve leant across to give her another hug, almost sending them both up in flames.

'Not near those trousers,' Daisy said, taking the lighter from her and dropping it in the ashtray.

Eve's energy went, her body slumped forward, her hair hanging down in a sheet, obscuring her face. Daisy tipped her head and sighed. 'Come on, Eve. Bed.'

They dropped down onto the double bed. Daisy made her laugh, reminding her about their schooldays when she and Rachel had nearly been suspended for smoking grass from the school playing fields because they thought it was marijuana. 'Thanks, Daisy,' Eve said, smiling into the dark, grateful to her friend for distracting her.

Just before she closed her eyes, it occurred to her that Daisy had seemed quieter than usual that night, the odd furtive look her way, an absent expression on her face when Eve had turned to ask her what was wrong. Eve promised herself she would ask her about it tomorrow. She would be a better friend; she had been so self-absorbed recently. She would focus on Daisy. She opened her eyes in the dark, giggling to herself as she realised she couldn't focus on anything.

'You okay, Eve?' slurred Daisy.

'I'm focusing on you,' Eve slurred back.

'Sounds scary,' Daisy said. And then there was breathing and then Eve was asleep.

Chapter 11

SHE DIDN'T know why she answered the call. She could see his name in big bold letters. Each one like four nails piercing her skin. L for LOVE BROKEN. I for I AM HURTING. A for AGGGGHHHH and M for MAN WHO BROKE MY HEART. It was too late, she had pressed it and now she was lifting the phone to her ear, and for a few seconds she knew she was excited about hearing from him. As if she could scrub the last couple of months from her mind for a moment and pretend she was going to answer a call about the milk he had picked up, or whether they should go out for dinner that night (yes), or was she aware that another *Transformers* sequel was out in the cinema and could they go (no).

'I want my dog back.'

His voice didn't sound like she remembered. He was abrupt, harder. Cold almost. It made her own replies sharper sounding.

'He's not your dog.'

'I paid for him.'

'And you paid for my tampons, but you never claimed ownership of them.'

'What?'

She regretted the tampons line, tried to get back on track. 'He's not YOUR dog, Liam. He was our dog. But now he is my dog because... because...'

She didn't have a reason. Well, not one she could say to him. The reason, of course, was 'he is my dog, Liam, because you slept with someone with very triangular pubic hair and I didn't and I was going to marry you and I loved you and wanted to have your children and trusted you and you were a complete pig and so I am keeping the dog because I know it hurts you. I can't think of another way to hurt you without involving your dog so Marmite it is.' But she couldn't say any of that so she just went with, 'Because I need him.'

Marmite came and rested a paw on her leg, as if he had heard her. It made her jolt and she looked at him. His brown wide eyes were staring up at her. Maybe she did need him. Then he jumped up and stole the biscuit from her hand.

'Marmite, don't...'

'Are you talking to him? Can I talk to him?'

She felt a brief flicker of guilt. He sounded desperate; it was sort of sad. She almost gave in, almost encouraged him. Then she thought of everything he had done, every promise he had made her, and her voice was frosty as she replied, 'No, and stop calling me about him.'

'I will if you give him back. I want my dog back.'

'I won't give him back. And he is not your dog.'

'Fine. Well, Eve, I will have to seek legal advice.'

'You do that,' she said in a rushed, high-pitched voice, trying hard not to instantly panic. Legal advice? That sounded serious. She swallowed. 'I was... I was going to seek legal advice too... Liam,' she tacked on as if it made it more true.

Was she? Yes, she could totally seek legal advice.

'Fine,' he said, his familiar voice snapping down the phone at her.

Eve's instinct was to soothe, to stop arguing, to see what

they could do. That was what she had always done when they had argued; she hated raised voices, she hated them falling out. She had often backed down; she had often apologised first. She gripped the phone tighter in her hand as a new feeling washed over her.

'Anyway, legal advice won't help you because I'm going away,' she announced triumphantly, her voice sounding around the living room and making Marmite cock his head to one side.

'What do you mean "away"? You can't steal my dog...'

'You can't steal something that already belongs to you,' Eve said, voice rising again.

'You can't take him away. Where is "away" anyway?'

'Wouldn't you like to know?' she said in what she hoped was her best Mysterious Voice. She didn't have a bloody clue, but she was damned if she was going to admit this now. She was enjoying the note of panic in his voice, the curiousity. Yes, ex-fiancé, little me, going away, just getting on a plane and travelling to who knows where because I am free now, whoop, free without you.

'This is outrageous.' Liam was spluttering now. She couldn't remember ever making him splutter before. He'd once spluttered after a mouthful of her first-ever attempt at 'Thai Curry' (the instructions should have been clearer – who the hell knows the difference between tsp and tbsp anyway?) but she'd never made him splutter in anger. This was new; this was different. She bit back the apology, forced herself not to cave in. 'You can't do that,' he said.

And, as if she were looking at herself from a long distance away, she said, in the most confident voice she could muster, 'Watch me.' And then she pressed her finger down on the 'End Call' button with a decisive huff.

She stared at the phone for a long moment and thought of all the times they had argued. She could practically count them on two hands. They had once rowed in the car on the way to his parents' house. Liam was a useless passenger, withholding vital information (e.g. turn left) long after the information was required (after the left turn). Then they'd had a fall-out because he always filled the bin with too much rubbish and then pressed it down until it all started to smell and the bag split. Then they rowed over the bread. Eve would leave the bread bag open and it used to really annoy him; he liked to use those plastic things that the bread comes with, twist the bag through it to keep the bread fresh. Yes, they'd got to the point where they'd shouted a bit at times. Silly things: she'd tripped over his shoes in the hall once and had gone back into the living room and thrown them at his head. He'd once yelled when she'd got so drunk she'd invited a country- and- western wedding band back to their hotel room for a line-dancing lesson.

Not much, though, nothing that had lingered, nothing that meant they had marched around the house slamming doors and hurling insults, nothing that had made her sleep badly or wake angry. They had always been over silly things, nothing to really worry about. She blinked back tears. How had it come to this? How were they arguing in this way?

And what did she mean 'away'? Where was she going? She couldn't very well take Marmite ski-ing. He loved a walk but she wasn't sure they let dogs on pistes and things. She couldn't leave him here and didn't you have to get passports for your pets now? Special jabs? She couldn't just fly off somewhere for Christmas. She had responsibilities. She was a mother, nay, a SINGLE PARENT. She had to make plans with her Dog Child.

Marmite rested his head on the sofa next to her, looking

up at her dolefully. She knew he probably wanted another biscuit but she let him stay there, one hand reaching out to rest on his head and scratch behind his ears. She wouldn't seek legal advice, she wouldn't have the first idea how to seek legal advice. Then, as Marmite nestled closer, she realised she didn't want to give him back; it wasn't fair, he had been *their* dog, not *his* dog. She had taken some persuading, but she had always been the one to walk him. She had allowed him to sleep in their bedroom; she had taken him to the vet's after he had eaten an entire chocolate Easter egg and nearly poisoned himself.

Marmite looked up at her again and she gave him a watery smile, nestling her head down onto his so that his rank dog breath wafted over her.

'There's a good boy. Do you miss him? I'm sorry. I miss him too.' She wiped a tear away. 'Just don't bloody tell him.'

Chapter 12

SHE KNEW she had to get away, but more than that she had to do something with the time off. December was only two weeks away and she needed a plan. She was off work on the 1st December and it was fast approaching. She didn't want to be sitting around at home; she needed to keep busy and stop herself being 'a tedious Misery Guts' (Mum).

This was confirmed a night later whilst squashed round a low circular table with her family in a sweaty pub in East London, staring at a man with a mouth organ who was mostly made up of facial hair, on a tiny square of raised stage. They were waiting for Gavin to appear at an Open Mic Night. Harriet had left Poppy with a baby-sitter and was drinking G&Ts as if they had just announced a drought, and swaying in time to the bearded man's tune, her mum was sitting straight-backed holding her white wine spritzer up like a shield and her dad was looking happily at his ale and well at home as an old rocker in a creased leather jacket that he had apparently salvaged from the attic. He'd decided to couple it with raspberry cords and pea-green Converse trainers. Mum had made him walk ten feet ahead of her once out of the car.

Gavin was apparently about to appear with Beard.

Eve leant across the table. 'How long has he been playing?' she asked, still wondering whether this was an enormous wind-up. To her knowledge, Gavin was an accountant who, fine, owned a lot more Take That albums than was normal for a thirty-seven-year-old man, but who couldn't play an instrument himself.

Harriet shrugged and smiled and drank more gin, and her dad spilled his ale trying to shout an answer back.

'Mum?'

'Um, a while, I think,' her mum said.

'Very precise.'

This was the first time they had ventured out to watch him and when Gavin appeared on stage, his head glistening in the spotlight, Eve suddenly wished Liam were here so she could grip his hand. How long would it be before she would stop automatically thinking of him? It was strange being with her family without him at her side.

Gavin stood in a small spotlight as the Beard played a note on the mouth organ, the crowd quietening as Gavin gazed around the room. Then he started to play, a gentle folk song, and he and the Beard sang in a lilting harmony.

They were pretty good and Eve felt herself relax as she listened. Five minutes later, when Harriet was leaning her head on her hand and looking glassy, it stopped. Dad, who had been nodding along to a non-existent beat, started clapping and we all followed in kind. Gavin took a bashful bow.

'Lovely,' Mum announced.

'Ace-ssh,' slurred Harriet confidently.

Dad was still clapping.

'Well, that was pretty good,' Eve said.

'Good man, good man.' Dad nodded, talking to no one.

'He has a talent,' Mum said, and Eve wondered whether the look she gave her afterwards had been pointed.

Did Eve have a talent? She was hopeless at sports, was

convinced that her coordination had been fundamentally damaged in some way after being hit on the head by a netball aged eight. She wasn't any good at domestic tasks, couldn't sew or knit, was useless in the kitchen, burnt anything she touched and was quick to panic.

She certainly loved to draw and doodle, was constantly filling blank notebooks with cartoons of mischievous squirrels, beady-eyed toads and lithe deer. She loved nothing better than breathing in the scent of a new, blank notebook, spending hours selecting the right one, a hardback (always) with an illustration or inspirational quote on the front. She created characters that frolicked through her imagination together.

Drawing cartoons wasn't exactly something a proper adult should do, she supposed, and over the years she had started to hide the notebooks away, in shameful piles, in boxes in the attic, amongst old photographs. She and Liam had been too busy going to drinks parties or friends' BBQs or watching box sets, and somehow she had neglected this part of her life. She felt a flicker of excitement as she thought of the time she had stretching ahead of her, a chance for her to fill a new notebook with sketches. Daisy had been right; she did want to do something with it.

Gavin came over then and they crowded round to congratulate him. He bent to kiss Harriet who seemed with it enough to give him a hug. 'Youoo wash exchellent.'

'You were excellent,' Eve translated.

Gavin laughed. 'Thanks for coming,' he said, sitting and accepting a beer from the Beard, who came over to clap him on the back.

'Good job,' Gavin said, half-rising out of his chair to shake his hand.

The Beard nodded and melted back into the crowd.

'Well,' Eve said, 'he seems nice.'

'Ha, ha, he is actually,' Gavin said, raising his glass.

'Are you going to do another gig together?'

'Not until the New Year, he's pretty busy over Christmas, touring in *Santa Claus: The Musical*.'

'Ahhhh,' Eve said, 'that explains the resplendent beard.'

The mention of Christmas had obviously been too much for Mum who had swivelled her whole body round to face them both. 'What's that about Christmas?'

'Oh, nothing much,' Gavin said.

'Nothing,' Eve said, knowing this wouldn't be enough.

'Well, I assume you were just making plans. Because we will all be at home for Christmas, won't we, Eve. We'll all be there.'

'I thought Eve wasn't coming,' Gavin said slowly, trying to provide some support as Harriet was currently slumped in her chair being no help.

'Of course she is coming,' Mum said, rolling her eyes.

Dad looked across at her and then at Mum. 'Eve is free to do what she wants to do,' he said, taking a decisive sip of ale.

Harriet looked up to contribute. 'Of courshe we'll misch her but okays by schme if she schan't.'

'Er thanks, Harriet,' Eve said, assuming the sentence was trying to help.

'Notsch at all yoursch my sishter.'

'Um, very good.'

Mum didn't let the interruption distract her, returning to the attack immediately. 'It is very immature of you, Eve, to dig your heels in like this when you don't have anywhere else to be.'

Eve found herself raising her voice. 'Actually,' she announced, with a lot more confidence than she felt, 'I do have somewhere else to be. I'm going to be working on a project.'

Project? Are you, Eve?

'What project, love?' asked her dad in this really sweet way that made Eve feel a lot worse for making something up than her mum glowering at her.

'Yes, what project?' her mum asked.

Gavin turned to look at her too, smiling automatically.

'I don't want to say,' Eve said, knowing she was sticking out her bottom lip and being petulant even without her mum pointing it out.

It was lucky really that the argument was diverted by Harriet, who chose that moment to fall off her stool.

Chapter 13

SHE'D SAID it now. She couldn't go back on it. They had all looked really excited for her and her 'mystery project'. Why did she have to lie? Why couldn't she just be quiet, or tell them she didn't want to spend another Christmas doing the same things with them while they all thought back to last Christmas and the celebratory Buck's Fizz in the morning, Dad's impromptu speech after lunch, toasting Liam, Mum taking photos of them standing awkwardly under the mistletoe in their matching jumpers as she shouted 'kiss each other, don't be shy' repeatedly, Scarlet pretending to gag just to the side while Harriet sat, cradling Poppy, a half-smile at Eve on her face, clearly happy to see her sister so content.

She logged onto the internet, tapping a range of ideas into Google. She wanted to do something creative, use her time wisely and take her mind off everything. She wanted to learn a skill or develop a side to her she didn't know she had. Like Gavin and his guitar playing.

'Become a Bee-Keeper', 'Make a Coracle' (note: find out what a coracle is). 'Produce Your Own Smoked Salmon – How to cold-smoke salmon', 'Basket Weaving – the basics'. There were so many things she could do and she felt a buzz as she moved from website to website. She didn't want to make baskets or keep bees, and a coracle was an old boat but she didn't live near water. She imagined a month of cold-smoking a salmon classes would start to get repetitive. Still, she knew she was on the right track; the idea of learning a new skill, creating something, definitely appealed. She could totally throw herself into it and turn the Christmas period into a real positive.

A website promising the finest artist breaks in Royal Berkshire popped up and a small photo of a crumbling mansion caught her eye: 'Pottery classes in a stately home on the banks of the River Thames'. They were running a 'Festive Special' – a daily lesson for the month of December (excluding weekends). The chance to learn this skill over the Christmas period. Perfect for beginners.

Pottery, Eve pondered. She had never done any pottery before, aside from painting a coaster in a painting café in London on a hen do. She had certainly never touched clay or learnt how to make it into a different shape on a wheel. She felt herself getting excited about the prospect. She was arty, she could draw, so maybe she could make pots and things. She imagined bowls in beautiful coloured glazes, vases with intricate designs.

Also, Liam had taken so many things out of her kitchen, she could replenish stocks, make her own set of dinner plates. She imagined her friends' faces as she nonchalantly pulled out a stack of plates she had made from scratch. 'What, these? Oh… it's nothing, I'm a potter.' Is 'potter' a word? She made a mental note to look that up before she described herself as one. She didn't want to be drummed out of the club before she'd even started.

She found herself filling in her details on the 'Enquiry Form', pressing 'Send'. The more she thought about it, the more she knew it was what she needed. A chance to meet new people, to develop a new skill, to live in a different place. For a few moments she had forgotten the original reason she wanted to get away and was simply gripped by a desire to do something entirely for herself.

She would need somewhere to stay if she went on it, but it turned out Royal Berkshire wasn't a cheap place. Having a palace in your county certainly hikes up prices. The local B&Bs were lovely but her heart sank as she did the maths. She simply couldn't afford to stay around there. She needed some local knowledge.

She searched the internet for an estate agent in the area and was surprised to see her own company had a small branch in the village, Pangbourne. She dialled the number, feeling more and more sure that this was fate and she was bound to find something.

A nasally voice answered, a man who sounded as if he needed to blow his nose. Eve explained what she was looking for, something near the postcode, something relatively affordable, a little cottage perhaps? She knew her voice was laced with expectation.

She heard shuffling and tapping and realised she had clenched her teeth as she waited for him to reply, her fist tight on the phone.

'We haven't got a cottage, no...'

Eve's heart sank, her shoulders slumped, her hopes fading fast. The little stone cottage with an apple tree in the garden, a bright wisteria climbing its walls, crumbled before her.

'We've got a room in a house in Purley? Lady tenant wanted, not bothered by smoking.'

'Oh, I'm not a...'

'No pets though...'

'I have a dog, you see...'

He wasn't really listening, just reeling the facts off, and Eve tapped her teeth and waited. She wasn't keen to share anyway, was hoping to remove herself from it all, and having a room-mate who could be any shade of mad didn't make her feel soothed, and she didn't have time to visit them all and vet them.

'Well then, if not that, we've got a lot of things in Tilehurst, or central Reading obviously...' The voice sounded bored, as if he were reading from a sheet, which Eve supposed he was.

'No, I'm going on a course in a house that overlooks the river just a short walk from the centre of the village,' she parroted from memory. 'And I don't have a car, you see,' she said, in her most polite voice. 'Are you sure there isn't anything suitable?'

'It's harder with a dog,' he said, sounding accusing.

'Well, er... I'm sorry, but...' She imagined her own office. They would never be this abrupt. Well Ed would, but that was precisely why they never allowed him to talk to clients.

'Anything at all? Please,' she tacked on, wondering if they had just got off on the wrong foot or whether he wasn't really a phone person.

'Not in that vicinity.'

That was it then; she sagged in her chair. She would have to get something further away, in town perhaps, and work out how to get into the course. It wasn't impossible but it would take more planning.

'We do have a short-term let for a houseboat for the month of December. They're normally really popular in the summer, but we do have people coming down for the winter months sometimes and we've just had a couple fall through as he's broken a hip and doesn't want to be getting in and out of it...'

Eve had stopped listening at 'hip'. A houseboat. She sat up, tucked a strand of hair behind her ear.

A houseboat was wonderfully romantic. She pictured herself now, out on the deck with her hair tied back, a scarf around her neck, an aperitif in her hand, watching the sun sink below the line of the water, fish zipping past, peace, alone on the water, just her and the great outdoors.

'Oh yes, please,' she breathed. 'Tell me more.'

Chapter 14

'**W**HAT DO river people wear?'

'What did you call yourself?'

'I am one of the river people.'

'Sounds like a terrible Irish band.'

They were browsing the rails in a big department store, Eve holding up a pair of frayed dungarees on the sale rack.

'There's a reason they're for sale,' Harriet commented, grimacing as Eve held them up to her body.

'Because they're so sexy.'

'No, that is not the reason.'

Eve poked her tongue out as she put them back, plucking a checked shirt from another rail.

'Very *Brokeback Mountain*,' Harriet commented as Eve frowned at herself in a full-length mirror.

'Well, what else can I wear? I'm on a boat. Ooh, how about stripes?'

'You're not a pirate,' Harriet said, holding up a plain black top. 'How about this?'

Eve looked at it. 'Not exactly memorable, is it?'

'Well, I thought you were doing all this so you could be alone with your thoughts and your pots. Why do you need to look good?'

Eve frowned at Harriet, realising that there was something

in her voice. 'You're annoyed,' Eve pointed out.

Harriet sighed. 'I'm not annoyed.' She raised a finger as Eve went to speak. 'And don't do that thing where you say "You are annoyed" and I say "I'm not" and you say "You are", and then I get annoyed.'

Eve had been about to do exactly that.

'It's not that I'm annoyed, I'm just sad, I suppose.' Harriet shrugged, not really meeting Eve's eye. Harriet rarely did big emotion so this was reasonably unexpected.

'Are you really going?' she asked.

Eve nodded. 'I paid the deposit yesterday.'

Harriet exhaled slowly. 'She'll miss you there,' she said, pointing to the stationary pram where Poppy lay, one arm thrown above her hair, her smooth skin so strokeable it took all Eve's willpower not to reach down and touch it.

'Hey, don't bring her into it. You know I can't resist her.'

'I was going to dress her as an elf,' Harriet said, a renewed glint in her eye.

Eve's head snapped up and she nearly cancelled all her plans. But she had made up her mind and she was sort of excited about doing something different. She knew she might miss them, Harriet in particular, she hero-worshipped her, and Poppy was just adorable. But she also knew she'd be a misery, moping and hopeless, remembering all the previous Christmases, remembering the proposal.

'I'd be a complete drain,' Eve said, pulling out a pair of red skinny jeans.

'They'd look good on you,' Harriet said begrudgingly; she could never stay stroppy with Eve for long.

Eve came and threw one arm round her neck. 'I'm sorry I'm being hopeless, I know it's all very me, me, me, but I just can't face it all.'

'I get it,' Harriet said, stiffening under her embrace. She wasn't brilliant at PDA. Gavin thought it was hilarious and always tried to grab her in restaurants.

'Hey, shall we both get reindeer hairbands?' Harriet said, passing Eve one.

Eve put it on, trying to make Harriet laugh. She had been such a grump recently and she didn't want to keep being a big stroppy bore. Bad things happened to people and in this case no one had died, it was just selfish of her to still be moping about. But she *was* moping about; she *was* having to make an effort to stay cheerful. She looked up to say more to Harriet and that was when it happened.

He was here.

She knew this moment was going to happen. She had been amazed in a way that she hadn't already bumped into him. Yes, London was made up of a population of eight and a half million and, yes, they lived on different sides of the river, and, yes, they hadn't arranged to meet, but she just knew, as if there were a Magnet of Doom, that somehow this moment was entirely inevitable. She wondered briefly whether she should buy a lottery ticket.

He looked irritatingly good, unshaven and sort of dirty, but she quite liked him like that. He was rubbing a hand over the cleft in his chin, a familiar Bench T-shirt in khaki, the bottom half of him lost to the clothes rail of denim skirts in front of him. Why was he standing by denim skirts? What was he thinking? She froze in the shop as he turned and saw Harriet and her only metres away.

He looked frightened of Harriet, his eyes widening in alarm, a little start in his shoulders as if someone had administered a small electric shock. He *should* look frightened, Eve thought; Harriet was frightening and now she was giving him the frostiest of frightening looks. If they were in the culinary section he should have feared for his life. Fortunately for him, unless she planned to smother him with denim skirts, he was safe. Eve was gratified to see he didn't take a step forward, although his eyes flickered to the pram. Eve knew he wanted to ask after Poppy, bend down and say hello. He had always loved Poppy when they'd been together, constantly telling her to say 'Uncle Liam' in a gooey voice despite knowing she was months away from her first word.

This thought made Eve feel nauseous, one hand resting on her stomach. They had teased each other about their own babies. They were going to make a family, have a child that was a wonderful blend of their best traits. The child would have inherited his straight teeth and her excellent hands (she had wanted to be a hand model for years). Their child would have been the best child. Eve blinked, desperate not to give anything away. Fortunately, Liam was looking around him as if he were hoping a large hole might suddenly appear in the glossy parquet and he might escape through it.

This made Eve stronger and she straightened and said, 'Liam,' with a nod. As if they were in a screenplay and she were about to pull out a long cigarette-holder and narrow her eyes as she smoked it.

Liam nodded after a momentary pause. 'Eve,' he said in a level voice.

'That's a new T-shirt,' she said, pointing at it to help demonstrate her sentence.

'No.'

Even his denial made her bristle. So she couldn't remember all his wardrobe, was that the reason that he had shagged someone else? He looked uncomfortable, tugging on said T-shirt, which at a second glance did look vaguely familiar.

Harriet hadn't said anything as yet, still staring at him as if she was hexing him. To be fair, Eve wouldn't put anything past Harriet. Then, as his eyes darted nervously around the room, it dawned on her that he might have been following them. 'Are you following us?'

He shuffled from one foot to the other. 'I wasn't following you,' he said in a voice that suggested he had definitely been following them.

'What are you here to buy?' Eve asked, hands on her hips, feeling strangely powerful. She had never really been like this around Liam. Always agreeing, nodding and acquiescing, in case she upset the barrel cart and he got fed up and slept with someone with really neat pubic hair. WELL, THAT TURNED OUT GREAT.

'Buy? I'm... here... to... buy...' Liam was slow. Clearly buying time. Buying time to make up more lies about why he was there, clearly stalking them, desperate to get another look. Eve brightened at the thought that he had grown so desperate, softening for a moment, a half-smile playing on her lips.

He was looking over his shoulder now. He did look really shifty, like he was planning his first shoplift.

Oh my God. It suddenly hit Eve. They were in the women's section of a department store. They were standing near clothes meant for women and Liam was not a woman. If he wasn't following them, there was only one other solution. He was here with... her. Eve looked over her shoulder, convinced now that she saw someone dive behind one of the marble pillars by the escalators.

'Is she here?' Eve hissed.

Liam frowned, his eyebrows pulling together as he asked, 'Who?'

'The vagina.'

Liam had the decency to look vaguely embarrassed; a flick of his lowered eyes to Harriet, a blush spreading from the top of his T-shirt. He shook his head, mumbling a 'no'.

'She better not be,' Harriet said in a low voice. She sounded exactly like the head gangster in a movie. In the next scene they'd definitely both be found dead.

Liam had pulled himself up taller now and had taken a step towards Eve. 'Where's Marmite?'

'Marmite doesn't like shopping,' Eve said, refusing to be diverted.

'I hope you haven't left him alone too long in the flat. That's cruel.'

Eve clenched her fists. As if he still had the right to be Bossy Boyfriend.

'Hmm,' she said, one finger to her lips. 'Cruel, I know what is also cruel.'

She could see Harriet bending over the pram, possibly to shield Poppy from the waves of fury rolling off her now. 'Cruel is you being here now lecturing me about our dog when you are shopping with your new girlfriend.'

'I'm not shopp... I don't have a gi... Marmite is my dog.'

'Seriously, not this again.'

'Don't make a scene, Eve,' Liam said, always quick to try and quieten her down in public.

'I'm not making a scene. There is no scene. I just don't want you lecturing me,' Eve hissed, her spittle hitting the row of denim skirts.

'I'm not lecturing you.'

'You are.'

'I'm not doing this here,' he said, trying to sound like the reasonable one. 'We need to talk about this again. I want my dog back, Eve.'

'Oh you go, you go,' Eve said, bordering on deranged.

He turned sharply and headed to the escalators, almost sending a rack of vest-tops flying in his haste to escape.

'You won't get him,' she called after him. She turned back round to Harriet, hoping she would be impressed. She had always told Eve to be more assertive with Liam, to stand up for herself a little more.

'You were almost scary,' Harriet said, stifling a laugh.

Eve frowned at her. 'I *was* scary. Well, I thought I was quite good. At least I didn't cry.'

'No, you didn't cry.'

'What then?'

Harriet pointed just above Eve's face and then it dawned on her. She pulled off the antlers in one smooth motion. 'Oh crap.'

Chapter 15

Prawn and Leek Linguine

4 whole leeks
Fresh linguine (50g per
person approx.)
1 pack of prawns
(defrost them as per
instructions)

200g Gorgonzola
1 small pot of crème
fraîche
Pepper

Method:

- Chop up the leeks and sweat them on a low heat in oil.
- Cook the pasta as per instructions.
- Add the prawns to the mixture and ensure they are cooked through.
- Add the cheese and crème fraîche and stir until the mixture is melted and bubbling.
- Season and serve on top of the pasta.

T HE NEXT couple of weeks flew by as Eve transferred the payments for the course and boat. She'd already taken the first two weeks of December off, assuming she'd be on holiday with Liam, so Ed hadn't minded tacking on a few extra days.

In fact she actually made him stutter a 'Happy Christmas' into the palm of his hand as, in a fit of gratitude, she bent to kiss his cheek.

The agency was pretty quiet at that time of year but Daisy made things easier, saying she was happy to cover the days. To return the favour, Eve found herself inviting her to her house for dinner the night before she left. Daisy had asked whether they would be getting a takeaway.

'I will be making dinner,' Eve had announced confidently, dialling Harriet to invite her and Gavin round too.

She'd been planning it all weekend. Weekends seemed strangely long and empty these days, no more snuggling under a duvet watching a movie, no more takeaways, no more sex on a Sunday morning. She didn't like the way the flat sounded as she padded round it alone. The other night she had made the mistake of watching *I Am Legend* and had slept on the sofa with a tennis racket by her side to brain the zombies that were going to get her in the night.

Liam and her had often hosted dinner parties. She was used to it, she assured herself as she stared at the kitchen tops, the oven rather too clean from its lack of use these past two months. Normally she would waft around the house in a dress lighting candles, laying the table, making napkins into swans (party trick), filling the fridge with wine and doing the washing up as Liam cooked. He'd been a brilliant cook, often talking about the meat he had bought from the butcher's or a new recipe he wanted to try out; he would record episodes of *Saturday Kitchen* and Eve would listen to him exclaim over the ideas.

He would have around five pans on the go; the sizzle of oil, the bubbling water, smells merging in the air so that when their guests arrived they sniffed appreciatively, stomachs rumbling. It worked as a set-up, the house looked fabulous and they sat and gushed over asparagus, Parma ham and poached egg with balsamic vinegar, or a cheese soufflé that he'd read would rise better because he hadn't over-whisked it. He had a Kenwood machine with about eighteen attachments, including a hook that apparently made bread. It was one of the industrial-sized ones, which he'd staggered under when he had packed up his things.

She didn't want to think about the day he'd packed up his things. It had been terrible. She'd planned to be out, to let him slope about the flat throwing his belongings into boxes and bags and leaving, his grey-faced dad helping him load things into a rented van. She hadn't left the house in time, though, had let them both in, a dreadful silence as she skirted round him, red-rimmed eyes, mouth clamped shut so she didn't beg him to stay, his dad opening and shutting his mouth as if he were about to apologise for everything, but then realising nothing he could say would make it better. She had given his dad a one-armed hug, stiff and awkward, the emotion blocking her throat and causing more tears to spring to the back of her eyes.

Why had he torn them apart? She had wondered as she stumbled out of the flat and down the stairs, forgetting her wallet, bag, her book, and then just walking blindly through Primrose Hill, unaware of the sunshine, the gambolling dogs, the shrieking, happy children. She had sat on a small patch of grass, willing herself to stay there, tempted to run back in, stop the unpacking, cancel the rented van, tell him they could work it out, see his dad's face light up, put a kettle on, forget it all.

But she couldn't do that so she stayed frozen to the grass, shivering as the sun disappeared behind banks of cloud. She'd returned, checking the street for the van, seeing the empty space outside the flat. As she'd pushed open the door she was instantly struck by the blank spaces, pictures that had left faded marks behind them, photos she had loved, bookshelves that now looked like gaping mouths with teeth missing, the kitchen scrubbed, two mugs left on the sideboard washed up. It had hit her then, so forcibly, that that was it and they really had separated, that it was absolutely over, no more jokes in the kitchen, no more hugging on the sofa, no more gentle ribbing from his dad.

So she was out of practice in the kitchen, a little rusty so to speak, but she could get back into the swing of things. Sure, she had never really shown much interest throughout university and afterwards, relying on meals out, invites from friends and a lot of sandwiches and wine, but she had seen Liam's logical approach to things and that must have rubbed off on her. She lived with him for four years so in that time, during the hundreds of meals he had produced, she would have learnt stuff. She remembered his favourite main dish, a pasta dish with some sort of cheese and prawns in. It had been really tasty. It was pasta: that was a good place to start.

Liam had taken all the recipe books. She'd only just noticed now, staring at the empty space in the kitchen with alarm. How dare he! She felt outraged. They had been his, fine; they had been gone for two months now without her noticing. FINE, but who takes ALL the recipes. At least leave her with one little recipe. What did he want? Her to STARVE? Rage replaced the melancholy and she stomped off to the supermarket, carrier bags balled into a tight fist.

In the supermarket she tried to feign confidence, nodding at a fellow amateur chef in the freezer section as they both stared dumbly at the peas. There were so many different bags of peas. Should she even buy frozen peas? Were fresh peas better? She felt a flutter of panic that peas (first thing on the list) seemed to be the undoing of her and confidently threw two bags of petits pois into the trolley. The man next door copied her and she wheeled away down the aisle feeling heartened.

They had frozen prawns in a big bag, grey and enormous, and she remembered Liam once telling her that it was better to buy them uncooked. She wasn't sure why; she did remember taking two of them in her hands and making them kiss. 'They're going to have prawn babies now,' she had said. He had laughed. She remembered that part, but not the bit about how he had cooked them and turned them from stiff grey frozen prawns to succulent pink edible prawns. She would ask the internet; there were bound to be answers there. You could ask the internet anything now and it would know. She then got home and lost thirty-five minutes to the internet, asking it things like, 'Can shellfish feel pain?' and 'How do fish have sex?' She learnt a lot about the copulation of crabs but not a huge amount about the cooking of prawns, and she was running out of time.

'You've defrosted them, though, haven't you, Eve?' asked Daisy down the phone. She sounded worried, as if Eve would have been stupid enough to...

'I'll call you back, Daisy.'

Shit, how long do prawns take to defrost? They had to go in pretty soon or the whole meal would be ruined. She was following exact instructions and wasn't confident enough to veer from the words in front of her. Why didn't she have a microwave? Who doesn't have a microwave in the twenty-first century? She ran hot water, filling the sink and throwing the bag into it, which instantly floated to the top until she weighted it down with the Fairy Liquid container. They were small; they wouldn't take that long. She had time to watch a YouTube hair tutorial; she really wanted to learn to braid her hair. It would make the front of her bob more interesting.

Gah, ten minutes later, and she was still waiting for the prawns. She remembered now that was why she had never liked cooking. She got bored. While something was bubbling she would check her phone; while something was simmering she would fetch a glass of wine, get distracted by turning the letters on the fridge into a funny sentence (it currently read DAISY WUVS NOEL). Suddenly the bubbling would get too much, the oven would be soaked, the simmering would emit a cloying burning smell and the stuff would have turned to sticky lumps. She would throw a strop, carry on drinking the wine and make a salad.

Not tonight, though, tonight would be a triumph. She would show them all she could do things without Liam, she would rise to the challenge. This would be the scene of her glory, her time to shine. She would not be defeated. She played a lot of rousing music to get her going.

She felt like mistress of her own kitchen. Liam had always banned her from his area, laying out the ingredients as if he were Jamie Oliver. He'd even bought a ceramic pestle and mortar which he actually used to grind things (Eve wasn't sure what). She had been happy with this arrangement but now she was in the midst of it all, taking back control, and it was going well. The cheese sauce looked right, the sort of consistency she had hoped for, the sticky Gorgonzola melting into the crème fraîche. She felt a prickle of excitement. She was cooking. Eve was being a chef! In your face, Liam the Loser. She giggled out loud at this name. She would have to put that on the fridge.

The time had come to throw the prawns in. They felt softer to the touch and she bit her lip, wondering if she had let them defrost long enough. The heat from the saucepan would finish the job, she thought, as she tipped them into the sauce and stirred them round. It smelt incredible and the doorbell was ringing, and Harriet and Gavin were arriving and Daisy was right behind them. She tripped out to press the buzzer, hearing them troop up the stairs inside.

'It's on the latch,' she called, hastily throwing an apron over herself so they could clearly see she was being a chef.

It had been a fantastic evening; in fact, it had been a triumph! Everyone had loved the prawn cheese dish, which was perfect. A few of the prawns were a little chewy but the leek and cheese sauce was perfection. Then she had pulled out a Sticky Toffee Pudding and they'd had coffee and sweet wine. Sweet wine she had found at the back of a shelf that would definitely make her look like she knew what she was doing. They had all held their glasses up in a toast to her, 'To Eve', the warm yellow liquid sticky and gorgeous.

She lay reflecting on the evening in bed that night. Harriet's surprised face as she dabbed at her mouth after the first mouthful, Gavin nodding and commenting, ''Tis really good,' as he ate, Daisy giving her a thumbs up. She had felt in control, the hostess, and hadn't thought about past dinner parties with Liam. In fact she'd barely thought about him all night. She realised then that maybe she could survive on her own; she didn't need to be so worried.

It came on quickly. One moment she was lying beneath her crisp white sheets running through the evening and the next she felt her stomach rumble, her muscles cramp, her skin break into goosebumps, her forehead start to sweat. She felt bile rise in her throat.

'Oh God, no...'

She ran to the bathroom and just made it in time.

Chapter 16

HE'D BEEN dreading this conversation since he'd seen the scan the day before. He stood behind the table; Pepper lay lengthways on it between them as they talked over her. Long grey hairs were sprinkled over Mrs McLaughlin's navy cardigan as she held her breath and looked at him with large, pale-brown eyes.

Greg cleared his throat, moved a hand up to his shirt collar underneath his scrubs. His tie felt tighter than normal. He knew he needed to maintain his professionalism, but there was something already broken in Mrs McLaughlin's expression that made him want to reach across and pull her into a hug. He hoped one of her grandsons was waiting in reception for her.

'Thank you for coming in, Mrs McLaughlin.'

'Not at all, Doctor, I'd been waiting for Karen's call. I knew it was her because she always seems to phone during *This Morning* and when it rang during their ad break I thought, "it'll be Karen" and it was.'

Greg waited for her to finish, knew she was probably talking to put off the inevitable. Pepper lay between them, so lethargic now. He remembered how when he had first met her, she'd been all claws. Wrestling her to get her out of the basket she'd been brought in, she'd given him a livid scratch and ruined a good shirt. Today, however, she was listless, her soft mewing pathetic and tiny, her chest barely rising and falling so you could only tell she was breathing by the long fur that seemed to quiver every now and again.

Mrs McLaughlin, Mrs Mary McLaughlin, had been coming to the practice since he'd first opened five years before. She had always come with Mr McLaughlin. They'd sit in reception doing the crossword together and their quiet chatter would leak under the door of his consulting room. Mr McLaughlin, Harold, would hold the door open for her and carry in the basket carrying Pepper. He would insist on Mary having a chair and she would tell him to stop fussing. Greg started keeping a chair in the room after that to make things easier.

They would write the practice Christmas cards and would send people to Greg who always sounded as if they'd had their arms twisted. 'Mary and Harold told us we must tell you they sent us.' When Karen had given them a card with the new Facebook page, Greg had been touched to see his first five-star review appear from Mary and Harold. 'A caring team. Mr Burrows is always wonderfully attentive to our Pepper. We highly recommend.'

Then, one day, Mrs Mary McLaughlin appeared at the practice on her own. A grandson, tall enough to need to duck into most rooms, wearing a baseball cap, sat awkwardly reading *Woman and Home* as Karen offered him a Fruit Glacier while he waited. Greg had looked around for Harold and been told in a small, level voice that Harold had died of a heart attack the month before. She didn't bring the crossword in any more.

Greg took another breath and began. 'Mrs McLaughlin, I'm afraid...' He could see the tears already filming her eyes as she stood defiantly staring at him. He could make out the powder she had brushed on, flecks of it in her eyebrows, and he blinked and continued. 'The scan confirmed Pepper has got a tumour. I'm afraid it is on his kidney.'

'Is it bad?'

'I'm afraid it is quite large and, because Pepper is fourteen years old now, it makes it quite a risky operation to remove it...'

She nodded as Greg carried on, knowing it was better to be really clear about things and allow his clients to make up their own minds with all the facts. '... I'm afraid I can't guarantee Pepper would survive.'

Mrs McLaughlin swallowed, colour flooding her powdered cheeks. 'Would it be costly, Mr Burrows?'

'I'm afraid without pet insurance it does become expensive...'

Mrs McLaughlin plaited her hands together, eyes scanning left to right.

'This operation would cost just over £1,000,' Greg continued.

A tiny intake of breath. 'Harold used to sort the insurance, but when he went I needed to find money. Funerals are very costly, Mr Burrows,' she said, biting her lip, perhaps feeling that was a treacherous thought, perhaps not wanting to think of the funeral at all.

'I do understand, I'm terribly sorry,' Greg said, and he meant it. He suddenly pictured Mrs McLaughlin dressed in black, a handkerchief up to her face, pale roses on the coffin she'd selected for her husband.

'Is there anything else we could do for him?'

Greg knew the answer to this question. He flicked his gaze over the cat who was still prostrate on the table. He knew he should have told her they could consider putting Pepper down. It was on the tip of his tongue; he just needed to say the words. He often had to broach this subject with his clients. It was never easy but, in this case, he found himself unable to speak. She was wearing a silver necklace with a bird dangling from it. His mother had a necklace like that.

'Perhaps, Mrs McLaughlin,' he said slowly, brain clicking into gear, and then he smiled softly at her, feeling himself grow in confidence as he spoke, 'there is something else we could do.'

Karen had stared at him as if he had lost his mind. She'd wondered why Mrs McLaughlin had left empty-handed with a smile on her face. Greg had put a hand on her shoulder and sent her on her way.

'Monthly instalments at what price?'

'Three pounds,' Greg said firmly.

'Three pounds,' Karen typed in, muttering, 'Soft-hearted, will go under...'

'What's that, Karen?' Greg grinned, standing over her.

'Well,' Karen said, 'it will take her twenty-eight years to pay it back.'

'Perfect,' Greg said. 'I'm going to scrub up then. Pepper needs to be operated on now.'

'Unbelievable, would sell the clothes on his ow—'

Greg poked a head round the door. 'Saying something, Karen?'

'Just wondering if you needed a tea,' she called.

'Love one after the op. Thanks.'

'Ridiculous man,' muttered Karen, shaking her head, a small smile slipping out as she tapped in the costs of the operation against the day's takings.

Normally Greg needed Karen to help hold the animals down for the anaesthetic, but Pepper was so still that, for a second, Greg panicked she had already gone.

'Come on,' he said, lifting her up and deciding it would be better to give her gas.

He hoped he hadn't raised Mrs McLaughlin's hopes. Pepper was even thinner than he'd imagined under all the fur. Would she be strong enough for the operation? He felt her side gently with two fingers. The lump was there, the lump he had first felt when she'd been brought in a few days ago. He hoped it would be easy enough to remove.

He loved surgery, the ability to be able to fix things, provide a solution. It was a large tumour but he thought he had got it all. He felt as he stitched her up that he might just have managed it. 'Come on, lovely,' he said, running a hand over her fur, 'you need to get better.' X-raying her to be sure it hadn't spread elsewhere, he left her to come round in one of the kennels, a dish of water next to her head, a drip on her leg.

Karen had kept her word, and a mug of tea and a ham and cheese sandwich waited for him in their small office. Checking his watch, he realised he only had ten minutes until afternoon consulting began and someone was always early for the clinic. He picked up the sandwich, taking a bite, just about to switch on the TV overhead and see what the score was in the cricket, and then it happened.

The ringtone went off.

For a moment, he didn't recognise it as it wasn't the usual sound. Then the tune it was playing seeped through his consciousness and he swallowed the sandwich quickly, the bread sticking in his throat. He had programmed it in for this moment so he'd react quickly.

It was time.

He didn't have a chance to think much more about it; he wouldn't be late. She wouldn't have to wait there without him. This was the moment. His heart sped up; he felt his palms break into a sweat.

'Karen,' he called, pushing open the door to reception, shrugging on his coat, car keys in his hand. He saw a woman waiting on one of the plastic seats, a white poodle sat up reading the magazine with her. They both turned as he appeared. 'I'm terribly sorry,' he said as Karen looked up too. 'Karen, I have to go, I've had the call.'

Karen blinked as if emerging from a long sleep and then roused into action, half-standing and then sitting abruptly back down again. 'Of course, of course, you go,' she said, shooing him and turning to the woman and the poodle. He didn't wait to hear what she said; his car was parked outside the back door. He didn't used to leave it there but he did now for precisely this moment. Karen would ring and cancel the afternoon appointments. He just had to leave, now.

He unlocked the car, dipping down into the seat, realising as he looked in the driving mirror he'd thrown his coat over his bloodied scrubs. No time to change, he thought, starting the engine, one hand behind the passenger seat, head over his shoulder as he reversed, changed gear and left the car park, the squeak of his tyres making one old man with a walking stick tut under his breath about the modern world. Greg didn't notice as he drove through the village towards Reading.

He just hoped he would make it in time.

Chapter 17

HARRIET: 'GAH, AM DYING.'

DAISY: 'So you didn't defrost them then?'

GAVIN: 'At least I can get off work
    tomorrow. Hash tag Every Cloud.'

SHE HAD taken the train to Pangbourne, her phone beeping with text messages from the others who had all been laid asunder by the prawns. Outside the weather was grey, rain dotting the windows of her carriage, droplets streaking sideways with the speed, blurring the view outside, and she hoped it wasn't a long walk to where she was staying. Marmite sat on the seat opposite, mesmerised by the views flashing past, his tiny head moving left to right.

They left London, past graffitied bridges, brick walls, the backs of people's gardens, and they gained pace speeding next to brown empty fields, trees stripped of their leaves, the river snaking in and out for much of the way. Stomach churning, she had tried to close her eyes and forget, the train's movements jolting her and making her head spin. She sat near the toilet, which was one of those new ones that she couldn't work. She was caught by two teenagers holding skateboards just outside Slough as the door slowly revolved to reveal her bending over the toilet, Marmite yapping at them as they rolled about laughing.

As they drew into Reading, she allowed herself a flicker of excitement. Her stomach was still cramping, although there was nothing left in it and she couldn't decide if it was the food poisoning or the butterflies caused by being so close to her final destination. She briefly shut her eyes again. They were only ten minutes away; two short stops and she would be there. The rain was heavier as they pulled out, the sky ominously dark for early afternoon, with enormous dark clouds overlapping each other; the windows seemed to be all running water.

She wobbled out at Pangbourne, gripping the bit of kitchen roll that contained the scribbled directions to the boat that was currently moored near the common there. It didn't look complicated, but she was definitely in no mood to get lost. It wasn't far so there was no point booking a taxi. The estate agent had been clear about that on the phone. It was a route that drew her down behind the village, skirting the weir and out by the iron bridge to Whitchurch. She glanced again at the kitchen roll and set off, head ducked down into her chest, eyes squinting as the rain soaked her head and ran down the back of her neck. Her suitcase was soaked as she bumped and rolled it down the path, avoiding the larger pools of water and navigating across a main road, Marmite bedraggled and whining as he splashed through puddles by her side.

The small path was thick with overgrown hedges on either side and muddy patches that forced her to wrench her suitcase up and over them. Her feet felt squidgy, her socks wet through. She had been assured that the boat had a woodburning stove in it; she imagined herself sitting in front of it, wet clothes hung up, feet drying. *Focus on that, Eve,* she thought as a roll of thunder sounded in the distance. Running alongside was the noise of the water in the weir, rushing and tumbling over a ledge, churning up the river, white froth moving past, raindrops pounding on the surface. She might as well have tumbled into it, she was so wet now. She sheltered momentarily under a tree, the rain drumming above her, leaking through the leaves that were barely able to provide cover. She examined the map on her kitchen roll, the blue Biro smudged as she turned right, then left, relieved to see a sign to the common: she couldn't be far.

Stopping by the side of the road, her heart lifting at the sight of the iron bridge up ahead, she didn't have time to react. The driver went past, splashing her decisively from the knees down. Gasping at the cold, her jeans dark with water, sticking to her calves, she wanted someone to sweep her up and away to somewhere dry. Marmite started barking at the back of the car, his fur dripping with rainwater. Gritting her teeth, she crossed the road, emerging into a car park with kayaks and canoes propped up in rows next door to an Activity Centre, its windows dark. Then the common stretching out and there, mercifully, sitting just off the stretch of common, a houseboat painted in navy blue, its circular portholes and painted lettering as she remembered it from the photo she'd seen.

Searching for the key under the flowerpot on the starboard end (she checked both ends for flowerpots, starboard was the kind of stuff she needed to Google), she unzipped a plastic flap like the outside of a tent and manoeuvred herself, Marmite and her suitcase through it, then down two steps leading to a door to the boat. The key turned easily and she pushed the door open, leaving behind the sound of rain thrumming on the deck as she shut it behind her.

She turned a light switch on her left and bulbs in half-moon holders all lit up the space. The boat was extraordinary, warm and welcoming, and she felt her face lift at the sight. The floor, walls and ceiling were all made of wood, polished and smelling of beeswax, framed pictures lined the walls and a vase filled with Michaelmas daisies sat on the table that was attached to the wall. There was a bench, a stool, rugs on the floor, a small kitchen beyond, a woodstove in the corner on her left, a television on the wall, a row of bookshelves inlaid below it. She walked through, her footprints leaving watery marks on the floor as she explored. The kitchen moved into a bathroom with a shower, separate loo and sink, and then beyond to a bedroom lined with shelves and cupboards, a double bed made up with fresh linen, and another vase of flowers on the side table next to a lamp. She could then reach steps to the back of the boat, the tiller and controls clear through the glass door. Marmite moved through each room, sniffing and yapping in delight.

6.34 p.m. She had been on the boat for less than two hours. She had unpacked and changed into dry clothes. The day had darkened and the portholes showed nothing but black, rain dripping like tears down them, an insistent drumming overhead as if tiny pieces of metal were cascading from the sky. She had washed her hands in the teeny square of bathroom. She had made herself a cup of tea, the tink of the spoon in the sink startling her. She bit her lip, rubbed at her palm, crossed and uncrossed her legs. Maybe she would have another cup of tea.

6.38 p.m. She got up to fiddle with the small television stuck on the wall. It remained stubbornly blank and she gave up quite quickly, selecting a dog-eared copy of *200 Unusual Orchids* and curling up on the bench to flick through its pages.

6.46 p.m. She tapped her teeth with her fingers, yawned, stretched. This wasn't quite how she had envisaged her first night – alone on a hard bench reading a book on botany and counting the hairs on her forearm. (She'd got to thirty-six – did she need to start waxing her forearms? Was that a thing?)

6.52 p.m. Dinner!

She'd make dinner. Normally she couldn't face making dinner after a long day and especially on an upset stomach, but it would definitely eat up some time. She only knew about three recipes but inspiration would strike, she was sure of it; she just needed the time and inclination. She hopped off the bench, leaving a bookmark in the page of the Lady Slipper Orchid in case she lost her place and missed something really unusual in the orchid world.

6.57 p.m. Oh dear. Ingredients were sparse. Pasta, rice, a can of anchovies, a digestive biscuit packet, half-eaten and tied up with a rubber band, a pot of half-full Dolmio. Her heart sank as she filled up the kettle. This was it, Eve. Pasta for one. She stared again at the black outside. The rain persisted and she couldn't face a trip out. Anyway, she wouldn't know which way to go to find a shop and she was pretty sure nothing would be open at this time.

7.02 p.m.

What had she wanted from her first night? There would have been no rain. And there might have been more people. She thought perhaps she would have been welcomed on board by some bandana-wearing Johnny Depp type with a mysterious tattoo that would be about water spirits or such-like. He would lead her to his boat next door to introduce her to his river-going friends, they'd fire up a barbeque on deck, bundle up into layers, sit out on deck looking up at a clear expanse spattered with stars, point out the Plough to her. They'd tell her boat stories, about life on board. Maybe they'd toast marshmallows, the crispy outer layer, the melt-in-the-mouth middle, sickly sweet, soft and delicious.

Bloody pasta. Bloody rain. Bloody lack of bandana-wearing men.

7.32 p.m. Her first meal on board! It was okay. No prizes for best meal of the year but edible enough. She'd kept a couple of mouthfuls down and her stomach seemed to have stopped protesting.

7.37pm. Was that a bird? Her eyes darted to the porthole. Black nothing, drops of water clinging to the surface. Had she locked the boat behind her? It didn't seem enormously secure. Did people break into boats like they broke into houses? Was it a bird?

7.42 p.m. She needed to do something about Marmite. He was yapping and racing up and down. Was it a bird? Did he sense movement out there? He wasn't exactly a trained guard dog but dogs could sense danger.

7.46 p.m. He needed to pee. Eve had lifted Marmite up over the boat and he had darted across the common, towards houses, the comfort of windows glowing orange, in the distance.

'Come on, Marmite, come on, there's a good boy.'

Marmite twined around her legs. The rain had stopped and scampering amongst the wet long grass, he obviously assumed it was playtime. She let him race out over the grass, looking left and right for another human being. Nothing. The blank snake of river sat behind her, the boat gently rocking as she climbed back on board, Marmite squirming damp and disgusting in her arms.

7.58 p.m.

She would give Marmite a shower in the small bathtub. The water trickled out and she sat on the floor resting her head on the cool of the bathtub as Marmite wagged his tail and yapped in circles behind her, growling at the water emerging from the tap. Eve held out a hand to place it on his head. His fur was still damp and the whole boat seemed to smell now of wet Marmite.

'In you go.' Marmite was not an enormous fan of baths and this one was no different. She was soon entirely drenched in water, droplets spattered up the walls, the thin towel to step on now a limp rag smeared in muddy water. Marmite barked, a huge sound in the empty space, again and again. She wrestled him into her towel, rubbing him all over so his curls dried in soft clumps and she could carry him through to the little living room.

8.24 p.m.

She could go to sleep. Or read more about orchids. She could... she'd call Daisy! It had been five hours and she should ring to tell her she had arrived safely.

'I've arrived safely,' she announced when Daisy answered.

'You're in Pangbourne.'

'Yes.'

'Less than an hour from London.'

'Yes.'

'Well... good.'

'Whatcha doing?'

'Nothing much.'

Eve thought she heard a voice in the background.

'Is someone with you?'

There was a pause before Daisy answered, 'Just the television.'

'Oh. Well, how's the stomach?'

'Better now.'

'Okay, well, sorry I nearly killed us all,' Eve said.

'That's okay.'

'Well, I just wanted to check in.'

'That's nice, what are you doing on your first night?' Daisy still sounded distracted, as if she wasn't really listening.

'I'm just chilling, reading about orchids and stuff.'

'Er... really?'

'There's one in the actual shape of a naked man,' Eve said, glancing at the book again.

'No, there isn't,' Daisy said, now appearing to focus.

'Seriously, Google it.'

She heard her rustling around, imagined her tapping on her iPad.

'Oh my God, you're right.'

Eve started laughing. 'I know.'

'That is one weird plant.'

'Totally.'

'Well, I'd better go, Eve, I have work tomorrow. Good luck with your class.'

'Thanks.'

Eve clicked her phone off, frowning briefly, having that same feeling that Daisy was holding something back. She re-dialled.

'Are you all right?' Eve asked, quickly, urgently.

'I'm fine,' Daisy said. 'Well, you have food-poisoned me but otherwise I am fine.'

'Okay, you're sure?' Eve asked.

'I'm sure.'

'Good.'

'Okay, Eve, so are you planning to do the "you hang up, no you hang up" thing because I don't think I can take that tonight.'

'No, I won't. Okay, I am really going now,' Eve said, feeling better as she heard Daisy's light laugh. 'So I'm going on three. Okay?'

'Okay.'

'THREE.' Eve hung up, laughing out loud and making Marmite lift his head in a question.

Chapter 18

8.42 a.m. – one hour and eighteen minutes till the pottery class.

The boat was muggy, the windows steamed up, the mirror in the bathroom covered in condensation too so that she had to rub a hand across its surface to see herself. She padded around the kitchen in bare feet, wrapped in a dressing gown. Sunlight poured through the portholes, slicing the air, dust dancing in the room.

Marmite weaved around her ankles, sniffing at the sideboard, looking up at her with his chocolate eyes. Eve laughed as he scuttled over to the door, then back to her, tail high, moving excitedly left to right. He barked up at her, his message clear. If he could, he would have taken the lead down from the wall, placed it around his own neck and handed her the other end. If he could, he would have undone the door and disappeared outside.

'I'm coming, crazy dog.'

Marmite barked a single response, impatient to be released from the hothouse, the kettle bubbling as she stepped across to the counter and poured the water into a mug.

Opening the door, she walked up the steps, grabbed a deckchair propped in the little landing area, unzipped the plastic flap and ducked under it onto the decking. Marmite joined her and she gingerly dropped him down across the thin sliver of water onto the bank, then returned for her tea before joining him. Her feet were encased in plimsolls and she could feel the dewy grass seeping through the canvas after seconds. She unfolded the deckchair and lowered herself into it, wrapping the dressing gown tighter around her and resting the mug at her feet, enjoying this unseasonably warm day. Marmite was off, chasing a swan in the distance before grinding to a halt and scarpering back to the boat the moment the swan turned on him.

The common looked glorious with the early morning mist, the grass steaming with the rain from the day before, the river silver behind her, the water moving quickly, carrying sticks and bobbing ducks along for the ride. Thistles and patches of nettles draped themselves along the bank over the water, the trees bare, lined up along the other side like sentries. The sky was opaque, streaks of hazy lilac running across the tops of the fields in the distance. The tea slipped down her throat, her ankles getting cold until she lifted them up, curling into the deckchair. She felt a momentary sense of absolute calm. This was it; this was the type of moment she had thought about as she had planned this trip. And later she would be attending her first pottery class. She glowed at the thought.

Finishing her tea, she stood, bounding over to Marmite, her dressing gown opening, her pyjamas exposed to pick up a stick and throw it for him. Marmite responded as he always did, sinking low to the ground, his breath held for the exciting moment when she would release the stick into the air and he would chase it, trotting back, nose in the air to return it proudly. Her hair was coming loose and she was racing across the common laughing. She felt free of all her worries, watching the stick twirl and plummet as if she was releasing all her pent-up anger.

Returning to the boat, breathless and rosy-cheeked, she fetched her phone. She had just over forty minutes before her pottery lesson; she smiled at the thought. She would have to leave pretty quickly to find the house, which was nestled behind the trees somewhere on the other side of the river. First, though, she would send a selfie to Daisy; she would take it on the deck, as captain of her ship.

Perhaps if she hadn't been rushing it wouldn't have happened. Or if she hadn't been leaning quite so far over the water trying to get the best shot. Or if she hadn't jumped when Marmite had started barking. She'd felt herself go before she started to fall, head first over the side, tumbling past the small line of rope that marked the edge of the boat, down into the river that was so cold she felt she had plunged straight into molten ice, her ears stinging, her mouth flapping open as she emerged gasping from the water, hair sticking to her forehead, her phone still in her grip. She kicked herself to the side, the dressing gown weighted down, the cord floating on the surface as if it were a tail. She threw her phone out and Marmite, deciding it was the next stick, gaily leapt on it, thinking this was all a game as he went to hand it back to her.

'Stupid dog, no.'

She struggled up onto the bank, shivering and filthy, and then shouted expletives as Marmite took off with the phone in his grip.

Racing after him, calling his name and most of the swear words, her skin entirely covered in goosebumps and already turning blue, it was moments before she realised he had stopped and was staring at something behind her. Turning in slow motion, hair plastered to her face, dressing gown and pyjamas soaked with brown river water, she took in the sight

100

of a man dressed in wellies, beige cords and a duffel coat, grinning unashamedly as he took in the state of her.

'An early morning dip?'

Marmite hadn't given up and she felt a momentary sense of smug as he stood before the man, dropping her phone to bark noisily up at him. The man was laughing now, hands held up in surrender.

'Your dog doesn't like me.'

Eve had wrapped her dressing gown around her, aware her whole body was arctic, and wiped at the hair on her forehead.

'I was...' She trailed away, knowing there was no good answer for why she had been floundering in the river.

'You look frozen,' the man said, stepping towards her until Marmite started growling and he stepped back again. 'Can I help?'

He wasn't laughing at her any more and she was bloomin' freezing, although the heat in her cheeks was fast warming her face up. She knew she looked absurd and she was painfully aware she had to get ready for her class. Her teeth had started to clash together from cold. The sun had disappeared behind a cloud and she rubbed at her arms, her skin numb with the shock from the water.

'Have you got any rice?' the man asked and Eve frowned at the conversational tangent.

'Your phone, you see...' He pointed to it, the blank screen facing up. 'It can fix it.'

She should have said no. She should have told him she was fine, but she felt so pathetically sorry for herself all of a sudden and he did seem to know about rice, so she found herself nodding.

Then, aware of her soaked clothes and the fact they were probably see-through by now, she walked as quickly as she could back towards the boat, aware of him trailing after her. Why had she invited him back to help? She just wanted to hide in a hole and forget the last five minutes had ever happened. She did need her phone, though, and he had a pleasant face, a small cleft in his chin, blue-grey eyes and thick dark-brown hair. He was also wearing a duffel coat like Paddington's and, frankly, no one could look threatening in a duffel coat.

'I'll put the kettle on and you er...' It was his turn to fade away as he waved a hand over her standing in the living room dripping water onto the woven rug.

It made her feel a teensy bit easier about it that he seemed reasonably at a loss too.

'Thanks, won't be long.'

She squeezed past him in the galley kitchen, not able to meet his eye as he pressed the kettle on. She disappeared into her bedroom, feeling soggy and disgusting, listening to him opening up cupboard doors as she peeled away her dressing gown and pyjamas and removed her soaked pants, heaping them all into a pile on the laminate floor, water already leaking out of them as she dived into a fresh towel, desperate for a shower but far too aware of the very thin wall between the kitchen and the bathroom.

When she returned, much warmer in a thick jumper, he was sitting on the bench looking at the orchid book, two mugs of tea in front of him and even a plate with two digestive biscuits on it. It was with a sort of slow-mo horror that she realised she had bookmarked the page with the naked man orchid. *Do not turn to that page,* she pleaded in her brain.

'A very unusual orchid,' she said, looking over his shoulder, relieved to see he was looking at the one in the shape of a duck.

'I didn't know how you took your tea but I added milk out of habit. I can start again.'

He seemed enormous in this tiny space, his long legs folded under the thin Formica table that could be folded up and hooked onto the wall. He had taken off his coat and was wearing a navy-blue sweater with a logo she hadn't seen before. Before she could ask, she noticed Marmite happily curled up at his feet. He shrugged as she saw her stare. 'He's come round.'

'I see,' she said, perching herself on the stool on the other side of the living room, aware that she didn't have long and this man seemed to have made himself well at home, while she had to find out where she was headed for her class, and she wanted to shower before she went there. All these thoughts were swirling around her mind and it was a moment before she realised he was talking to her.

'... Your boat?' he asked, looking around him and taking a sip of his tea.

'No, I'm renting it for a few weeks.' She slapped the back of her neck, feeling something crawling there. Didn't people catch diseases from the river? Hadn't that been a problem for David Walliams?

'Can you get diseases from the river?' she found herself asking into the space.

The man sipped his tea again. 'Unlikely to. Unless you are planning to make a habit of it.'

'I'm not.'

'No, I didn't think so. Unusual swimming get-up.'

'I wasn't...'

He put up a hand. 'No need to explain. I often see interesting things on my walks, although so far you have been this week's highlight.'

'This week's?'

'Last week I saw two swans mating. Noisy.'

103

'Oh.'

It was only then that she noticed he had poured rice into a bowl and her phone was sitting in it on the counter behind him.

'Does that really work?' she said, getting up to peer at it.

'Apparently so. You'll have to see. Right...' He scooted up off the bench and took a last sip of his drink. 'I think I'd better go. You seem drier and I have made real headway with your dog, so best to leave on a high.'

'Marmite.'

'Sorry?'

'His name... it's Marmite.'

'Oh, very good. Well.' He bent down and stroked Marmite between the ears. 'I'll be off.' He looked back at her as he stood up. 'I hope your phone does come back to life and I hope you don't contract anything horrible from the river.'

He had picked up his coat and was now through the door, ducking through the flap to the outside.

'Well, thank you,' Eve said, feeling wrong-footed and silly as he nodded and disappeared out onto the common.

The clock told her she had less than twenty minutes to be at her pottery class. She couldn't phone ahead to say she was going to be late and she couldn't very well not appear. She had come all this way to do the course and do it she would. Loading up Marmite's bowl with food, she swept through to the bathroom, standing hunched in the bath as she turned on the shower, staring at herself in the circle of mirror over the sink, a leaf in her hair, eyes smudged with eyeliner, hair straggly, dripping down onto her top. No wonder he had escaped after five minutes. She felt relief as the water cascaded down her body.

She hastily dressed, then squeezed water out of her hair and scraped it back into a wet bun.

The clock told her she had less than ten minutes. Locking the door, leaving Marmite curled up in his fleece basket, she pounded across the common and over the iron bridge, past the toll booth and along a path to the right that she had been told led to the class, which was held in a house just overlooking the river. Her ears were cold as she placed both hands over them; she wished she'd had time to dry her hair.

She hadn't asked him anything; she could have discovered more about the village. She thought back to his kindly face; his blue-grey eyes had crinkled at the edges. He must have been around the same age, perhaps a little older. He seemed tanned for this time of year. She wondered whether he was local or just passing through. He had seemed friendly enough. Then she reminded herself she was here to learn a skill and to be alone, and anyway, she didn't even know his name.

Chapter 19

9.12 a.m. – forty-eight minutes till Greg needed to leave for the game.

He was heading home to get changed into his kit, they were playing at home this morning and the drive wasn't far. He was trying to remember where he had left his Astro turf boots when he noticed the woman on the common. For a second he thought she must have been released from an institution, running around in pyjamas, her dressing gown flapping, trainers on her feet, one lace trailing. Who did one call in this situation with a crazy woman running around dew-soaked grass in her nightwear? He paused and watched as she bent over, her short hair falling around to obscure her face. She picked up a stick from the ground and flung it for a dog. It looked like a terrier, maybe some kind of cross, grey curly hair, tail wagging as the stick looped over his head and he spun to fetch it.

He had spent so long looking at the dog he hadn't noticed the woman was actually really pretty, as she stood, her dark hair rich in the morning sunlight, grinning after the dog. Her cheeks were pink with running and she seemed almost sane from this distance, normal but for the pyjamas. He walked nearer as she continued to chase the dog, her laugh reverberating around the common, aware suddenly that he was intruding.

She started walking across the common to a houseboat moored up by the square platform on the common. The pyjamas made sense and he felt a rush of relief that she wasn't mad at all. He found himself smiling then, watching the dog trot after her. The early morning mist still clung to the top of the water, refusing to budge from the surface. He stayed for a moment more and then checked his watch, back to wondering where his Astro boots were and reckoning he had time to grab a coffee on the way.

Then there was a splash and a gargled scream of surprise and he craned his neck in the direction of the noise. He had been sure that it had come from the boat but perhaps he was imagining things. Then, covered in turgid water, a dripping dressing gown that stuck to her legs, hair now plastered to her face in loose strands, stood the stick-thrower. Before he could make his escape, the dog, carrying something in his mouth, was running straight for him and the woman was shouting after him and in hot pursuit. Then they were both there, panting. The dog had dropped the thing in his mouth – a phone – and she was standing before him, all her clothes sticking to her. Greg panicked, which is why a bubble of laughter spilled out of him.

'Early morning dip?'

God, Greg, make her feel worse, why don't you?

The dog started barking in short, sharp bursts and Greg's laugh stopped as abruptly as it began. He wanted to reach down and pat him but the woman was staring suspiciously. Dogs usually liked him, unless he was intending to castrate them, then they seemed to have a sixth sense he was the enemy. He could normally calm them, though. But he didn't recognise this dog, hadn't seen it in the practice.

'Your dog doesn't like me.'

He sounded defensive, he knew he did. *Greg, stop talking to her and leave.* The woman had wiped some of her hair back from her face. Her skin was smooth and she had wide eyes, an extraordinary colour, a mix of greens and yellows. He was trying not to stare at her too hard, her outline clearly visible through the thin layers. Then he realised she was shivering and stepped forward. 'You look frozen. Can I help?'

The woman put a hand up and he noticed her arms were covered in goosebumps. He wanted to help her, make her feel better.

'Have you got any rice?'

She looked startled, a line forming between her eyes.

'Your phone you see, it can fix it.'

Rice, Greg? Leave the woman alone; she is clearly not interested in your help. She has just fallen in a river. Would you want to talk to someone about rice five seconds after you had fallen in a river?

He found her nodding, though, and felt strangely happy that he caused it. Then she turned round and headed for the boat, her soggy clothes sticking in patches to her. She had this energy about her when she walked, bouncing on her heels, and he found himself two-stepping unevenly to keep up. As she stepped onto the deck, he felt a curiosity steal over him.

The boat was more spacious than he had first thought. Everything had its place. A wooden stool in the corner, a TV fixed to the wall, a folded chair hooked to the other wall to keep it out of the way, a bench with hinges that clearly doubled as a trunk, a rug on the floor in a faded design, a woodburning stove tucked into the corner, a low shelf of books running below the television, and then a galley kitchen and beyond to the rest of the boat. Small, square picture frames of pressed flowers were dotted around, in between the occasional circular portholes that showed the water and other side of the river, a sprig of lavender in the nearest.

He hadn't been on a houseboat before and he found himself ducking as he entered, hunching his shoulders as he stood there, feeling that if he stood up he would bang his head.

'Thanks, I won't be long.'

He shrugged off his coat and moved over to the kettle. Unable to find the coffee, he took down two teabags and poured water over them, uncertain as to whether she wanted milk or sugar. Most people liked milk in their tea at least, so turning to locate the fridge, he added milk to the mugs. He saw a pack of digestives and tipped two of them onto a small plate on the side.

The rice was next to the biscuits and he tipped most of it into a bowl, taking apart her phone and submerging the different pieces in it. Then he stood in the kitchen waiting, tapping his teeth with a finger. He could hear her moving around in the room beyond, although nothing was really separate – he could see the sink with her toothbrush resting on it, the toothpaste still open, it was strange. He stepped away, taking the mugs, not wanting to intrude.

On the small table next to the bench a book was left open and he picked it up idly, realising it was about flowers. She must really be into plant life. This was confirmed when she emerged once more in jeans and a thick olive jumper, her wet hair neatly combed back from her face, and peered over his shoulder.

'A very unusual orchid.'

He didn't know anything about orchids, or flowers, and the picture had slightly thrown him, so he pushed one of the mugs towards her, feeling idiotic and in her space. 'I didn't know how you took your tea but I added milk out of habit. I can start again.' Her dog had sneaked under the table and was now lying happily rested against his legs. The woman raised an eyebrow as she noticed and Greg shrugged quickly. 'He's come round.'

She took her tea and walked over to the stool on the other side of the room, sitting down and watching him. There was a moment's pause as they both drank their tea, the gentle tilt of the boat reminding them of the water beneath them.

'This is a cool place to live. Is this your boat?' he asked, looking around him and taking a sip of his tea. She looked like the kind of person who would rent a boat, the laidback clothes, the way she looked completely comfortable on the stool next to the stove. She seemed free of things, ready to hop up and disappear. He thought back to her running around the common after her dog.

'No, I'm renting it for a few weeks.' He wanted to ask more then. Where had she appeared from? Did she often rent boats? But she cut him off with her own question before he could ask.

'Can you get diseases from the river?'

Greg sipped his tea. 'Unlikely.' She looked a little worried, that line again between her eyes, her fingers rubbing against the other. 'Unless you are planning to make a habit of jumping in it.'

'I'm not.'

It burst out of her and made him smile.

'No, I didn't think so. Unusual swimming get-up.'

'I wasn't...'

He put up a hand. 'No need to explain. I often see interesting things on my walks but you have been this week's highlight.'

'This week's?'

'Last week I saw two swans mating. Noisy.'

110

'Oh.'

Two swans mating, Greg? He internally put his head in his hands. Why had he mentioned that? She was definitely looking at him warily now. Of course she was. She had got up from her stool, clearly wanted to move on, walking over to look at the bowl on the side.

'Does that really work?'

He cleared his throat, trying to move on from the mating swans comment and seem confident and in control. He didn't actually know if it worked; it was one of those things he'd heard. Danny had told him once, it was rice or an airing cupboard, and he wondered momentarily whether he should have made these wild promises.

'Apparently so, you'll have to see...'

Something about her unnerved him, and he found himself rushing, tripping over his words. *Leave, Greg, leave now.* He checked his watch; he actually did have to leave now. He'd be late for the warm-up, although he consoled himself that was no bad thing – he often played better just heading straight onto the pitch after a quick stretch.

'Right...' He stood up, feeling again too big for the space. 'I think I better go. You seem drier and I have made real headway with your dog, so best to leave on a high.'

He added a bark of laughter that didn't sound like his usual laugh at all.

'Marmite.'

'Sorry?'

'His name... it's Marmite.'

'Oh very good, well.' He bent to stroke Marmite between the ears. 'I'll be off. I hope your phone does come back to life and I hope you don't contract anything horrible from the river.'

111

He crossed the small room, opened the door and pulled back the sheet of plastic that reminded him of a tent entrance.

'Well, thank you.'

He nodded at her, worried now he had stayed too long. He stepped across onto the bank, careful not to trip and end up in the reeds too. There were a few people now on the common and he headed home through the park at the back, wondering whether she would still be there later or whether she would be further upstream chasing her dog around another patch of grass. He kicked himself for a second. Marmite was the dog's name but he couldn't believe he hadn't even asked hers. As he rushed home to change for the game, he briefly conjured up the image of her dripping dressing gown and startled eyes and laughed out loud into the empty room.

Chapter 20

THE HOUSE was at the top of a sloping lawn, a wooden gate with an arrow sign directing Eve off the river path as the website instructions had suggested. She walked slowly, her head moving left to right as she took in the gorgeous honey-coloured facade, the enormous mullioned windows, the wide stone terrace that was crammed with pots and smart wicker garden furniture. Ivy clambered up and around the windows and smoke rose from one of the four chimneys. It was an idyllic place, with a view of the river below from the many bedrooms. Eve cast about in the direction of the houseboat but the line of trees blocked out a great deal from where she stood. She imagined living in a house like this, her palms dampening as she skirted the house, moved up steps, past two stone pillars to pull on a large brass bell.

The sound was greeted by barking and she was grateful that she had left Marmite on the boat. He always went crazy around other dogs, jumping, yapping and generally showing up how little control she had of him.

'Coming,' a female voice hollered. 'Down, boy, stop it now, Sandy, down.'

Eve felt marginally better that the authoritative female voice was clearly struggling to control her dog too.

The latch slid across and the woman revealed herself,

standing at the entrance of an airy hall. White panels with bold pictures of flowers in a row made it seem as if it were the entrance to an art gallery. The woman was draped in a multi-coloured shawl, pearl earrings hanging like tear drops from her ears, hair twisted into a bun, strands of iron-grey hair escaping, blue eyes sparkling behind pink-framed glasses.

'You must be Eve,' she said, stepping towards Eve and startling her by enfolding her in the most enormous hug. She smelt of pancakes and lemon. Eve wiggled in her grasp, desperately aware of the damp tendrils of hair, the river still clinging to her.

The dog, a golden retriever, chose that moment to surge forward and for a second it seemed that Eve was encased in a massive hug: limbs, noses, arms everywhere. 'It's always wonderfully exciting to meet a newbie to the group. The others have all been on similar courses before but there are two new members this time, it is just so exhilarating.'

She released her and told her to follow behind, and they moved down the hallway and right into the most gorgeous living room painted rose pink, a tattered chaise longue next to the window seat, a Jackie Collins book face down. Through the living room, they moved into a conservatory, which overlooked the garden and was set up with eight potter's wheels. Various people in aprons moved around the room, filling up bowls with water, chatting in corners, looking at the shelves which lined the walls and were cluttered with half-finished egg cups, bowls, mugs and all sorts. The winter sunlight was weak and hazy, blocked by bare vines that criss-crossed above their heads. She caught a glimpse of silver river through the trees at the bottom of the sloping lawn. It was gorgeous. Eve felt her muscles relax; it would be great fun. She would sit in this incredible house and become an expert potter.

'Everyone, this is Eve, Eve, this is everyone.' The woman waved a hand, ten silver bracelets clattering down her forearm as she did so. 'The most important person, of course, is Raj — you absolutely must meet Raj.'

Did Eve imagine it or did the woman's blue eyes soften as she said his name?

A smooth-skinned man in a rolled-up white shirt, looking as if he had just stepped off a beach and wasn't sitting in a conservatory at the start of December, flashed her a smile; his teeth bright and even, his eyebrows perfectly manicured. Eve found herself stumbling over her hello.

'Raj is our potting maestro, our leader, our ceramic chief. He is very in-demand, hence he could only do this month this year.'

'No need to go overboard, Minnie, hey? Set up there, you'll need an apron and I'll sort you the rest. Have you ever made anything before?'

Eve shook her head, embarrassed to have temporarily lost the ability of speech, grateful to be thrust an apron by Minnie, who was throwing one over her own head. 'Raj here is a magician. He taught me and my school reports clearly stated I was unteachable. Unteachable. And yet Raj here manages to break through.'

'Sounds good,' Eve said, sitting in front of a wheel.

Raj appeared in front of her, holding a lump of clay in both hands.

'So, Eve, there isn't much to it. You can just follow my lead today and see how you get o—'

He was distracted by the arrival of a couple shyly holding hands in the doorway, the drawing room behind them framing them in rose pink.

'It's the lovebirds.' Minnie clapped, springing out of her

seat before her bottom had touched down. 'Aisha, Mark, this is Eve, she's new, be nice.'

Aisha and Mark stepped into the room, holding hands, small half-smiles on their faces as they said hello. They looked strangely similar, the girl with raven-black hair in a long plait, the man with dark curls and a wide, easy smile, a gap between his two front teeth.

Minnie turned to Eve to explain. 'They're getting married next July. They're making all their wedding guests a little something, isn't that amazing?'

Eve didn't react to the question, too busy replaying the previous sentence. July. Next July. Liam and she had planned to marry in July next year. That was just over six months away. A summer wedding. Clear blue skies, flowerbeds bursting into colour, the sun high overhead, their guests sipping Pimms, eyes hidden by sunglasses. She had scoured the internet looking for the perfect venue. Now there would be no wedding for them in July; she'd be alone in July. She blinked, realising she was still sitting at her potter's wheel staring at the couple, Minnie frowning at her vacant expression.

'Are you Pisces?' Minnie asked.

'Sorry?'

'Pisces, they are dreamers, you seem to be a dreamer. Not to worry,' Minnie continued, holding up a finger and pointing it at her own chest: 'I'm Cancer, us water signs are all the same really, rivers run deep and all that.' She looked over at Eve curiously. 'Are you all right? You look as if you've had a bit of a scare.'

'I'm fine, fine, sorry, just thinking about something else.' Eve busied herself with her apron, retying the back in a bow, trying to focus on Raj who was now sitting at his own wheel two rows in front of her, facing towards the class, his brown

116

hands glistening with water, holding firmly onto a lump of clay.

'Right, everyone,' he said once they had settled and Minnie had double air-kissed another new arrival, a woman with tight brown curls and an ancient lined face, as if you could count how many years she had been around by counting the different lines. She bustled over next to another lady with a dark-grey bob, who took her lilac handbag off the potter's wheel seat next door now that her friend had arrived.

'So welcome to a new set of classes gearing up for Christmas. I know some of you are regulars...' Raj really did have the most melt-in-the-mouth voice, Eve thought, his voice suitable for a night-time chat show on the radio, '... but we have some new recruits to this class so do all welcome Eve.' He pointed a hand towards Eve. 'And Danny...' A man next door to her raised a hand grinning, foppish blonde hair falling into one eye, a thinner Boris Johnson.

'Some of you will be continuing with where you left off but for those of you who want to start something from scratch, just follow my lead.'

He got up and walked over to stand between her and Danny. Eve stared up at him from the wheel.

'Eve, Danny, welcome. Normally I would spend some time teaching you how to get the air out of the clay but, today, why don't you just dive in, get yourself excited about pottery.'

'Sounds good,' Danny said as Eve nodded.

'I've already got the air out of these,' he said, handing them both balls of clay. 'So you just need to slap them down in the centre of the wheel and follow me. All right?'

Eve nodded again, taking the cold, slippery ball of clay offered to her.

Danny grinned at her as he took his. 'Should be fun,' he

said, slapping his into the centre of the wheel with relish.

Eve felt a warmth spread through her as she replied, 'Damn right.' Grinning, she slapped it down too.

Raj was back at his wheel, dipping both his hands in the bowl of water on his left and pressing down on the pedal on his right. The wheel started rotating and he smiled over as Eve copied the action. 'Lots of water, there you go. Now you need a good steady pace,' he said, holding her gaze and making her foot slip momentarily from the pedal. She felt the water running through her fingers, the outside of the clay slippery to the touch. Raj added more water. 'You need to get it really wet,' he said. Eve noticed her breathing thicken. *Get a hold of yourself, girl, he's talking pottery not sex*. Still, as her hands held the clay firm and she continued to press on the pedal, she could feel the heat steal up from her neck to her cheeks, warming her face as she worked.

Everyone else seemed to be happily doing the same thing, apart from Mark and Aisha, who were both turning smaller lumps of clay, Aisha placing a finger on the top and watching as the clay spread out and away from her touch.

Minutes passed and, gradually, Eve's lump felt smoother and more rounded to the touch, the wheel spinning steadily, and she felt a momentary excitement that she was in the middle of making something all on her own.

'Right, now start to gently encourage the clay up, squeezing gently with both hands into the middle to make it taller... Keep throwing water on it, Danny, or it will dry out and stick.'

Eve pressed the clay evenly as she was told, watching it start to rise in her hands, an inch above them, thinner now so that, as heat prickled her face, she realised her clay was taking on a decidedly phallic shape. Danny was openly laughing next door and Eve found herself distracted, clay wobbling and slipping from the centre.

Raj was standing above her then and she thought she might die as he looked down at her clay that was now definitely in the shape of a penis.

'I, er... I think I pressed too hard.'

Danny was chortling as he continued to press on his clay, a tall, neat cyclinder rising out of the centre of his wheel.

'Not to worry,' Raj said, bending to take a look. 'It's meant to look like that, well sort of, it should have better girth.'

Danny lost it again and Eve bit her lip, darting her eyes over at him as he innocently pedalled away.

'Let's start again, shall we?' Raj said, picking up the clay from her wheel, scraping it into a ball and pressing it all together again. 'Try again and this time, keep it steady and don't press too hard.'

'Right.' She nodded, determined to make it work this time. She pressed down on the pedal again.

She lost track of time, working quietly to smooth and shape her cylinder. She wasn't sure how long he had been there but she looked up to see a face pressed up against the glass to her right, staring at her as she smiled at her clay. The surprise caused her foot to release, her clay to wobble precariously and her thumb to press into it, creating a wobbling juddering lump.

'Oh,' she exclaimed looking around to see if anyone else had noticed. There was no face now, but she was certain that she had seen someone. A weathered man, in a flat cap, nose pressed against the glass. She blinked and stared at her clay, straightening as Raj came to stand over her.

'All okay, Eve, that's not a bad start, here.' He encouraged her to press the pedal down and, wrapping his hands around hers, poured water on them. 'That's good, that's the right

119

pressure.' He helped her to get the piece back into a perfect symmetry. She desperately tried not to think about that scene in *Ghost*, expecting Raj at any moment to whip off his shirt and seat himself behind her, feeling her face flaming again as she tried to focus on what he was saying. *Eve, woman, get a grip on yourself.*

'That's better. Now, what we're going to do is draw it up carefully, just a little more. Good, that's good. Okay, I'm going to take my hands away now, are you ready?'

She tried not to look entirely deflated as he removed his hands and stood up again, Minnie calling over her shoulder, gaily poking her thumbs into her clay that still seemed to resemble a giant lump of nothing. 'Raj, darling, what have I done? Why does it still look like a terribly deformed cock?'

Danny made a sound next to her. Eve's eyes widened. Raj flashed his smile and turned away from her, his well-oiled voice wafting around the room like a balm. 'I'm sure it doesn't,' he soothed.

'It's like he has a dreadful disease...'

Eve was working well, the lump starting to smooth out so that it had started to resemble a pot. That was the plan, she thought, a pot for pens would be an excellent starting point. Everyone needed somewhere for their pens.

Then she felt something again, looked to her right: the face was back. This time she kept pumping the pedal but she found herself calling out to Minnie in front of her. 'Minnie, um... there's a man staring at us through the window.'

Minnie huffed, 'Not again,' instantly removing her foot from the pedal, to get up and march across to the side door. Flinging it open, she called in an imperious voice, 'Gerald, I have told you not to disrupt the class.' Then she closed the door with a second huff and marched back across the room, all jangling bracelets and exhales.

'Bloody husband.'

Eve turned to see Danny, one eyebrow raised, clearly as confused as she was. Was this normal? Why was Minnie's husband lurking outside the conservatory windows during the class? No one else had really reacted to this interruption, aside from Danny who shrugged his shoulders, blond hair falling in his eyes as he returned to his lump. She thought it was probably rude to ask but she was fired up with curiosity. Still, her lump of clay was looking so like an actual thing now from all the pressure she'd been applying that she didn't want to lose control of things and returned to focusing on her clay.

'Right now, Eve, Danny, you're ready to push down into it. Keep hold of the sides like this; take it slow and keep it steady.'

Eve enjoyed the gentle sound of the pedals, the splash of water and Minnie's insistent muttering that everything she tried turned out the same shape. The room was warm, the heat seeped in from a crackling open fire in the living room next door and became trapped by the canopy of vines that Eve had since learnt would be grapes in the summer.

Raj was helping the lovebirds with two napkin rings, Aisha resting her head on Mark's shoulder as she listened to him. Eve felt a sharp stab of pain in her stomach. She would have rested like that unconsciously for years, a dip on Liam's chest that seemed to fit her head perfectly, his aftershave tickling her nose as she breathed in.

It had been a great hour in the class; she had loved meeting Minnie, Danny and Raj and couldn't wait to come back but, as she waved goodbye, she felt an overwhelming loneliness. She left, skirting the house once more and down the path, the wind forcing her to wrap her arms around her body tightly, the sky awash with grey cloud, the early morning sunshine long gone.

She turned right along the river, traipsing past roots in the ground, skirting brambles and patches of rainwater and churned-up mud, picturing how it had been with Liam, her draped over him in wordless bliss and him making a ball of his jacket, sticking a pillow under her head for her to rest on, a light kiss on her forehead. How could he have kissed her like that, with all that sweet affection, and do what he did to her? How could he have talked to her in his low-level voice, all the while knowing he had spoken to another woman in the same way?

By the time she had reached the boat and Marmite's wagging tail greeting her at the door, she felt filled with tears. Scooping him up and burying her face in his fur, she let herself cry for a moment in a hopeless, empty way. Marmite struggled, not happy with her returning mood and keen to get out and explore the surroundings once more. So with a weary 'I'm coming,' she deposited him on the bank, clambering over to watch him race around the grass, skipping and yapping at the air as if he didn't have a care in the world. She felt her mouth lift a fraction as she watched him, smiled as he growled at a nearby crowd of ducks and then, taking a breath, trying to recall her mood in that conservatory, she raced after him, feeling her feet slapping on the grass as he looked about him, barking gleefully at his playmate.

When they returned to the boat, it was clear there was a problem. Roaming up and down the bank like a sentry guard on duty was the largest, grubbiest goose Eve had ever seen. He had a filthy white belly, light-grey wings and dark markings up his neck. His beady eyes swivelled in his head as they approached. Marmite started to bark, racing forward, then thinking better of it, pausing, legs astride, his fur on end. The goose lifted both wings and hissed in their direction, his bright-orange beak letting out a terrible noise. Eve started, unused to geese anyway but definitely unsure how to react to one intent on being this unfriendly.

He seemed hell-bent on stopping them getting up onto the boat and each time they moved closer, hissed another time. It was a stand-off, a strange confrontation, and Marmite looked up at her as if asking her what they should do. She found herself shrugging helplessly at him. She was as clueless as he was. She tried shooing, she tried darting in another direction, but the beady-eyed goose simply stood his ground, following them all the time in his gaze, heckles up the moment they neared.

She felt as if an hour had passed when, with no warning, the goose set off in a half waddle, half soar, away from them and down the common.

'Quick!' Eve shouted, fumbling with the key, racing to the plastic flap and nearly smashing her shins as she stepped into the boat. She turned to lift up Marmite, who looked terrified to be left alone with the impending return of the goose. Allowing himself to be bundled into her arms, as her cold fingers searched for the lock, Marmite yapped at the common and Eve noticed with alarm that the goose was stalking BACK TOWARDS THEM with what she could only assume was a determined glint in his eye. She dropped the key.

'Shit,' she said, feeling her voice rise in panic. 'Guard the boat, Marmite, guard it.' Marmite was now running along the wooden deck away from the goose, under no illusions who was the tougher character and not planning to guard anything.

123

With the key back in her grip, she opened the door. The goose was gaining on them, wings raised, wingspan intimidatingly wide, mouth open.

'Marmite,' Eve said desperately, hoping he could do something to deter their unwelcome visitor. But the moment there was a gap in the door, Marmite had raced back and dived on it, straight in, scurrying down the steps to the safety of inside. He wasn't hanging about to take on a deadly goose. Eve quickly followed him, shutting the door behind her, leaving the goose outside their boat, mouth open, the sound of his hissing only just muffled as she turned the key in the lock with a decisive twist.

Chapter 21

Boxing Day Polish Salad

4 tablespoons mayonnaise
salt and pepper
1 teaspoon caster sugar
2 trimmed leeks

2 apples (Cox or
   Braeburn best)
Optional: small handful
   of walnuts and a few
   chopped dates

Method:

- Mix the mayonnaise with seasonings. Add very
  finely chopped leeks and apple. Combine and
  leave in fridge till required. Best eaten on
  same day as made.

'IS THIS absurd little experiment over now?' On Skype, her mother peered down the lens at her; Eve could see every pore on her face.

'Mum, you're quite close to the lens.'

'I was going for threatening.'

'Well, you nailed it,' Eve said, taking a sip of her tea and leaning back a little more. 'Where's Dad?'

'Not sure. I last saw him at breakfast wearing a purple turtleneck and white jeans. He looked dreadful, like a pornographic sailor on leave, so I refused to let him sit down at the table and he took his breakfast into the living room.'

'That's not very nice.'

'It's the only way he'll learn.'

'Mum, you've been married nearly forty years, shouldn't you just admit defeat on this one?'

'Some of us believe in fighting on,' she said pointedly, glaring down the lens again so that Eve hit the back of her head on the ledge of the porthole.

'Ow.' She rubbed at the patch. 'So,' she started, determined to get Mum back onto happier topics, 'I started my pottery classes yesterday.'

Mum tried to look disinterested, brushing an imaginary speck off her crisp white collar. 'Oh, right.'

'I really enjoyed it, Mum, I met some really nice people.'

'Well, that is good,' she admitted begrudgingly. Normally she would be firing questions Eve's way. Who had she met? Were they related to anyone the family knew? Were they interesting? Did they have all their teeth? Eve smiled at her mum's tight lips, pressed together firmly to ensure no stray questions sneaked out.

'The woman who owns the house, Minnie, I think you'd like her.' Eve wafted this nugget in front of her.

Her mum looked ready to burst, eyebrows raised, nothing escaping her lips.

'The house is spectacular, overlooking the river on the way to Purley.'

Her mum couldn't take it any more. 'That was where the Lewises moved to. Do you remember the Lewises? Girl about your age? Always had very severe haircuts?' She clamped up again after that last sentence, but the damage had been done and she knew it. She capitulated, allowing Eve to tell her more about the class, the conservatory, the other people in it, the rose-pink living room, the ivy creeping up the house.

'Well, it all sounds lovely for a few days but, really, Eve,' she said, edging closer to the screen, her eyes enormous as she swivelled them towards the lens, 'you will be home for Christmas. This ridiculous jaunt is all very well and good, but you can't stay there for ever.'

'Mum,' Eve sighed, feeling a wave of despair; 'I told you, I don't want to be reminded of it all.'

'But he's not here any more. He's not even going to be around at Christmas, he...' Her mum stopped abruptly, a hand lingering on her throat as if it were about to cover her mouth. Eve felt a prickle of confusion. How would her mum know that?

'Have you heard from him?' Eve asked slowly and carefully, her voice steady, but desperate to reach into Skype and shake her mum's shoulders, shouting, 'TELL ME EVERYTHING.'

'Well, no, not exactly.'

'So what exactly?' Eve said slowly, determined not to let her mum squirm out of this one.

'He was in Millets,' she announced.

'So you saw him? Did you talk to him?'

'Well, it was hard not to really.'

'Mum... what did you say?'

'Well, he helped me, I had to say something...' Mum raised both hands, appealing to Eve.

'Helped you with what?'

'A cagoul. I was taking it back for your father because he'd bought it in hot pink and I told him I would rather die than walk in the rain with him in it...'

'And. Go on,' Eve said, eyebrows lifting.

'Well, I was swapping it at the counter and the man there

127

was being most difficult because, of course, your father, being a completely hopeless individual, hadn't thought to keep the receipt. Of course, the tags were still on and it was clearly never worn but the young man, whose attitude by the way I really didn't like, was being very sniffy about the whole thing and then Liam was there talking to him, very kind really, and he helped convince the young man to allow me to part-exchange it.'

'What was he doing there?'

'Doing? He was holding walking boots.'

'Walking boots. Liam doesn't like walking.'

'Well, he wasn't wearing them, he was holding them. I wasn't sure if he was planning to buy them.'

Eve wanted to know everything. When had Liam taken up walking? He always complained about walks, always needed a ball to keep him entertained, like a dog. Eve thought savagely. She had always wanted to go for long walks with him, take in scenic views and have deep chats. Had he taken up walking? Had he just been holding the boots for no reason?

'Was he with anyone?'

Her mum paused a fraction so Eve pushed her again. 'Mum?'

'Possibly, I wasn't sure. There was someone trying on a hat but she might not have been with him, I just thought I heard a laugh. It was odd actually because...'

Her mum trailed off. Eve was gripping the cushioned seat in one hand, feeling hot, her palm sweaty. She licked at her lips. 'What was odd?' she asked, jumping on the sentence.

'Odd?'

'You said it was odd.'

'Did I?'

Her mum wasn't looking at the lens any more, and Eve

128

thought she could make out two spots of colour high on her mum's cheeks, a sure sign she was lying, or had drunk more than two glasses of wine.

'I suppose...' her mum said carefully, 'I thought it was odd... seeing him there... in Millets, and he still looked the same, as if he hadn't done anything terrible.'

'I wish you hadn't spoken to him,' Eve said in a voice she knew was a throwback to her teenage years; unreasonable and whiny.

'Well, I couldn't really avoid it, Millets isn't a big place and I really was rather grateful for the help with the cagoul.'

'What did you talk about?'

'Nothing. I went to show him the cagoul I had found, a lovely one in navy blue – your father doesn't know the difference, of course, but it is a lovely looking coat – and he had left.'

'Just like that.'

'Yes – poof! – gone.'

'Poof! – gone,' Eve repeated, feeling her breakfast churning in her stomach, rising in her throat. Why did any mention of him cause this reaction? Why couldn't she hear about him buying boots without it torturing her? Why couldn't she just shrug these things off? Here she was, in the middle of nowhere, getting on with things, staying busy, signing up for classes, meeting new people, and he was there, always, lurking on the edges of her vision, his sandy hair and his amber eyes, his distinctive laugh that had always tugged her own mouth into a smile.

She didn't remember saying goodbye to her mum, had tried to read more about orchids but even the ones that looked like dancing girls failed to rouse her interest. Marmite had nudged her tentatively and she had taken him outside, watched him chase a butterfly, watched him chase his tail. That had always made Liam laugh; he had loved Marmite. She felt a flicker of satisfaction; at least she had Marmite. He might be off walking with new boots but she had the dog that he had so loved. She had that at least.

She put away the laptop and looked around the boat, feeling restless and irritable. This month away wasn't focused entirely on not being reminded of her old life. Now that she was here she was determined to learn a new skill, make friends, remember how to function without checking with someone else. She wanted to regain some confidence, remember how to be herself.

Pulling down the recipe book she had noticed the night before, she thumbed through it. Liam had always told her that cooking was a way of him switching off after a long day. Perhaps it would work for her. She idled through the pages, pausing to look at the glossy photographs and imagining herself being able to cook up what was inside. With a renewed determination she threw on her coat, hat and scarf, popped the recipe book under one arm, Marmite on a lead, and, pausing to check for wildfowl, quickly left the boat.

The temperature had dropped again and the grass on the common was crispy with cold. She could see her breath in the air as she headed towards the centre of the village with a purposeful stride, sighing as Marmite nearly garrotted himself barking at a nearby squirrel, both relieved to see the goose had definitely departed.

'Come on, Marmite,' Eve said, pulling on his lead and not keen to take any chances.

Turning down a road towards the shop, she noticed fairy lights winking on Christmas trees in bay windows, fresh laurels on front doors. Up ahead a woman wrestled with six bags of shopping, her toddler holding a roll of wrapping paper, wielding it like a sword. The sky was thick with cloud and Eve could smell a bonfire somewhere in the distance. She hugged her coat around herself and tramped down the road, careful to avoid the puddles that overnight would turn to ice. As they emerged into the centre of the village, she saw a large Christmas tree had been erected outside the pub, the tables pushed back to make room for it. Silver fairy lights in the shape of icicles were strung up over the road at intervals and Eve felt a spark of excitement, before remembering. She scowled at the tinsel lining the windows of the shop, the fake snow sprayed into the edges.

Tying up a bemused Marmite outside, she grimaced at him, patting his head. 'Won't be long, boy.' She tried to block out his pathetic whining as she scuttled inside. She would be lightning fast, she thought, seizing a basket and heading down the first aisle, following the recipe book.

'Eve,' boomed a voice as she was holding up a bag of pine nuts. Were they made of gold? Why were they so expensive?

It was Minnie, wearing a large fur coat and a pair of sunglasses. She looked extraordinary in the small village shop, surrounded by ketchup bottles and cans of tuna.

'You look like you are planning a dinner party,' Minnie said admiringly, taking in Eve's overflowing basket.

Eve didn't have the heart to say it was a meal for one and half-nodded, half-shook her head.

'Pine nuts, amazing, make any salad,' Minnie commented, noting the bag in Eve's hand.

'Oh, I know,' Eve said, trying to win back some cool and popping them on top of the other items.

'I'm here buying things for the class tomorrow. Raj just loves those dark chocolate ginger biscuits so I must keep him happy.'

'Of course,' Eve said, smiling.

'Well, I don't want to hold you up, lovely to see you here, though. You made such a good start today. I am so glad you've joined. See you tomorrow. Raj says he is going to show me how to do a completely different type of glaze. So marvellous.'

'Really marvellous,' Eve agreed, wondering if Minnie's accent was already rubbing off on her.

Her run-in with Minnie had given her a renewed confidence. She was cooking with pine nuts; she was following a recipe. Nothing needed defrosting. This would turn out fine. She would make sure she followed the instructions to the letter.

Back in the boat she laid out all the ingredients on the sides; surrounded by food in the tiny square of kitchen, she filled up the kettle and lit the hob. She wedged the recipe book open behind the taps, the glossy image of the final product making her mouth water. She started putting things on to fry. The recipe was long but she could keep up. She was enjoying herself, it was working, she was focusing on the bubbling sauce and enjoying the smell of cooking chicken and she had only thought about Liam a couple of times, a few times, well hardly at all.

She was impressed with herself, using every pan she could find, grating, cutting, slicing, boiling. She was stirring and sniffing like an expert. Then, in the midst of it all, Marmite left the space between her legs where he had been lurking for any fallen pieces and ran to the porthole, legs apart, fur up, growling. Turning, she yelped as there, in the circle of window, was one beady eye belonging to a disgruntled goose. He was back! Marmite was racing up and down the living room now, yapping at both portholes as the goose disappeared from view from one only to reappear at the next, staring in at them. Eve rushed over and banged on the thick glass with a wooden spoon.

'Shoo,' she called ineffectually, running back over to the hob as she heard the sizzling sound of water on flame. Marmite was on high-alert, growling, jumping and running, and Eve was beating the windows with other pieces of cutlery. Then, just as she thought he had gone, the smoke alarm she hadn't even realised was there started sounding, filling the whole boat with its wailing. Marmite increased in volume and then, as if they were in a horror movie, the goose was now back and joined by a second goose. It was like the end of days.

The water started bubbling over and leaking down the stove and when Eve opened the oven door, a cloud of thick smoke and the smell of burning encompassed her. Why was the chicken a chargrilled mess? The recipe clearly said it was ready in twenty-five minutes and yet she hadn't reached that time at all. Her eyes stung from the smoke and she knew she had to open up the flaps of the boat to let some of it out, but the geese were out there waiting as if they knew and were biding their time. Marmite had now manoeuvred himself up onto the strip of Formica table and was barking straight at the porthole window, neck stuck out, mouth open.

There was so much smoke Eve couldn't see through the doors any more but could only assume the moment she opened them up, the boat would be invaded by wildfowl. With her heart hammering, her arms out in front of her to guide her towards the handle, she fiddled with the latch, opening up the plastic flaps and stumbling out into the shocking cold of the day, the mist on the common mingling with the cloud of smoke released, and she coughed and spluttered on the bank, looking all about her for menacing geese who were already probably inside and taking over her houseboat.

It was no wonder she started screaming in a piercing way as he approached her across the grass.

His eyes widened in alarm and he paused, clearly deciding whether to run away. She stopped screaming, licked her lips, coughed her last and straightened.

'Are you, is there a fire?' he asked, jogging towards her and taking in the scene.

'No, but geese and chicken and...' She knew she was babbling and she couldn't hide her relief at seeing another human being. He hadn't heard her, though, and was poking his head inside the boat searching for flames, stepping back with his arms full of Marmite, who started licking his face in gratitude.

'Where are the geese?' Eve asked, spinning round, searching everywhere. But the water was calm, the sky was a puff of white and the smoke had dispersed as if it had never been there.

'Geese?' the man asked uncertainly, looking at her as if she were unwell.

'There were...' She faded away, holding out her arms for Marmite, who was now over his rescue and wriggling furiously, clearly determined to be released. He set off over the common as she put him down.

'So you're sure you are all right,' he checked, readjusting his coat; it was a nice camel-coloured coat, now dusted with dog hair.

'I was cooking,' Eve said, the lingering smell of something burning in the air, the sound of the alarm still ringing across the empty evening.

'Were you?' he replied. Did his lips twitch then or was it her imagination? 'I might just...' He indicated the boat. 'If I may?'

She nodded hopelessly, calling to Marmite and scooping him back up and inside, then following in his wake. Marmite's fur was cold from the outside as she clutched him, watching the man reach up and remove the battery from the alarm. When the noise stopped, she felt a wave of relief wash over her, a persistent ringing in her ears like a ghost of the sound.

The boat was still full of smoke and the smell of burning hadn't subsided. The man put on an oven glove and opened the door again, another wave billowing out. He turned the dial another notch to the left and then pulled out some blackened pieces on a tray.

'Grill was on,' he coughed, wiping at his eyes.

'Oh,' Eve replied, mentally kicking herself. What an idiot.

'Was that what it was going to be?' he asked, indicating the propped-up book with its taunting photograph.

'Supposed to be,' Eve said, biting her lip and staring at the indistinguishable chargrilled chicken lumps on the tray.

'Well, it looks delicious,' he said. 'You are obviously a decent cook,' he added generously, overlooking the last five minutes.

'Er...' Eve hung her head, too humiliated to lie. 'It was an experiment. I thought if I could get this recipe right I could do it, but I don't have the first clue how to cook.'

'You did go for something very complicated,' he said in a reassuring tone and she was grateful, feeling herself relax a little in his presence.

'Was it?'

'Well, I am always wary when the title is in French. And you would have had to make the Sauce Velouté from scratch, which is definitely not a beginner's meal. I mean, who even knows what a Sauce Velouté is?'

She felt lighter as he went on, watching as he looped an

apron over his head.

'I don't know how to make anything, it always passed me by, you know?'

'Well...' He took in the rest of the ingredients on the side. 'We could make something from this,' he said, his voice filled with an enthusiasm that was new to her.

'Oh no, I'm sorry, I didn't mean to well, um...'

He had already rolled up his sleeves and was undoing the catch on the window above the cooker. 'Well, look, I have nowhere to be for a while, you have clearly gone to some trouble to buy these things, so I'll teach you how to make one simple dish.'

Eve looked at him sideways. His cheeks were flushed pink and he had the same expression Marmite wore when he knew there was a walk in the offing. 'What do you say?'

'But I couldn't...' Eve didn't know what to say. Suddenly the idea of being alone in her smoke-filled boat with geese stalking up and down outside and the world's most useless guard dog to protect her didn't seem like the best alternative. A smile crept over her face and she picked up the oven glove to show willing. 'That would be really kind. Thank you...'

She left a pause for his name and he added it, 'Greg,' holding out his hand as he did so, still dressed in her apron.

'Eve.'

Greg beamed and, walking her through it, handed her things to peel and chop as he discreetly threw the burnt remnants out and scrubbed at the dirty pans.

'This is a recipe for a salad my mum used to make every Boxing Day. Best with potatoes and cold meat. My brother Danny is pretty hopeless in the kitchen, but even he can make this, so now, Eve, I pass it on to you.' There was something in the way he said it that made her pause for a second, as if he were going to add something but had changed his mind. His eyes clouded over for a moment and she thought his mouth sagged down before he turned to her, clapping his hands and continuing his instructions.

'It's apple and leek salad, essentially. You can still make an ordinary salad, we'll do that too, but this is special.'

'Special?' Eve's eyebrows shot up.

'Very.' He laughed, raking a hand through his hair. 'Right, chop that,' he said and threw her an apple. 'Good catch,' he said.

Eve happily accepted his guidance and together they stood at the counter, chatting aimlessly and putting the meal together. She could feel the warmth from him on her right, his reassuring presence in her kitchen, taking up so much space but skirting round her, never making her feel crowded. He showed her how to make a simple dressing from the oil, mustard and other parts in the cupboard, shaking it all up in a cleaned-out jam jar. The new potatoes were boiling and it seemed like only seconds had passed before they were mixing all the items in a large bowl together, scattering nicely toasted pine nuts on the top and standing back to admire their handiwork.

With her concentrating on chopping, stirring and timings, she didn't have time to think very much, lost in the tasks. She realised as she stopped that she was really enjoying herself. Greg had shown her what to put in the apple and leek salad and she hadn't been able to burn it or ruin it and it looked delicious.

'You must stay,' she said, automatically fetching cutlery from the drawer.

'Oh no, I really shouldn't,' he said, looking at his watch, still wearing her apron.

'Do, absolutely, I insist,' Eve said, laying another place at the small table and dragging the stool over to it.

'Well, I can't be long, I have to be somewhere.'

'Very mysterious.' Eve laughed and then turned her back to him to get two plates, wondering whether his own laugh had been a few moments too delayed.

Chapter 22

'**W**HERE WERE you today?'

Danny looked up at him from above his pint. 'I told Andy I couldn't make it.'

'Yeah, he told me, but where were you?'

Danny looked awkward for a second in his chair. 'Busy,' he said, indicating to the barman to bring them two more beers.

Danny wasn't a busy kind of guy. Not when it came to sport, he was always there at any training, got Greg out in the shittest weather.

'Busy where...?'

This was unusual; Danny didn't normally skirt around things. Greg waited it out, knowing it was simply a matter of time. He leant his head to one side.

Danny sighed, realising there was no point avoiding it. 'I've started on a course.'

Greg shifted in his chair, enjoying watching his little brother redden. 'A course in what?'

Danny picked up the beer mat, shredding one corner in deft movements. 'I wanted to make stuff.'

'So... you're making?' Greg couldn't help smiling. This was news, his little brother, the mechanic, the lad about town, wanted to make things. He imagined it would be something oily to do with machines that Greg wouldn't have a hope of understanding.

'Pots and things.'

Greg nearly spat his beer on the table. 'Pots.'

Danny looked up. 'Ssh.'

'Pots.' Greg couldn't lower his voice if he tried. 'What, like pottery pots?'

Danny nodded miserably, ready for the inevitable axe to fall. Greg paused a moment, his lips twitching and then pursed his lips together. 'Cool.'

Danny looked up sharply, clearly still waiting for the piss-taking to begin.

'What?' Greg asked, finishing his beer. 'Sounds good.'

The barman deposited two more beers in front of them. Greg looked up. 'Thanks.'

Danny watched the barman leave and then leant forward as if he was worried the rest of the pub might hear. 'It is, actually, we're going to make a whole load of things in one month, and I'm pretty good, well...' He coughed, shredding more of the beer mat. 'I think I am all right.'

'Sounds interesting, mate, good for you.'

Danny sat taller in his seat, pushing his blonde fringe back with an oil-stained hand as he took the first swig of his new beer. Greg was impressed, not sure what had happened to his brother who normally only ever wanted to talk about cars and girls. Greg lumbered through any car chat, an owner of a Vauxhall Astra, so not qualified really, and was then left gaping at the girl talk. Danny knew a lot of women.

'What brought it on?' he asked, looking over at the corner of the room where the rattle of pounds meant someone had won on the cash machine.

'I just wanted to do something a bit different, you know,

can't keep thinking about things and not doing them.' It was the last sentence that prompted Danny to look away.

A slow realisation of why he'd suddenly decided to take up pottery crept over Greg and he felt a rush of affection for his little brother. 'Fair enough, mate. What about work?'

'I was owed a load of holiday so I'm taking mornings off this month. They've been good about it.'

'So, pottery. Looking forward to seeing what you produce.'

'Pool?' Danny suggested, clearly not wanting to linger too much more on the subject.

'Cool,' Greg said, searching through his pockets for a pound and letting his brother off the hook.

'Loser buys the next round,' Danny said, getting up, a confident look on his face.

This was a pointless statement really as Greg always paid for the round, he also always lost at pool to Danny; who could clear a table in one go.

'You're on,' Greg said, pushing back his chair with a scrape on the stone and nearly hitting his head on the heavy oak beam that ran through the middle of the ceiling.

They'd played for an hour and then Danny was off, out to take a girl to dinner. Greg couldn't get a name out of him. He waved as he left, round the corner and onto the high street. The common wasn't on his way home but he found himself weaving his way there, the street lights on and the village quiet in the darkness. He stuck his bare hands in the pockets of his coat, the cold seeping through the thick material.

He didn't need to walk towards the iron bridge, could join the common further up, but he found his legs taking him there, wondering if the boat would still be there, feeling a flicker of curiosity as he saw circles of yellow light in the distance. Then, maybe it was the four beers, he was sure he saw smoke belching out of the back of it, followed by the high whine of an alarm. He started ambling towards it. It was her boat; it was definitely the same boat. Then suddenly she was there, a silhouette really, hunched over herself on the bank, boot slippers at the end of bare legs.

Maybe it had been the beers that gave him the confidence to approach her. He regretted it the moment he saw her. Still bent down, her head whipped round, she took one look at him and started screaming.

Fair enough, Greg, you have just emerged from the shadows like you've been lurking outside her house and now you are making an unsteady beeline for her.

'Are you, is there a fire?' He realised he was running at her still, the beers making it harder to tell how fast.

'No, but geese and chicken and...' She was gabbling something at him and he was trying to concentrate on what she was saying. She was either pretty incoherent or he was more drunk than he thought. He swept past her and poked his head through into the boat, looking for a fire. It was then that Marmite launched himself up into his arms and started licking him as if he had rescued him from certain death.

Stepping back onto the bank, he looked worriedly at the girl, who was turning in a slow-circle, asking, 'Where are the geese?'

Maybe she was a little nuts. He noticed for the second time she was wearing pyjama shorts and top. He was often finding her in nightwear on the common.

'Geese?'

'There were...' She stopped quickly as she noticed him clutching her dog. He sheepishly handed him over, aware of his beer breath as he leant towards her.

'So you're sure you're all right?' He put up the collar of his coat and tried to hear her over the sound of the alarm.

'I was cooking.'

He couldn't help smiling. She seemed impossibly young in her pyjamas, goosebumps breaking out on her arms, her hair sticking out in different directions.

'Were you. I might just, if I may?'

He returned to the boat, stepping into it and finding the alarm on the ceiling. Pulling it back to reveal the square of battery, he let it dangle from two wires. The noise ceased and he turned to check the oven, opening it with an oven glove, coughing as he released more smoke into the room and into his face. He was holding the black remains of something on a tray and set it down on the side.

'Grill was on,' he said, trying to look at her but his eyes were streaming. Wiping at them, he noticed the open cookbook on the sink. 'Was that what it was going to be?'

'Supposed to be.'

'Well, it looks delicious.' The photo looked tasty, the ingredients long and complicated-looking. 'You are obviously a decent cook.'

'Er, it was an experiment. I thought if I could get this recipe right, I could do it, but I don't have the first clue how to cook.'

He heard the uncertainty in her voice and wanted to reassure. 'You did go for something really complicated.'

'Was it?' She looked up at him fully then and he took in her smile, her green eyes warm in the light.

'Well, I am always wary when the title is in French. And you would have had to make the Sauce Velouté from scratch, which is definitely not a beginner's meal. I mean, who even knows what a Sauce Velouté is?'

He suddenly felt the overwhelming urge to stay, shrugging off his coat, taking the apron off its hook and putting his head through it. He knew this was one area where he could help. He wasn't a man of many talents, but he had been taught to cook as a child by his mum and he had always loved it, experimenting with different recipes, buying stacks of cookbooks. He looked at the piles of food on the counter.

'We could make something from this.'

He barely heard her next word, running through what he could make as he rolled up his sleeves, too quick to realise she was protesting. Normally he would make his excuses and take the hint, but something stopped him; he wanted to try.

'I'll teach you how to make one simple dish. What do you say?'

She went to refuse and then he saw with a relenting smile that he had won. 'That would be really kind. Thank you...'

She raised both her eyebrows at the end of the sentence and he realised he had yet to introduce himself. 'Greg,' he added, feeling ridiculously formal as he held out a hand.

'Eve.'

It was a simple, elegant name and he felt himself smiling again as they shook hands.

He knew exactly what he was going to make and he talked her through what to peel, passing her things to chop and quietly scraping the ruined food into the bin before she could really notice. As he was scrubbing at a pan, he felt an overwhelming sense of familiarity as he talked, as if he was back in the kitchen at home but instead of learning the recipe he was passing it on.

'This was a recipe for a salad my mum used to make every Boxing Day. Best with potatoes and cold meat. My brother is pretty hopeless at cooking, but even he can make this now, so, Eve, I pass it on to you.'

Mum had always loved this recipe. He had a strange urge to tell her more about himself now, here in her kitchen, feeling like he had known her for a while when in fact he had only just learnt her name. She had that kind of face, a sort of child-like expression, easy smiles and wild hand gestures as she spoke. He turned his back and busied himself with turning on the gas oven and putting the potatoes on to boil. He rattled on. 'You can still make an ordinary salad, we'll do that too, but this is special.'

'Special,' she teased and Greg couldn't help but laugh, lobbing an apple at her as she grinned at him.

It was easy. Watching her amused him – she seemed to be enjoying learning and was just lacking confidence, clearly expecting the leeks to start burning, or to chop off a finger. He remembered his mum teaching him to cook after Dad left; it was something they'd done together. Greg had always liked making things. He'd been the science geek at school, while Danny had spent all his time in the drama department because he said that was where to meet the best girls. Greg had liked concocting things in the kitchen in the same way that he enjoyed the lab and, later, veterinary surgery. Now, as he was balancing and slicing, it seemed to him the same skills. He felt himself switch off, relaxed in the warmth of the little boat, making dinner.

He looked sideways at Eve, bent over some leeks, frowning as she ensured she chopped them into precise 1 cm slices. He nearly started teasing her again but found himself unable to, happy to smile as she turned to him with a triumphant grin and a curtsey.

'You must stay.'

She moved past him to get knives and forks; she smelt of apples.

He knew he had to go; he shouldn't have stayed this long, knew where he should be, back with her. 'Oh no, I really shouldn't.' He checked his watch.

'Do, absolutely, I insist.'

He heard himself reply without another thought, liking this life on the boat, his life out there somewhere behind the portholes, beyond the common. 'Well, I can't be long, I have to be somewhere.'

'Very mysterious,' she said.

He nearly told her, right then, wanting to share it all. The thought was gone as quick as it came and he laughed back, a little higher than normal.

Chapter 23

SHE WAS completing the pen pot today. It stood where she had left it and Raj was showing her how to slice it off the wheel using cheese wire. It was smooth around the edges and, as she balanced it on a wooden board, she felt an absurd rush of pleasure; her first potted item, ready to be fired in the kiln. It was smaller than she'd imagined it would end up, but she had scraped and pummelled and the clay hadn't quite worked in the way she had envisaged. Still it was a pot, it could hold stuff in it like pens and things. She pictured herself in her flat, surrounded by her pottery, offering guests a pen and being all 'this old thing' about it, nonchalant laugh, ha ha, I am soooo creative.

It wasn't relaxing starting a new piece, a bowl which she was told would be straightforward. She was hunched over the wheel, teeth biting down on her lip with every false turn, the watchful presence of Raj, quick to step in and help her. He was wearing a black T-shirt and faded blue jeans today, and Eve had tried not to stare at his forearms, which seemed large, probably from carrying lots of heavy pots around the place. Halfway through the class a cough came from the door and Minnie called out without looking up. 'Gerald, don't loiter there, come in and make yourself useful, we need more ginger biscuits.' And, moments later, Gerald had sidled in huffing, carrying a plate and lowering it with a clatter on the table.

He was wearing very tight-fitting trousers and Eve had been forced to look away as Gerald had stood in front of her, looking at Minnie's wheel and trying to engage her in conversation.

Minnie swatted a hand behind her. 'Thanks, darling.' And Gerald stood there looking lost.

'What's all that about, do you think?' whispered Eve to Danny, who was at the wheel next to her.

He shrugged, one hand pushing his blond fringe back, leaving traces of clay clinging to individual strands. 'Not sure, think he's a bit uneasy about...' Danny indicated towards the front of the class where Minnie was gazing up at Raj from her wheel, one hand on his arm as he helped fix her egg cup.

Eve nodded, giggling a little conspiratorially. 'I see.'

Minnie turned then, Gerald still standing there lost. 'Darling, could you get Raj a green tea, you know I told you he doesn't drink caffeine.' Gerald had turned, muttering to himself. Eve's new pot wobbled as she bit down on a laugh.

'I think he's worried about the competition,' Danny confirmed, waggling his eyebrows and setting her off again.

Sure enough, the week was spent with Gerald wandering into the lessons feigning interest and sometimes asking Minnie random questions under the clear guise of spying on Raj. Lowest points: 'Do you know where I put my secateurs?' and 'There is a squirrel on my car.' Danny had hidden under his wheel on that one, shaking with laughter, as Eve had got up pretending to go and hunt for more clay on the other side of the room. When the visits caused Minnie to banish him from lessons, Gerald could be spotted walking across the lawn peering in sideways, pruning trees that didn't need pruning and suddenly emerging from the dining room at the end of lessons, at one point making Eve jump and step straight back onto Danny's toes.

Eve loved the lessons, was sad not to have her phone so she could call her friends and tell them more, relying on emails to keep her in touch and make her laugh. She hadn't seen any more of Greg after that first night and, later in the week, she found herself walking into the village, hoping on the off-chance she would bump into him.

Too cold to wait around for long, she had sat on a bench next to the enormous Christmas tree with a hot chocolate, the air smelling of pine needles, her shopping bags around her feet, Marmite trying to steal her marshmallows when she wasn't looking. Various men walked by bundled inside winter wear but no sign of Greg. She had prattled on while they'd cooked and she hadn't thought to ask him more about himself. There were no sightings and, as she waved goodbye to her potter friends for the weekend, Marmite in tow this time, sad to be leaving Sandy who had already become his Best Dog Friend, she wondered idly what she would do on her first Friday night alone in a long while.

She thought she was seeing things as she picked her way across the common back to the boat. She was feeling a little lost without her mobile so perhaps her mind had conjured up friends? If it was an optical illusion it was a pretty brilliant one.

'Surprise!' the optical illusion called.

Eve stared at the two people standing towards the front of the boat. One dressed in a bright-blue duffel coat, fluffy hat with bobble on her head and a sheepish smile on her face, the other in a slate-grey cashmere coat and heeled boots, clutching a handbag to her chest as if a little unsure how to hold it.

'Dais', Ro-Ro,' Eve said, feeling her face break into the most enormous grin. She couldn't believe it. Marmite couldn't believe it either, spinning and yapping at their legs, jumping up on Ro-Ro's cashmere coat until Eve noticed her expression and rushed forward to sweep him away. She apologised all the way into the boat, suddenly aware of the smell of algae and wet dog.

'Sorry, gosh, wait...' Eve started patting the cushions, clearing half-empty mugs and her crumb-covered plate from breakfast into the sink.

Inside the tiny space there suddenly seemed no room to breathe, and as Eve raced about, putting the kettle on and showing them the bathroom and bedroom beyond, she felt a strange defensive feeling. She wished she had known; she might have put fresh flowers in a vase or been sitting waiting with a chilled bottle of wine. She wanted them to think this was all a wonderful idea but she could see Ro-Ro standing strangely suspended between the bathroom and kitchen, bag still clutched to her, looking around at the miniscule kitchen, taking in the drying underwear on a string in the shower, the damp shoes in a heap by the door, and almost tripping over Marmite's food bowl.

'It's so small.'

Daisy, however, had already browsed the small bookshelf underneath the television that Eve still didn't know how to turn on, had topped up the crackling remnants of the woodburning stove and had curled up with the orchid book on the bench.

'There's a flower in here called a Dracula simia that looks just like a monkey's face.'

'I know, the Orchis simia look like dancing monkeys. Cool, eh? Also, Dais', go to page 78. You *won't* believe it.'

Ro-Ro rolled her eyes. 'Christ, you two. Right, where is

the wine, and tell me why you have felt the need to abandon the real world, i.e. London, and come and live like a river rat.'

'Very to the point.'

Ro-Ro shrugged and held out her hand to accept the glass that Eve had found.

'I can see his penis!' Daisy had turned the orchid book on its side.

'I know, brilliant, isn't it?' Eve said, laughing at Daisy's face. 'An actual naked man. Nature is naughty.'

Ro-Ro relented, walking across to Daisy and snapping her fingers for the book, her face barely moving as she examined it. 'Not very well endowed.'

'Well, he is just a flower.' Eve shrugged, feeling sorry for her orchid. 'So are you staying the night?' Eve asked them, propping up a fold-up chair that hooked onto the wall and settling herself into it.

'I am.' Daisy nodded. 'If that's okay?' she checked.

'I can't stay,' Ro-Ro said in her booming voice, still standing, the top of her head nearly touching the ceiling of the boat. 'Anyway, there is absolutely no room, how does anyone live like this?' she asked in disbelief, holding out her arms to touch both sides of the boat. 'You basically have to be a hobbit.'

'I think it's cosy,' Daisy said quietly, eyes quickly returning to the orchid book.

'Cosy, I suppose. Daisy told me she was coming down here and I wanted to stop by.' Ro-Ro put her head to one side, which Eve knew to be her 'sympathetic pose', and pressed her lips together. 'I hear you are escaping down here over Christmas. Totally understandable.'

Eve felt a flush of surprise. This was pretty empathetic of Ro-Ro. It didn't last particularly long.

'Anyway, I'm heading home for more wedmin. I'm getting Hugo to pick me up at Didcot, his mother is meeting us at the house as she wants to see where the cake will be set up and my mother is completely dreading her being there as the house is a state, boxes everywhere, so I need to be there to act as go-between. Weddings are soooo stressful.' She mopped her brow in a cartoon gesture and Eve tried to look like she was nodding along, but she couldn't help being reminded of her own wedding plans. When Liam had asked her, Eve had been keen to tell Ro-Ro quickly; she was engaged too and Eve thought she might have advice. She'd talked about swapping mood boards and promised her they'd go wedding dress shopping together.

None of it had really panned out, Ro-Ro hadn't wanted to go to any of the sample sales Eve had earmarked, and then Liam and her had broken up and Ro-Ro had stopped ringing. Now she was walking up the aisle in less than two weeks and Eve was on a houseboat in the middle of nowhere with no man, no wedding and no mood board (Liam had taken his laptop; it was saved on there).

They sat and talked about Ro-Ro's wedding plans, listening in mystified awe as she discussed the arrangements. It all sounded suitably complicated and Eve said a quick prayer of thanks that she didn't have a role in it. Hugo's sisters were bridesmaids, Ro-Ro had made a big fuss about it, but in truth Daisy and Eve had drifted apart from her in recent years. Eve secretly thought there was no way Ro-Ro would have entrusted her with any responsibility even if they had still been close. Woe betide the bridesmaid that failed to march in front of the wedding party scattering flower petals.

They walked along the river, Ro-Ro sticking to the path, skirting puddles in her heeled boots, sighing as Daisy stopped to take another photograph.

'It's water,' she said, arms folded. 'God, what makes people move to the country? Literally NOTHING happens here.'

The village seemed almost comically quaint as Eve saw it through Ro-Ro's eyes, the row of pastel-coloured cottages leading to the ivy-covered railway bridge, fairy lights in their windows, icicle shapes stuck to the glass. The delicatessen painted cherry-red, a blackboard outside advertisintg artisan bread and freshly baked mince pies nestled next to the shop selling antique furniture, where china dolls in velvet clothing were propped on a rocking chair in the window.

'It's gorgeous,' Daisy enthused, her neck craned up taking in the lights draped across the road, the Christmas tree in the square beyond.

'It's no Oxford Street.' Ro-Ro sniffed.

They traipsed back to the boat, past another idling narrow boat and a man in a flat cap and tweed coat huddled on the bench feeding ducks that waddled around his feet. There were still just under two hours before Ro-Ro's train to Didcot.

Eve's stomach rumbled. 'Shall I er... make something?' Eve said uncertainly, opening a cupboard that she knew to be bare.

Daisy started to speak. 'There's no need to—' But she was soon cut off by the sound of Ro-Ro's laughter filling the whole boat. 'Cook, Eve, honey? No, I am not in the mood for a Pot Noodle and Daisy told me you nearly killed them all at a recent dinner party.'

Daisy protested quickly. 'Wait, I didn't say that! I... okay, fine, I did sort of say that.'

Eve bristled at the assumption that they both thought they were in mortal danger with her in the kitchen or that a Pot Noodle would be the fare on offer, and then realised, with a sinking heart, that they were both right. She couldn't remember ever cooking for them all, always relying on Liam, something from the freezer or a takeaway from one of the many restaurants around them in London.

'Anyway, I'm on the 5:2 diet and it is one of my starvation days.'

Eve wrinkled her nose. 'That sounds awful.'

'Awful,' Ro-Ro admitted, then patted her stomach, which seemed practically concave. 'But really effective. The wedding is in two weeks,' she sing-songed.

'Good point. Well, we can walk back into the village, grab something and drop you at your tr—'

There was a noise then, familiar, sinister. Eve looked nervously over her shoulder. 'Oh no,' she whispered, watching as the goose led his friend straight towards them.

'What?' Daisy asked, turning round to look in that direction.

Eve pointed a shaky hand towards the geese. 'They come here all the time. Marmite is scared of them,' she said, not wanting to admit she was bloomin' petrified of them too.

'What? Those geese?' Ro-Ro said, her grey eyes swivelling until she found them. Then she sucked in all her breath and stood up.

'Ro-Ro, don't!' Eve half-shouted rather dramatically, as if Ro-Ro was preparing herself to run outside and take a bullet for her.

Marmite was whimpering, utterly hopeless, between her legs. Daisy had curled herself into a ball on the bench, as if she expected them to march onto the boat and start snapping at her ankles.

Ro-Ro, however, had moved to the door. The geese were gaining pace, their eyes trained on the small group inside, their beaks moving into slow smiles (Eve imagined). Eve watched as Ro-Ro slid the lock across, pushed open the flapping door and stepped gingerly onto the deck of the boat, an imperious, Chanel-wearing boat captain. The geese wavered.

'Be gone!' Ro-Ro boomed in her most authoritative voice. She had been like that at school on the netball court, striding down the sidelines with her long-standing knee injury that had forced her to stop playing for the season, marching past their timid teacher Mrs Harris and directing them as if she were the Manchester United manager. 'Wing Attack, cover the corner, can't you see number 6?' 'Christ, team, keep an eye on that Centre, she's all over the place. Defence, stay on them, tight, don't give them an inch.' Mrs Harris had been breathing into her asthma inhaler as Ro-Ro had stalked over to take the team talks. Now here she was, as if directing traffic, pointing to the geese and sending them on their way.

'Be. Gone,' she repeated, slower now but with the same tone, adding a pointed finger to indicate where they should go to.

The ridiculous thing was, it worked. The geese stopped twenty feet from the boat, took one look at her long arm, painted talons shooing them away, pivoted and turned back, waddling quickly over the long grass and further along down the path up the river, with one resentful last look before diving through a patch of reeds and gliding away. Ro-Ro nodded, satisfied, and returned to her seat.

'Er... thanks,' Eve said, raising a mug at her.

Ro-Ro stepped back into the boat, turning the lock once more, and with a dismissive shrug added, 'It's how I stop Hugo trying to have sex with me.'

She didn't smile afterwards so Eve wasn't absolutely sure if she was joking. She couldn't help it, though: catching Daisy's eye, they both started to laugh, Eve snorting and covering her mouth, which only made Daisy worse.

'What?' Ro-Ro said, sitting down. 'It is... he is a very persistent lover.'

Daisy held her sides and Eve's eyes started watering as they both tried to stifle their giggles. Ro-Ro was still looking as if she'd missed the point.

Their mood only grew sillier and, by the time they had polished off both bottles of wine from the small fridge on the boat, deposited a slurring Ro-Ro onto her train with air kisses and promises to call before the Big Day, Eve had really cheered up. The boat adventure seemed to have really started here; what she was doing was terribly romantic and exciting. She should be patting herself on the back. She waved at the back of the train as it grew smaller, the tracks twisting and taking it out of sight.

Daisy put a hand on Eve's shoulder. 'Sorry, Eve, I tried to stop her coming, but she insisted, and you know what she's like when she insists.'

'Fucking terrifying.'

Daisy nodded. 'Fucking terrifying.'

'Why are we friends with her again?'

'Habit,' Daisy said, her voice low and sad.

'Oh, she wasn't that bad,' Eve said, throwing an arm round Daisy. 'But I'm glad you're staying the night. Can you stay more?' Eve knew she shouldn't really ask; she was meant to be branching out on her own, getting used to NOT relying on someone else.

'I've got work tomorrow,' Daisy said ruefully.

'Working Sundays sucks.'

Daisy sighed. 'It does.'

Something in the sagging of her shoulders and the weary look made Eve squeeze her closer. 'Come on.'

They stopped to buy fish and chips, starving now, before weaving back down the high street of Pangbourne, the

Christmas lights twinkling over their heads. They moved past the pub, clusters of people drinking steaming mulled wine next to the Christmas tree, under the railway bridge and along the narrow strip of pavement to the common, past the iron bridge, the lights from it shimmering in the water below, back to the boat. Opening up the bag, it seemed the whole space smelt of vinegar. Eve unravelled the chips, the newspaper soggy with oil.

'Amazing,' Eve said, dipping one in some ketchup.

Daisy, mouth too full to make a comment, nodded.

They weren't tired and there were no more sightings of any geese, so when Marmite whined to be taken out, Daisy and she grabbed two of the blankets from the inside of the bench and trailed them outside onto the small platform that stretched out into the water. It was cold, their breath forming clouds in the air, but it was a still, clear night and above them the stars were out and bright in the purpley darkness. They sat together beneath the blankets, glad to be snuggled into them as they gazed onto the black quiet of the river as it quietly moved past them. Marmite wriggled inside the blanket too and lay, his little body pulsing between them as they sat.

'Are you glad you did this?' Daisy asked, her head dipping to rest on Eve's shoulder.

'I am,' Eve said, and realised it was true. 'I think I needed to do something completely different, learn to be on my own again. Ridiculous, isn't it? Me, an ardent feminist, completely floored without my man.'

'It's not like that,' Daisy protested, straightening up again. 'You can cope, you just loved him,' she said simply.

'I did, I do, I suppose, gah, it's grim,' Eve admitted, putting a hand on Marmite's head and feeling his tongue licking her in sympathy.

'Well, you wouldn't have done this if you were still together,' said Daisy, obviously trying to remind Eve of the silver lining.

'Liam wouldn't like it here at all. Do you remember he had a thing about water? I think he nearly drowned as a child or something,' Eve said, clutching the blanket to her.

'His mum saved him,' Daisy added, stopping abruptly then, as if her remembering details from Liam's life made her somehow disloyal to Eve.

'Oh yes,' Eve said softly, recalling the story then. Eve missed his mum, his softly spoken mum who made enormous casseroles and was a member of about eighteen local committees. That was the awful thing about breaking up with someone. You didn't just lose them you lost the whole network that you'd fallen for, the mum you were able to chat with over a cup of tea, the dad that teased you like you were his own daughter, siblings who gossiped with you, told you funny stories about their brother, brought you immediately up to speed.

'God.' Eve put her head in her hands, feeling the familiar tears sting her eyes. 'I'm pathetic, Dais'.'

'No, you're not,' Daisy said, rubbing her back. 'You're going to be okay, you're brilliant,' she said, one arm round her shoulder.

Eve sniffed. 'I am kind of brilliant,' she said, a ghost of a smile on her face.

'Ace.'

'And pretty,' Eve added, now with a full beam. Then she stopped suddenly, the question she had asked for months still on the tip of her tongue.

'Do you think he still sees her? I can't stop wondering who she was, he wouldn't say...'

'Who was who?' Daisy asked, a frown in her voice.

'The girl, in the photograph, the, you know,' Eve said, not wanting to be reminded of that image but picturing it anyway. It was like being haunted by a really well-tended pubis.

'He told me it didn't matter who she was, but there was something about it. Dais'?'

Daisy didn't answer, just sat there, turned a fraction towards Eve, opening her mouth as if she were about to hazard a guess. Then the moment passed, her eyes slid from Eve's and she said in a too-bright voice, 'It wouldn't matter, I'm sure. Gosh, it must be late, shall we go to bed?'

Eve agreed, standing up and clutching her blanket to her. It was too dark to see Daisy's expression but Eve felt something niggling at her. She didn't know why. Daisy had never kept anything from her before, so why should she start now? They traipsed back to the boat, trailing their blankets, Marmite sleepily following behind them, before they fell asleep in the swaying boat, the stars still bright through the portholes in an inky sky.

Chapter 24

HE HAD always run along the river and he needed to keep fit for the last match before Christmas. They were middle of the league now, but they'd played some of the stronger sides so things were looking hopeful. He hadn't always run along the common. There was a shortcut that led to the recreation ground and park behind that he normally took, but it would be nice to run along the water's edge, the iron bridge was always worth a look since it had been repainted.

He was kidding no one as he neared her boat. He could feel his palms, damp already from the run, his heart racing. Would she think it was weird? He supposed she would; she had probably come here to get some peace and quiet and he was now pounding down the common towards her again. The portholes were dark and there seemed to be no signs of life. Still, it heartened him that she was still there. There was something comforting about the thought that she was still in the village.

He turned to go back along the road past the doctor's surgery, feeling his legs burn with the exercise, his muscles aching with effort. As he mounted the pavement and made his way under the railway bridge and into the village, he heard an excited barking in the distance. This wasn't unusual, as the local vet he tended to bump into his clients and their pets all the time. It was only at a second glance that he realised the barking was coming from a certain Morkie and on the end of the leash was a grinning Eve, who held up one hand in a wave, nearly choking Marmite in the process.

He stopped in front of her, aware of his red cheeks, his sweat-soaked T-shirt, wiping at his face with the back of his hand. It suddenly seemed very warm for December.

'You look very sporty,' she said with a laugh. She seemed more relaxed in this setting, wearing a woollen dress and knee boots, her face flushed from the cold.

'And you're not wearing pyjamas,' he replied.

'This is true! Although give me an hour. Do you want to come back with me – there's a Christmas market on all afternoon.'

She pointed a gloved hand behind him.

He tried to look surprised, as if he hadn't just jogged past it.

He did want to walk with her but he thought of the plans he'd made that afternoon; he needed to shower first.

'How about I meet you in a bit? I need a shower first, I'm pretty gross.'

He could call, move the plans; she would be used to it, he often had to race off for work anyway.

'Of course,' she said. 'I can drop Marmite back on the boat. I'm not sure he can be trusted at a Christmas market.'

Marmite whined as if he could understand.

'Brilliant, I won't be long.'

'Lovely.' She really was extraordinary-looking with her greenish eyes with flecks of yellow set off by dark-brown hair that seemed to glint in the sunshine. She had a Biro mark on the side of her face, which made him feel better.

'I'll see you in a few minutes then,' he said, smiling, hoping she wouldn't watch him jog off. Danny always said he ran like a twat – although Danny told him he looked like a twat most of the time.

Chapter 25

HE APPEARED quicker than she'd imagined, his hair ruffled by the wind, the ends still wet.

'That was fast,' she said.

'I live on the high street,' he told her. 'Here.' He handed her a pack of chocolate digestives. 'One up from your last lot,' he said, placing them on the counter.

'Thanks,' she said, feeling as if there was suddenly no room on the boat with him in it. She squeezed past him, her back curved into the wall to put the kettle down.

'Coffee before we go?'

'Sure.'

He had taken a moment to reply and he had that faraway expression again. It was like there were two Gregs, the one she had bumped into earlier and this more guarded guy. She sneaked a glance at him as she waited for the kettle to boil. He was looking at one of the pictures, reading the inscription underneath the dried flower. His mouth curved downward and when he met her gaze she had the sudden urge to reach a hand over to him; he looked impossibly sad.

'Are you interested in plants and things?' she said instead, indicating the picture.

'Oh no, I don't have a clue. It was just... well, it reminded me of something.'

She glanced at the sprig of lavender behind the square of glass, something in his voice telling her not to probe any further.

'So do you run a lot?' she asked, wondering why she suddenly felt the need to fill the silence. She always had this desire to fill a gap; Liam had told her it was infuriating. Why couldn't she be still?

'I just run to keep fit. I play hockey.'

'Very impressive,' she said, handing him a coffee. 'I was rubbish at hockey at school, more of a rounders player because that was basically an excuse to sunbathe.'

He had sat on the bench again, making room for another person, but Marmite had taken that as a green light and had jumped up first, his head resting on Greg's knee as he scratched behind his ears.

'He really has taken a shine,' Eve said, lifting the folded chair from the wall and finding the cushion for it.

'I'm a vet,' Greg said. 'He probably knows to keep me sweet.'

'A vet? Really?' Eve said, surprised perhaps and remembering then the logo on his sweatshirt when they met.

'What did you imagine?'

She paused for a moment, playfully putting one finger to her lips. 'Hmm, I suppose I thought... woodsman or carpenter.' *Eve, are you flirting?* The thought made her stop short.

'I don't have the beard for it.'

'So do you see lots of dogs then?'

'Lots.' Greg nodded, his hand around the coffee mug making it look miniscule.

'What is your best dog-related story?' Eve asked, again wondering at the playful tone in her voice.

Greg tipped his head to one side before answering slowly, 'There was one man who brought his puppy in for his first vaccinations. I thought it was odd because he brought it in a cat basket, must have been small. He said he'd bought it the night before in the pub.'

Eve enjoyed watching him tell the story, his slow smile spreading across his face, one hand resting on the table.

'He opened it up to show me and pulled out a black and tan guinea pig. I said, "I'm sorry, we don't vaccinate guinea pigs", and he just put it back in the basket, no reply, and left.'

'What, he really didn't know?'

Greg shrugged. 'I was never sure. Didn't see him again.'

'Odd,' Eve said, draining her coffee.

'How about you?' Greg asked, one hand stroking Marmite's body. Eve couldn't stop looking at his knuckles.

'Me?'

'Work stories, what do you do?'

'Oh,' Eve said, dragging herself back, surprised by this old familiar feeling, she hadn't felt it in years, 'I'm an estate agent, but I'm not allowed to tell you any stories about my job because you will explode with laughter, they are so funny.'

'Really?'

'No, really not. The funniest thing that happened in our office recently was that someone put the staplers in upside down so the stapler wouldn't work.'

'I can see how that might be amusing.'

'So, shall we go?' Eve stood up, placing her mug in the small sink, the movement causing Marmite to scramble up and look at her expectantly.

'Oh dear, he definitely thinks he's invited,' Greg said, grinning at her.

Eve sighed and rolled her eyes. 'Fine, but you have to behave.' She dropped to her knees. 'No embarrassing me in public.'

Marmite walked over and licked her nose.

'That definitely means it's a deal,' Greg said, shrugging his coat back on and holding out the lead. 'What?' He laughed. 'Trust me, I'm a vet.'

She clicked the lead into place and stood. 'Woe betide you if he eats all the sausage.'

Marmite yapped once.

'Sausage?' Greg said, and for a second Eve felt her whole body flush.

'There's always sausage at a Christmas market, German thing,' she mumbled, busying herself with putting on her gloves.

They stepped out onto the common, the day already darkening, a couple of stars out. The wind was whipping around them, flattening the long grass and lifting their hair. The sky was a deep blue, ribbons of blacks and greys cutting across it, the river moving past making its silent progress. They walked across the common in companionable silence, Marmite racing round their legs, growling at a dandelion clock and randomly sniffing the ground as if picking up the scent of Christmas-market sausage.

In the distance they could hear the sounds of laughter, children's shouts and the noise of sellers. As they approached, they could make out the stalls lining one side of the common, emitting steam, their windows lit up yellow and inviting, children queuing for cookies warm from the oven, candy floss on sticks, bags of doughnuts covered in sugar, the doughy scent making Eve's stomach grumble. In the centre was an enormous Ferris wheel, with a couple of other rides, all lit up with flashing bulbs, tinny music clashing and competing. A siren went off, a shout, some jeers from a group of boys nearby as one of them walked away with an enormous giant stuffed panda, his cheeks flaming.

Greg raised an eyebrow. 'I hope you don't expect me to win you one of those,' he said.

'Why do you think I invited you?'

They bought a bag of peppermint creams to share, the sweet, mint smell making her nose wrinkle. They melted in her mouth, 'Amazshing,' she said through a mouthful. She swallowed, giggling at him. 'Um... you've got icing sugar on your nose.'

Greg reached up and rubbed at it. ''Course I have.'

They were interrupted by Marmite, who decided to make a run for it, strangling himself on the lead as he came up short, barking and yapping like a mad thing so that people turned to stare.

'Marmite!' Eve hissed.

His barking was joined by a lower, longer bark and Eve looked up to see Sandy straining on his own lead, Minnie wrapped in a charcoal shawl, purple leggings underneath, waving at her frantically, 'Eve, darling, Eveeeee.'

Eve gave her a wave back and watched as Marmite and Sandy jumped and frolicked, clearly delighted to see each other.

'Darling, isn't it wonderful, I just love this market...' She stopped with one hand to her mouth as she took in Greg standing next to Eve. 'Oh, hello, I doooooo apologise,' she said. 'I'm interrupting,' she continued in a way that made it sound as if Eve and Greg were busy doing something disgusting rather than eating peppermint creams.

'Oh, not at all. Minnie, this is Greg, Greg, Minnie,' Eve said, motioning between them and wanting to add 'we were just eating mints, it was nothing', but felt that would be strange.

Minnie stepped forward to kiss him on both cheeks as if she were at Ascot races. 'Greg, I know Greg, darling, he's the heavenly local vet.'

'The heav... oh!' Eve nudged him in the arm. Greg seemed pinker beneath the thin layer of stubble.

'How's Sandy?' he asked, bending down to pat the golden retriever on the head.

'Oh, how gorgeous you remembered. He's fine, long in the tooth obviously, but fine. Actually, I was going to come in and see you last week because he was doing these very strange poos, but turns out he'd been at Gerald's Braeburns.'

'Well, that's a relief.' Greg laughed, his face splitting into an easy smile, one of his front teeth slightly crossing the other. Eve felt a bubble of warmth rise up through her at the sound.

'And how is...'

'Oh look, isn't that amazing,' Greg said, pointing quickly towards the trees where the sun was now streaked with lilacs and pinks. Eve was surprised; she hadn't pegged Greg as a sunset man. Minnie had spun round to look, both hands flying up to rest over her heart. 'Just glorious,' she said, her face glowing orange from the last of the sun.

'So, Eve and I were just about to head off actually, to the Ferris wheel...' Greg said, his mouth in a thin line.

'Were we...? We were, sorry, we were,' Eve confirmed, noticing Greg's expression, her thoughts whirling a little.

'Well, I best get on too; I want to head back. Gerald is out tonight with the darts team so I have a whole evening to myself. Baileys and Jackie Collins. Bliss.'

'Sounds ideal.' Eve laughed.

Minnie turned to go, waving an arm behind her as she left them, weaving her way through the crowds, Sandy looking wistfully behind as he left.

'So the Ferris wheel?' Eve asked, turning to Greg and putting her hands on her hips, her eyebrows raised in a question.

'Definitely.' Greg grinned and offered her his arm. She went to link hers through his, wondering why she felt as if she should be wary. What was it about the moment Greg had said it, as if he was trying to distract her? What had Minnie been about to ask? As they stepped over in the direction of the Ferris wheel, with the sight of the gently rocking carriages, the bold colours, the lights, she found herself growing excited and the questions were already fading.

Chapter 26

Mulled Wine

1 Bottle of red wine
75ml French brandy
60g Demerara sugar
1 lemon (quartered)
1 orange (quartered)

1 cinnamon stick
Optional: Grated nutmeg
Small handful of cloves
  and glacé cherries

Method:
- Put all ingredients in saucepan and slowly heat.
  Serve just before boiling point.

THE MARKET noises faded as they returned to the boat on the common. The tinny music tripped on the wind as they left the magic behind them. Eve had loved the market; as the day had darkened and they had moved around the stalls, the light falling in pools on the grass in front of them, people smiling and nodding, she had really felt part of the village. Large lanterns were stuck in the grass to guide people back into the centre and the meaty scent of roast-turkey baps and stuffing made her think of her mum's Christmas lunch.

She was quiet as she made her way back to the boat, Greg walking beside her, a small stuffed panda under one arm. Marmite drooped on the end of his lead, over-excited by the sights and smells of the market. The turkey-bap man had given him a sausage.

They got to the boat and moved inside, Eve not wanting the day to end, suddenly bereft that he would leave.

'That was fun,' she said in a hearty, Head Girl voice.

Greg smiled and sat down, still in his duffel coat as if he would make his exit at any moment. She didn't want to beg him to stay, felt she had taken up enough of his day. She sat opposite him, casting around her for some inspiration.

'Do you know what I really feel like?'

Eve leant forward, feeling herself growing pink. 'What is that?' she asked in a husky voice. Gosh, where was that voice coming from? That wasn't the voice of a heartbroken woman who was hurting from her fiancé. 'What is that?' she repeated in a newer, louder voice that made him frown a fraction.

'Mulled wine. I've had a craving for it since I saw the Crosskeys put a board outside the pub.'

'So shall we go there?' Eve asked.

'It's the pub quiz tonight, you can never get a seat. But...' he paused. 'We could make it here?' he said. 'It's not difficult.'

'I don't know how, and I don't have any ingredients,' Eve said, knowing mulled wine probably wasn't made from tea and dried pasta.

'I'll tell you what, I'll make you a list of what we need and get things ready here.' He reached into his coat pocket and pulled out his wallet. 'My treat,' he said, handing her a twenty-pound note before she had time to take things in.

'Well, that's kind,' Eve said, confused now as she clutched the twenty-pound note. 'Don't you want to come?'

'No, I can sort things here so we're ready to go when you get back.' He was writing a list on the counter, pen tapping his mouth before his eyes lit up and he was done, thrusting the list at her like it was homework he wanted marking.

'Okay, if you're sure,' she said, holding the list and the twenty-pound note. 'I'll just get my scarf, it's colder now,' she added, taking a step forward to squeeze past him and doing a sort of half-dance as they side-stepped each other. Her eyes met the top of his jumper and she focused there, suddenly afraid to look up.

'Brilliant,' he said, his laugh a little strange, faster and higher than normal.

She shrugged on her coat and wondered whether she should go. It felt odd leaving him in the boat on his own. It wasn't that she didn't trust him but something felt wrong. Did he not want to be seen with her?

When she moved back through to the kitchen, though, he was washing up at the sink and as she went to say something, he gave her a slow smile and she found herself saying, 'I won't be long.'

She stepped off the boat and walked away, still feeling thrown by this last development. She clutched the list in her hand. Had she made a mistake about him? Should she be more suspicious? She didn't know him very well yet and couldn't necessarily rely on the fact that she thought he had a trustworthy face, a lovely laugh. Look where that had got her with Liam. Something was going on. Then perhaps she was just being silly. Maybe mulled wine required quite complicated preparations and when she returned he would have transformed the kitchen into an elaborate staging area.

*

When she got back, he had cleaned up, put a saucepan on the hob and had the chopping board and a knife out on the side. He had wiped down the table in her absence and took the bag from her peering into it with false enthusiasm, a muscle going in his neck.

She felt heat on her legs and turned. 'You lit the stove.'

Greg's eyes widened, the muscle still pulsing. 'I hope that was okay?'

'Of course, I love it,' Eve said, listening to the pop and fizz of the logs inside, the smell filling the boat, warming her up immediately. It was fantastic, pumping heat into the space, crackling and spitting as the flames flickered behind the door. She moved over to the counter as Greg started to lay out what she had brought: spices, fruit and red wine.

She took a breath, ready to ask him whether he was all right. She had psyched herself up to probe on the way back over the common, but as he lined things up on the counter, his face relaxed, he looked like the easy Greg, the one who smiled readily, who absent-mindedly scooped up Marmite to ruffle his hair, the one who lit up when he cooked.

She let him walk her through the recipe as he instructed her to keep stirring at a steady pace. He poured in red wine, brandy, sliced up oranges, opened up the container of cherries and popped one into her mouth automatically.

'You won't look back once you've tried this,' he said. 'It's a real winter-warmer, perfect.'

He ladled it into two wine glasses and handed her one, raising his glass at her before he drank.

'This is incredible,' she sighed after the first taste, leaning back against the counter.

'Told you.'

Eve moved through to the living room, curling herself up

onto the bench and watching him sit on the stool, Marmite quick to nestle at his feet. The room smelt of bonfires and cinnamon and Eve felt herself feeling festive for the first time. In this space, with the orange glow from the woodburner and the tartan blanket she had flung over her legs, the mulled wine warming her from the inside.

'We just need an old movie,' she said, nodding ruefully at the television, the stubborn blank screen staring back.

'Do you want me to try and fix it for you?' Greg asked, getting up and putting his wine on the counter before she could protest.

He started looking behind the television, his head resting on the wall to peer at the back of it. Reaching behind it, he fiddled with some wires as Eve called, 'I've tried that, I really think it's broken.'

Not saying anything, he followed the lead down to the wall, clicked the switch to On, picked up the remote and grinned at her as it sparked into life.

Eve rolled her eyes. 'I'm an idiot.'

'Or I spend too much time watching television,' Greg said, handing her the remote and settling back in the chair.

She scrolled through the channels, half-wishing he hadn't got it working. The jarring voices filled the boat and drowned out the gentle sound of the logs and their quiet chatter. They watched partway through a film, Greg topping them up with mulled wine, the portholes turning from dark blue to black. It was easy, familiar and, for a panicked second, she wondered what she was up to. Greg was stroking the top of Marmite's head and when he drained the last of his wine glass, he suddenly rose from the stool, his head almost bumping the top of the boat.

'I'd better get home,' he said, perhaps as thrown by the domestic scene as she was. He looked about for his coat as she stood up, feeling her legs wobble from the rocking of the water, and the brandy.

'Thank you for the recipe,' she said, feeling strangely shy, her mouth all tongue as he leant across to place his empty glass on the counter.

'My pleasure, work tomorrow, probably shouldn't do surgery after too many of these.' It was the second Greg, the one with the tense look in his eye.

She went to ask, to see if everything was okay, and then bit down the question. *He's fine, Eve, he just wants to go home.* Some people have actual real lives to live rather than pottery classes and lie-ins.

She followed him out to the door, a strange moment, a half-hug, an 'Okay then,' as he left. She watched him step onto the bank, cross the grass, hands in his coat pockets, head down. Leaning against the wall, she felt her body relax. The mulled wine seemed to have flushed her cheeks, warmed her toes and fingers, reached into every part of her and heated her up. She watched him until he left the common, turning down the high street, wondering where he was headed and whether he was still sad.

Chapter 27

HE KNEW he'd been acting strangely, could see it as he wrote out the list in a hasty scrawl, Eve's uncertain lingering as she wondered whether she should leave him there on her boat. Seeing Minnie had reminded him again; he spent the day with clients from the village and those who knew her often asked, so he was on guard. When he was out in the village, though, focusing on the shopping or getting a quick pint, the enquiries floored him for a second and he didn't want to answer. It got to the point where he couldn't face going to his usual haunts because of the questions.

What had he been thinking? Turfing her out of her own boat and sending her into the village like his skivvy? The moment she'd walked off he'd wanted to run after her, walk to the shop, be *normal*. Instead he pulled things out of the cupboard, cleaned and wiped the surfaces, lit the stove, fooled himself into thinking he was just preparing for her return when, in fact, he was just being a coward.

He was relieved when she had come back, glad to find the stove on and the kitchen wiped down, watching closely as he got all the ingredients prepared. She seemed genuinely interested, writing down the recipe so she could make it again. And he'd loved watching her face as she'd taken that first sip, the brandy hitting them both at the same moment so they gave each other sleepy smiles. It suddenly felt like Christmas then and, for a second, he was looking forward to it. Then the thoughts came crashing in and when they started watching that film his mind wandered like it often did now. He didn't want to share it with her and, anyway, talking about it wouldn't help.

He'd had the most surprising afternoon, though, wanted to be walking round a Christmas market with her every day, exclaiming over the stalls, watching her face flood with embarrassment every time Marmite ignored her. She had sat on the Ferris wheel, as it rocked gently at the top, the black ribbon of river winding out of sight, the bridge in the distance peppered with lights, and pointed out the boat, one porthole lit up. He had a sudden urge to take her face in his hands and kiss it. She looked so adorable in her hat, hair sticking out under it, her coat buttoned right up to her chin, her nose and cheeks pink with cold, her green eyes sparkling and shifting in the lights from the Ferris wheel. Then the mechanics had kicked in and they were falling past the treeline, down towards the ground, and that moment had remained up there, with the shadows of themselves.

As he reached to turn off his bedside lamp, he felt the urge to open his curtains and look out across the village in the direction of the river. He couldn't see anything and a light drizzle had started up, smattering the window, making it impossible to make out even the houses opposite, but he felt better doing it. Getting his e-reader out, he started to read, losing himself in another world.

Chapter 28

DANNY WAS standing next to the table with the teapots and mugs, talking to Raj. She noticed the backs of his hands were smeared with black and wondered whether he was a painter. She reached across for the cafetière, sun bursting through the conservatory windows, making the glass sparkle.

'Morning,' she said as she poured.

Raj gave her a devastating white smile, a Colgate advert, and Danny swiped at his blond fringe. 'Hey.'

The lovebirds were already at their wheel, discussing something in low voices, their heads bent towards each other. Aisha looked up and gave her a gentle smile; Eve raised a hand in greeting.

Minnie could be heard shouting at something in the distance and Eve guessed either the dogs or Gerald were on the receiving end. She appeared in her usual clash of jewellery, a sequinned kaftan and a turban perched on her head, looking like the Genie of the Lamp. She swept across the room, air-kissing Eve and fluttering around Raj.

'Good morning, good morning.'

'Eve, your pot has been fired,' Raj said, turning to a shelf over the tea table and bringing down a pot, a similar size but lighter in colour with hard, even grooves on its surface. She studied it as closely as if it were a Ming vase, turning it over, feeling her eyes widen in amazement. Scratched into the bottom were her initials. It was strange seeing it in this form, no more a malleable piece of clay but an actual thing. She grew excited about the prospect of painting it, wondering what designs she could create.

Eve settled herself at a table in the front lined with tubes of paint, determined to get going. Raj stood in front of her and explained what she needed to do.

'I would draw something in pencil first,' he said. 'And remember that some of the colours will need two or three coats. It's like watercolour, you tend to start with the lighter colours. Happy?' The two white rows of teeth flashed at her again; a perfectly manicured eyebrow was raised.

Eve swallowed, letting out a high, 'Very.'

'Ha, good.' He laughed.

Danny joined her, pulling a stool out from under the table, his pot a little higher and narrower.

'That's really good.' Eve nodded at him and she giggled to herself as he blustered a reply, clearly not used to taking a compliment.

They chatted quietly as they worked, bent over their pieces, carefully drawing shapes onto the surface. Eve thought back to the river, to the boat, and then, shoulders hunched forward, a slow smile spreading over her face, she started to sketch.

'You're an artist,' Raj said, looking over her shoulder.

Eve felt herself burn and she almost dropped the pot. 'I like cartoons,' she said in a quiet voice, as if it were something to be ashamed of. She had drawn a goose, waddling around the bottom of it, wings behind him, beak up, eyes wide. She couldn't wait to fill in the lines with paint, wanted to make the silvery blue of the river the first colour to go on.

Danny was having less luck, muttering at his as he rubbed

out another line. After a few more minutes he threw his pencil down on the desk and folded his arms. Eve couldn't help noticing his biceps as she turned to ask if he was all right. His pink lips were in a pout and he really did look like a cross cherub.

'Can I help?' she asked.

'I just want a wavy line splitting it in half but I can't make it meet up.'

'Do you mind?' she asked, picking up his pencil and holding out a hand for the pot.

He shrugged and unfolded his arms, pushing it across. 'Be my guest. I like making stuff but I can't draw to save my life.'

Eve carefully drew a line round the middle of the pot, making smooth waves and joining the line back up as she rotated it.

'You made that look so easy,' Danny said, the pout back.

'Well, your pot is much smoother than mine so it's easier.'

Danny seemed to sit up straighter at that, jutting his chin out.

They painted in relative silence and Eve loved the industrious atmosphere, the wheels around her rotating, the quiet brushstrokes as Danny covered his pot in layers of blue glaze, Raj's gentle instructions, Minnie's occasional puffs of irritation. Mark and Aisha were making small pendants for some of their bridesmaids, and their quiet voices and occasional laughter was like the babble of a stream beneath it all.

She nearly missed it, completely absorbed in her work, but it caused her to turn and frown through the conservatory window. There was movement in a tree in the garden and she craned her neck to the side to see if it was something interesting, expecting a squirrel or a bird, eyes widening when she latched on. It was Gerald, binoculars clamped to his face, looking straight into the conservatory rather than at the sky.

'Oh,' Eve said, which was enough to make Danny pause in his glazing. 'Can you see?' Eve said, waggling her eyebrows and indicating the tree. 'We've got a bird-watcher,' she said, lowering her voice and glancing at Minnie, who seemed entirely oblivious.

Danny looked through the window and then frowned, lines appearing between his eyebrows as he took in the twitcher. 'He gets weirder,' he said with a small laugh.

'Shall we say something?'

'Nah, let him have his fun.'

'But hasn't it gone a bit far?'

Danny shrugged, slapping on another layer.

Gerald was still there ten minutes later, scooting down a low branch to lean forward and rest there. Eve worried he might tumble off it at any moment. Minnie still seemed completely engrossed at her wheel, Raj leaning over to show her how to create different effects with the glaze. He had a clay handprint on his white shirt. Eve bit down her question, returning to her painting, adding the fine lines around the picture now in black; her hand had to remain absolutely steady.

She soon forgot too and, as she left the class that day, Raj promised her he would put her pot back in the kiln and she would see it the next day. She wasn't sure she could wait that long, felt light as a feather as she skipped off through the garden, no one now in the tree as she passed, no one in any of the bushes. The sky was a light blue above her, weak sunlight dancing on the surface of the river, the gentle chug of a long boat as it passed, the ripples slapping the sides of the bank.

Returning to the boat, she was desperate to talk to someone

about it all, energised by the lesson, feeling excited about the progress she had already made. She had neglected a large part of herself for years and spending hours focusing on being creative, allowing herself to indulge in something she had always loved doing, was an incredible feeling.

She headed to the kitchen counter, picking up the pieces of her phone and praying that it might work now. She was amazed to see it light up and then listened to continuous beeping as messages and emails popped up. It was a deluge of love and she grinned at the screen.

'You have eight new messages.' Granted, most of them would be her mother asking her to come home, but eight was still a lot.

She was wrapped in three jumpers, the sun brighter now but the day still decidedly chilly. She stepped out onto the square wooden platform over the river, careful as the wood was still slippery after last night's frost. Placing a large cushion on the ground, she sat cross-legged, her hat on, her coat wrapped round her, as she listened to her sister shouting at someone else on another phone. 'It's only 11 p.m. in Hong Kong so bloody well wake him up. Hi, Eve, darling,' she said, her voice impossibly soft.

'Er, who's in Hong Kong?' Eve laughed, always astounded by Harriet's dual personality.

'A little prat we are paying too much. Anyway, very boring, how are you, how's the pirate life?'

Harriet had an incredible knack of focusing on you, blocking everything else out and making you feel at the centre of her universe. She was probably in the middle of dismantling someone's company, or feeding Poppy lunch, or both, but for that moment it was simply all about you.

'It is pretty good actually,' said Eve, telling her sister about the small victories: the pot she'd painted, the meal she had helped make, and then felt a little silly. This was her cool big sister who did million-pound deals.

'That does sound idyllic.' Harriet sighed and Eve was buoyed up again.

'How's home?' Eve asked. 'How's Mum and Dad?'

'Fine. I had to take Dad Christmas shopping yesterday as he wanted to buy Mum something for Christmas that she wouldn't hate. He really does have appalling taste. I had to steer him away from all sorts of things. At one point he was about to buy her a hot-pink onesie because he thought she would like new pyjamas.'

Eve grinned, picturing her dad's enthusiastic face. 'So what did you plump for?'

'A silver locket.'

'She'll like that,' Eve conceded. Harriet was great at buying presents and could wrap anything perfectly. Eve always handed over lumpy gifts with Sellotape everywhere; Harriet found bows and sticker things and ribbon. 'And Scarlet's asked to borrow more money so she doesn't have to make everyone gooseberry jam again.'

'Oh thank God, lend it to her,' Eve said, remembering everyone's faces last year as they clutched their jars to their chest.

'I will, I will. I gave mine to my highly efficient PA just to freak her out that I had a newborn and was making friggin' jam at home. She was terrified.'

Eve was laughing as Harriet talked, picturing her back in her kitchen in Clapham, the polished white surfaces, the bar stools and the artful pictures, imagining Harriet move around the space in her high heels.

'So any other news?' Eve asked, and she wondered for a

moment whether Harriet paused for a little bit too long before answering.

'Not from me,' she said. Was her voice a fraction too loud? 'Look, Eve, I'd better go. I need to sort out this situation in Hong Kong or I'll get the sack.'

'I totally understand,' Eve said, not wanting to distract her.

'Keep enjoying it all, remember why you're there,' Harriet said in a quiet voice. 'I'm pleased for you, Eve, sounds like you are really embracing it all.'

Eve felt choked as they wished each other goodbye, Harriet back off to shout down the phone at someone on the other side of the world, Eve looking out onto the still river, a heron in the distance preening himself as he bathed in the winter sunshine.

She clicked on the email icon on her phone.

Daisy had sent her a photo of herself in the office doing a sad face, a photocopied picture of Noel Edmonds next to her and a Post-it note as a bubble coming out of his mouth: 'We Miss You'.

Eve giggled at it.

When she'd finished her emails, she returned to her answerphone messages. Two were simply dropped calls, a momentary sound of someone breathing and them changing their mind. The next, however, made her suck in her breath as the drawling voice of Liam came over the line. He sounded distant, as if he were in a car or on speaker phone.

'And this is the fifth time I've called so stop ignoring them. Your sister won't tell me where you've gone but I want Marmite back by Christmas Eve. It's not fair.'

She loitered over the keypad, knowing she shouldn't press 'Reply'. *Why do it to yourself, Eve?* But unable to resist, she found her finger moving to the button, the ringtone sounding.

It was too late to go back now.

'Hello.'

'Liam,' she said quickly, trying to remain businesslike, trying to channel Harriet as she spoke. Harriet would tell him to effing well get a grip on himself. But she would actually swear. Eve licked her lips. 'I told you, I'm not giving him back. Marmite is staying.'

'Where are you?' Liam asked. 'You're not at the flat.'

She felt a little rush of pleasure that he had been there.

'I'm not, and I'm not telling you,' she said, feeling strangely powerful, her voice confident.

'God, Eve, you are being so selfish,' he said. 'You don't even like Marmite.'

'I do, I really do,' she said, picturing Marmite's bewildered face, expectant eyes. She realised with a lurch that she really did love him now.

'Well, how convenient for you,' Liam said with a whine, a new tone to his voice. 'I want him back.'

'I want never gets,' Eve said, wondering where that sentence had come from.

'There's no need to be a cow about it,' Liam said, making her bristle with his words.

'Liam,' she said slowly, 'I am not being a cow about it. You cheated on me, remember. You left and it took you a couple of weeks to even remember you left Marmite too...'

'Yes, but I want him now.'

'Well, so do I, and I really think it is the least you can do—'

'Permission to join,' a voice called from behind her.

Eve frowned, her body twisting round on the cushion. It was Greg, standing on the bank, his hand in a salute that wavered as she turned. He obviously hadn't seen the mobile clamped to her ear and put a hand over his mouth, a silent

'Sorry' mouthed to her as she stared at him.

He looked impossibly awkward standing on the bank as she spoke into the phone quickly, 'I have to go... there's nothing I can say anyway... what? It's no one,' she said, riled at Liam's whining questions on the end of the phone.

She pulled the phone away, aware her face was set in a line, and jabbed at the Off button.

'I'm so sorry. I thought you were just staring out at the river.'

She tried to rouse a smile but felt the weight of the call on her mind, her mouth refusing to lift at the edges.

'I brought you these,' Greg said, handing her a Tupperware container.

Her earlier happiness had evaporated like that morning's mist and she was shivering now despite the three jumpers. Worried that she could feel tears build at the back of her eyes, she tried to look more enthusiastic, shake off the black gloom that wanted to descend.

'Mince pies.' She clicked the container closed again. 'Thank you.' She knew her smile was strained but she suddenly couldn't face anyone being kind to her. Maybe she was being a selfish cow? Maybe she should give Marmite back? She hated hearing Liam's voice, cold, as if the last four years had never happened and they were strangers.

'I'll go,' Greg said, turning to leave. 'Keep the container. I'll see you soon.'

Marmite started barking excitedly from the boat, more welcoming than she was being.

'No, I'm sorry, I... Come in, I'll put the kettle on.'

'Are you sure?' Greg asked, his body half-turned away.

She swallowed, forcing a smile. 'Yes, absolutely.'

Chapter 29

MAKING MINCE pies seemed to help. As he stirred the mincemeat together, the raisins and currants sticking to each other, the smell of the brandy coming off it in waves, he felt that soothing release that cooking gave him. The mindless stirring, concentrating on heaping ingredients into a bowl, measuring, stirring, tasting. He could lose himself in it and simply follow the familiar recipe on a notepad in her handwriting.

He'd been over there again this afternoon after work and he had left with this terrible hollow feeling, this hopeless knowledge that they wouldn't ever get back to where they had once been. They'd sat in the sitting room, him in the armchair he had always sat in, her perched on the end of the sofa. They had talked about Christmas, skirted round it really. He would go there for the day; she couldn't face coming to the apartment and he agreed hastily.

He had made too many. He was sure he had a Tupperware container. It sat at the back of the bottom shelf, behind flan dishes and a glass stand that he was pretty sure wasn't his. Running it under the tap, he felt a relief steal over him. He would get out of the flat, take them to her. He didn't want to head anywhere else. He pictured her face as she saw the mince pies. The image made him smile as he closed the Tupperware container.

It was colder today, his car still covered in a layer of thin ice, the sky a baby blue, the high street full of people wrapped in hats and scarves, slivers of faces peeking out, red noses, hands in pockets. He walked with a purpose, glad of his collar up, his enormous scarf obscuring his face. On the other side of the road he spotted Mr Parker and Lennie, his black Labrador, white whiskers on both their faces. He sped up, not wanting to be spotted. He felt a flash of guilt as he did; he couldn't keep avoiding the villagers like this.

Once he was under the railway bridge and could see the frost-covered common, he felt his body unclench, his arms swing more freely, his chin lift a fraction. As he opened the gate he saw the boat in the distance, the portholes seemingly dark. He hoped she was in; he didn't want to simply leave them at the entrance. Then, as he crossed the grass, he felt like letting out a whoop. She was there, sitting cross-legged, bundled into a hundred layers so that her body was hidden under jumpers, hat on, hair almost touching her shoulders as she looked out across the river. He felt something fall in his stomach as he took her in.

He opened his mouth, raised his hand in a mock salute, already feeling lighter than he had done all day. 'Permission to join.'

When she turned, he found his hand falling. Her face was set in an expression he had never seen before, her mouth an angry line, her eyes dark, eyebrows knitted together. He mouthed an apology at her. He was encroaching, he could see that immediately.

He could hear her conversation. The words 'It's no one' snapped down the receiver, brittle and certain. He was a no one; they'd only just met. He wasn't sure why it hurt so much.

As she turned the phone off, the frown still on her face, he started to speak. 'I'm so sorry, I thought you were just staring out at the river.' Nothing he said seemed to help; she seemed to be looking through him, her mouth still set. 'I brought you these.' He handed her the container, wanting to get out of there quickly. He felt awkward and foolish. She clearly didn't need him descending on her out of the blue. She didn't need to get tied up in his problems too. He had been right not to share anything with her.

'I'll go.' He heard her thanks and then, spotting Marmite's face leaping up in a porthole, a quick flash of face then nothing, a second flash. At least someone was happy to see him.

'Keep the container. I'll see you soon.'

He hadn't expected that look. He had hoped to appear on the common and be swept along in her enthusiasm, hear her light laugh, listen to her stories, watch her hands moving in the air as she told them.

She tucked her hair behind an ear and stood up, the lines between her eyebrows still there. 'No, I'm sorry, I... Come in, I'll put the kettle on.'

He wavered. *Greg, mate, go, she is just being polite.* But then he thought back to his flat, not wanting to be there in the empty space. Seeing her face start to return, a suggestion of a smile, her green eyes brighter as she waited for him to respond.

'Are you sure?'

'Yes, absolutely.'

He saw her pause before it but couldn't walk away now. There was an energy about her that made him want to stick around. He didn't want to be anywhere else. He nodded and watched her walk into the boat, Marmite flying out to greet him as she opened the door. *You can't hide for ever, Greg.* He hushed the voice and picked up a stick to throw.

Chapter 30

Mince Pies

Block of shortcrust
  pastry or homemade
Homemade mincemeat (see
  below) but could be
  shop-bought

Ideally, mincemeat
should be made two
weeks before you
use it

Method:

- Roll out pastry. Cut a larger base and a smaller one for lid.
- Put a generous teaspoon of mincemeat inside.
- Put lid on top, holes in top of lid.
- Glaze lid with beaten egg or milk (optional).
- Cook at 175°C for 15 minutes or until golden.

Mincemeat

500g each: currants, sultanas and raisins

250g very finely chopped Bramley apples

125g mixed peel

125g red glacé cherries

125g dark-red (natural) glacé cherries

185g vegetarian suet

Juice of 1 lemon and 1 orange

220ml brandy

Optional: 125g finely chopped walnuts or Brazil nuts

½ tsp each salt, cinnamon, nutmeg, cloves, mace, ginger and mixed spice

Method:

- Mix all ingredients together, finishing with the lemon and orange juice and brandy. Cover bowl and leave in cool place for 36/48 hours. Sterilise jar. Spoon mixture into it. Should mature for at least 10 days before using.

SHE WAS glad that Marmite was providing entertainment as she left Greg tussling with him and a stick. She cleared the table in the small porch area of the boat and put the mince pies in the middle, heading inside to make them tea to go with them. It gave her time to try to push the phone call to the back of her mind, smiling through the porthole at Marmite, who was eagerly standing at Greg's feet, tail wagging, as he prepared to chase another stick.

Greg looked completely at home with him, bending to rub at his head as he removed the stick. As he walked over to the boat, face relaxed, his dark-brown hair swept up from running around, she couldn't help smile at him, as if she had known him for years. He had the kind of face that made you feel calm, as if he were permanently ready to be amused. You felt like making an effort, trying to rouse the smile.

The kettle whistled and she busied herself with mugs, tea bags, a jug of milk, a pot of sugar, carrying it out to the porch on a tray. She sat down on the lip of the boat that acted as a bench on one side of the table, calling over to Greg, 'Tea's ready.'

He turned, his cheeks flushed. 'Coming. Marmite. Heel,' he called and Eve giggled as Marmite lay down on the grass.

'Heel, boy, heel,' Greg repeated.

Marmite started licking his paw.

Greg walked over to her, one hand in his hair as she looked at him. 'Great job.'

He stepped into the boat, shrugging and reaching for his mug. 'Animal's a liability.'

Eve stood up. 'Marmite, here, boy.'

Marmite jumped up and bounded over in an instant as Greg mumbled something into his tea.

'What's that?' Eve grinned, lifting Marmite up onto the deck of the boat and ruffling his fur affectionately. 'Good boy, who's a good boy.'

She joined him back at the table, picking up a mince pie and exclaiming as she took a bite. 'Sho goooood,' she said through crumbs.

'You're such a lady,' he laughed as she brushed pastry off her lips.

Wrapping her hands around her mug she looked out across the water, the reflections of the clouds still on its surface: every shape mirrored perfectly, the weeping willows bent over themselves, the trailing leaves obscuring the bank. Another narrow boat approached, causing gentle ripples to nudge the side of the boat.

'It is beautiful here,' she said, breathing out.

'I run here all the time but I never get bored of looking at it,' Greg said simply, his eyes crinkling as they met hers. 'Cheers,' he said, raising his mug.

The other boat passed and a man in a white flat cap, one hand on the tiller, waved as they cruised by.

'Have you taken it out yet?' Greg asked, biting into a mince pie, crumbs falling onto his brown jumper, staying there like tiny yellow dots.

'What?'

'The boat,' he said, indicating with his hand.

'Oh.' Eve made a face, not sure whether she should admit to not knowing how to start it. She'd lived on it for over a week and she had started to think she would never take it out.

'You are going to take it out?' he checked in a slow voice.

'Of course I am,' Eve said, nodding her head quickly. 'Just you know...'

'Waiting for the perfect conditions?' Greg smiled, the sun glinting on his teeth, the icy blue sky a brilliant backdrop.

'Yes, that and, oh... I don't know how, okay,' Eve admitted, biting her lower lip. 'There's no manual or anything. And you probably need a boating licence or something which I don't have.'

'You don't,' Greg said, his voice animated. 'We took one out on a stag do. It's pretty straightforward actually. Shall we?' he asked, leaning forward.

She had to smile at his reaction; he couldn't disguise his eagerness. She took a breath out slowly. 'Where to?'

'We could do one lock, maybe take it up to Goring, that's a great bit of river. Not too far.'

'I'm not sure how to do the locks and things – do you know?' Eve asked, starting to catch his enthusiasm, remembering

193

the metal windlass that was sitting unused at the front.

'I do,' Greg said, uncrossing his legs. 'Well, actually, some-one just opens it up for you at Goring, but I still do.'

'Okay then.' Eve laughed, feeling like she was in safe hands, a bubble of excitement at the prospect of doing something new.

'Let's go boating,' Greg said, standing and hitting his head on the lower-ceilinged porch. Eve grimaced for him. 'Are you okay?'

Greg rubbed at his head, eyes blurring with unshed tears. 'Ow. Not funny,' he said, turning as Marmite started to bark. Eve hid a smile behind a mince pie. 'I can totally see you laughing,' Greg said, still rubbing his head.

'I'm sorry,' Eve mumbled.

In the end it didn't take them long to work out how to turn it on, the engine churning into gear, the water frothing beneath them as the blades turned. They untied the ropes on the side and threw them onto the deck. It was harder to manoeuvre it out onto the river, the steering a little wobbly at first, but they took it slowly, moving through the water at a snail's pace as they both took turns on the tiller. You had to stick to the right side of the river, but seeing as most traffic was going at around 3 m.p.h. you had plenty of time to get into position.

It was incredible feeling the breeze lifting her hair, the cold biting at her ears and nose as they moved down the river. She soon warmed up as she moved along the deck of the boat, the sun high above them. Marmite, delighted at the journey, was racing up one side of the deck, yapping at them both, yapping at passing birds, eyes bright, tail wagging. Eve stood looking out over the length of the boat, marvelling at kites dipping out of sight, walkers ambling along as they passed, the river opening up before them as they rounded corners to be faced with the wide expanse of glittering water. She felt her palms dampen as they approached the lock at Goring, hoping it really would be as easy as Greg promised. Hopping out to talk to the lock-keeper she sat on the hunk of wood as he opened the enormous gates to the lock, laughing as she peered down at Greg's face as the water drained out, the stone sides streaked with algae, rusty chains looped along the walls. Taking the steps down to the bank on the other side, she walked along by the side of the boat, ready to hop back on.

'Let's moor up,' Greg said, choosing a spot by a dense patch of reeds and steering it slowly to the side. They secured the boat with ropes so it wouldn't disappear on them and high-fived each other as they switched the engine off.

'Great work, Skipper.'

'Thanks, Cap'n,' he replied, dipping his head and making her laugh.

She had forgotten about the phone call from Liam, forgotten about the last few months. Her chest felt lighter as she moved around the boat, patting Marmite on the head as she forked food into his bowl and waited for the kettle to boil.

The sun had disappeared behind a haze of cloud and the whole sky looked like a layer of gauze had covered it. They sat on the top of the boat draped in blankets, drank coffee and played backgammon on a wooden board, the dice rattling on the surface, Greg's shout as he threw a good roll causing a flock of birds to disappear en masse from a nearby tree. Eve knew they needed to get back but she wished the afternoon could stretch on forever, smiling to herself as she watched him move the counters around, his grey-blue eyes glinting as he looked at her.

'We need to get back,' she said, her voice filled with regret as she saw the sun quivering over the treeline. They didn't have long until it was dark and she didn't trust their boating skills without light.

Greg, deciding that they should talk in pirate all the way back to Pangbourne, was refusing to recognise any sentences that didn't end in an 'Arrrrrrrr'.

'Ready?' Eve called from the engine.

'Ready who, Cap'n?'

Eve pretended to sigh and roll her eyes. 'Ready, Skipper.'

Greg nodded, satisfied, setting back off towards the lock and hopping out on the bank himself to talk to the lock-keeper.

Eve stayed by the tiller, watching the water bubble and rush in beneath her, lifting the boat inch by inch, the smell damp, the sun blocked from her position inside the lock. She was pleased to pick up Greg on the other side of the lock as she steered it carefully through the lock gates, calling a goodbye to the lock-keeper. She left him at the tiller and headed along the deck, the sun setting ahead of them, the sky full of pink and purple strips, wisps of cloud.

'How faaaaaarrrrrrrr?' Eve hollered from the other end of the boat.

'Not too farrrrrrrrrr, me hearty,' he tacked on, the weather turning his cheeks pink beneath the stubble.

Eve nodded and disappeared inside, emerging moments later through the door at the back of the boat. 'Would you like a beer?' she asked Greg, craning her neck up to him, his hand clamped to the tiller. He deliberately turned to the side and stared out at the water. She sighed. 'Would you like a beer, me hearty?'

'Is it from a barrrrrrrrrr?'

'I'm getting you a beer,' she called, giggling and moving back through to the kitchen to fetch one, hearing his belly laugh following her there.

They clinked and stood on the deck as they moved under the iron bridge and back into the spot where the boat was moored, scattering ducks in their path. Greg had grown quieter in the last few minutes and for a moment she had the desire to ask him if anything was wrong. The sight of the village seemed to sap his energy and his blue eyes were troubled again. Eve frowned, wondering whether she was just imagining things. Liam had always hated it when she had probed, teasing her that she read something into every look and every sentence. She clamped her mouth shut, convinced she was just over-thinking things.

As they drew alongside the bank, he leapt out to bang the large iron nails into the grass, securing it to the side by lashing it with ropes. He was breathless by the time he had finished, only looking up once as a goose honked from the far side of the common and he raised a fist in a comedy gesture. This wasn't enough to lift Eve, who suddenly felt really sad the day was over. The clouds were thicker now, a blanket of white overhead, and the temperature had dropped again as the sun sank behind the trees.

'Do you want to stay for dinner?' she found herself blurting.

'Actually,' Greg said, banging in the last nail and looking up at her, his eyes crinkling, 'that would be great.'

She felt instantly lighter, blushing and hiding the fact with an 'I better see what we have in the boat yaaaaaaaarrrrrr'.

'Hmm, that doesn't really work.' He hopped back on the deck and followed her inside.

They stood in the kitchen staring at the cupboard of ingredients. She turned to admit she didn't have the first clue what to make.

She wasn't sure how it happened, but the kitchen suddenly felt a lot smaller and she was aware of his body in front of her. He was close. When did he get so close? Their eyes met in this wordless moment and the next moment he had leant down towards her and they were kissing, clashing at first and then melting into this amazing, prolonged kiss. She felt her whole body react, leaning into him, his hands were on her face, the sharp sting of the cold outside a shock. Then the warmth of their skin as they melted together, as she moved her body into his.

She and Liam had never in four years kissed like that. She hadn't had a second thought, the whole day had seemed magical and the kiss felt absolutely right. As she'd tiptoed to meet him, feeling the warmth of his chest, she found herself letting go, legs weak as the kiss went on and on. She felt her body being nudged backwards, her hands reaching for his hair, her bottom pushing papers to the floor. Then she felt her back against the wall of the boat, the spice rack behind her, pots falling to the floor around them, showering their feet with spots of spice and dried herbs. Envelopes, a tea towel, nothing made her pull away.

They finally did, both breathing heavily, laughing, looking down at the mess they had made. Cinnamon and parsley streaked across the floor.

Eve touched her mouth, almost shocked by the strength of the kiss, still able to feel it.

Greg's hair was sticking up, his chest rising and falling. 'Shit,' he said, looking down too and stepping in some stray dried basil. 'I've got cumin on my shoes.'

Eve laughed again, her breathing shallow. She felt herself burn with the shock of it all, the silence now as they stared at each other. She wanted to kiss him again but now suddenly, sobered up and standing surrounded by scattered papers and spice, she felt embarrassed at the way she had let go.

Somehow, instead of laughing again or making light of things, she found herself over-reacting to the scene, staring at the spices as if he had thrown them on the floor in a rage.

'I'll clean it up,' Greg said, perhaps noticing the change in atmosphere, perhaps not.

'No, don't,' she said, pressing herself away from him, stepping back. She needed space from him, in her head, thoughts now jostling one in front of another.

'I'll... God.' He raked his hand through his hair.

'I'll sort this,' she said, her voice high and loud. She squeezed past him to the sink, not wanting to touch him again, running the cold tap and feeling the relief as the water gushed out, seizing a cloth.

He had walked into the living room as she bent to scrub at the debris, feeling foolish as she mopped at the floor. *Say something, Eve, make it right again. It wasn't such a surprise. Was it?* Why was she behaving like this person? She found herself unable to look up, circling the floor furiously.

'That was quite...'

'Look, Greg.' She stopped circling, sitting with her legs stuck out in front of her, suddenly overwhelmed by it all, the reasons she had come here, the phone call from Liam, the mess of the last few months, that afternoon, the kiss. He had stopped, his mouth slowly shutting as he looked at her. He still had spices on the top of his trainers and it seemed to act as a prompt. She didn't need confusion and complications.

'I think maybe it would be best if we just...' She didn't know what she wanted to say. *Just what?* Her cheeks still burnt from where he had held them, the memory of his stubble as his skin pressed against hers. *What the hell did she want?* Standing looking down at her acting like this, he looked remarkably composed, all trace of the tension disappearing as he rubbed at his chin.

'I'm sorry,' he said, straightening his jumper. 'I don't know where that came from.'

Oh God, you've done this, Eve. Don't guilt-trip the man, you kissed him back.

'Look, I...'

'I'll go. I didn't mean to, you know, jump on you. I just, well...'

She was nodding miserably from the floor. He would go. Of course he was going. She would go if he was behaving like this. And yet she couldn't shake it.

'Right, so...' He looked about him, patting his pockets as if he could find a Time-Turner and send them back ten minutes.

'Thanks,' she said from the floor. Neither of them seemed able to form a coherent sentence but she didn't have the energy to try. He had been the only other person she'd kissed in four years. He hadn't kissed like Liam. It somehow felt final then, stupid really, as she had made him leave immediately, but now it really felt like that part of her life was over. She hadn't expected it, she hadn't wanted it. Or had she? She watched him get his coat, shrugging it on, seeming on the verge of saying more. She struggled to her feet, holding the cloth up against her like a shield guarding her from him.

'I'm sorry, I just, the thing is that I came here to get away from things and, well, I wasn't planning on...' She wanted to try to put her thoughts into words, try to make sense of them.

'You really don't need to explain, and thank you for the trip out, it was brilliant.'

'Of course,' she said, her voice a whisper. Half of her wanting to reach out and stop him from leaving, fix this strange new atmosphere. Half of her wanting never to see him again. Why hadn't she been able to laugh things off?

How had they gone from that moment to this? She felt an overwhelming urge to cry, blinking slowly as she watched him let himself out, heard him step from the deck. Marmite barked after him almost like he was chastising her for letting him leave like that. What had she done?

She turned to the kitchen counter, absently picking up a mince pie. She bit into it, the pastry soft and buttery, the mincemeat rich and smooth. It was delicious. It would always remind her of that kiss.

Chapter 31

HE STUMBLED out of the boat, tripping in the dark, the common all shadows now, filled with rustling, insects, night-time sounds. Looking back over his shoulder, he saw the portholes yellow, a shape crossing one of them. What was she thinking?

Pulling his coat tighter around him, he walked away still feeling shell-shocked by the kiss, the urgency he'd felt, the way she'd responded. It had been this blissful day and he'd just totally stuffed it up by lumbering in and leching all over her. No wonder she reacted like she did. *God, Greg, what an idiot.*

He wasn't even sure how it happened, where it had come from. They had been staring at the measly offerings of the kitchen cupboard and then suddenly they'd been staring at each other and the whole boat felt like it was charged with this extraordinary energy and everything had just taken over. He pictured Samantha, his ex-girlfriend, caramel skin, smaller than Eve. He had never felt the same electric charge run through him, the need to hold her, wanting to stay there. It had felt completely right and then, as if someone had dialled the lights up and switched the noise back on, it had gone into freefall.

As he passed underneath the railway bridge, skirting a puddle that dripped off the wall into a tangy smell of rotting rubbish, he pictured her face as she sat on the floor surrounded by spilt pots and chaos. She had looked at him as if he were a stranger, as if he had just appeared in the boat at that moment, as if they hadn't spent the day together. He felt terrible as he stood there, realising he'd blown it, something in her expression warding him off asking too much. He had known at the start of the day that she was distracted by something, had seen it as she had turned on the platform, her body disguised by a hundred jumpers. He'd wanted to hug her then, she had looked so adorable in the cold, bright day. He wasn't even sure if she was single, married, divorced, hadn't asked anything, had just presumed. *Stupid Greg*.

He couldn't shake the kiss, always in the back of his mind as he got back to the flat, half-heartedly made himself dinner, sat unseeing in front of the television, aware of his solitary existence and for the first time in years, missing having someone next door to him. He pictured her curled up under his arm on the sofa, the awkwardness forgotten, the joking and the teasing back, the atmosphere from the boat that day, remembering her walk briskly along the bank calling to him, her head appearing to ask him if he wanted a drink, her laughter, her hand on the tiller, her expression as she steered the boat into the lock, the excitement on her face as the water had risen around her, pushing the boat higher and higher.

Christ, Greg, you've blown it, jumped in way too fast, too heavy-handed. He raked a hand through his hair and tried to force himself to look at the screen. He stared at his mobile, knowing she wouldn't call or text. They hadn't even swapped numbers. Two weeks ago he had no idea that she even existed and yet now every time he closed his eyes all he could see was her face right in front of him, in that moment before he'd stepped forward and drawn her towards him.

Chapter 32

Gingerbread

185g soft dark brown or
   molasses sugar
220g golden syrup
125g butter
2 large eggs, beaten
250g self-raising flour

2 tsp ground ginger
2/3 pieces of chopped
   stem ginger
150ml boiling water
1 tsp bicarbonate of
   soda

Method:

- Pre-heat oven to 160°C.
- Melt sugar, syrup and butter in saucepan. Add this to beaten eggs and flour and ginger. Pour boiling water over bicarbonate of soda and add to mixture. Combine and put in 20 cm square or similar tin. Bake for about 50 minutes. Can ice with thin lemon icing if wished.

SHE HAD twitched all night, throwing off the covers, turning and slapping at the pillow, trying to get comfortable. She would close her eyes and then she would be back there in the kitchen, sitting on the floor staring up at him as if he had done something terribly wrong. She sighed and reached out for Marmite, idly stroking him as he lay curled into himself on the bed. She didn't think about the kiss, blocked it from her mind the moment it strayed there. His face had started to morph into Liam's and she could feel herself spinning with the confusion.

Bleary-eyed, stirring coffee, she clattered round the kitchen, the spice rack still needing to be returned to order, the boat clashing with the smell of spices and sugary sweet cinnamon, reminding her of the day before. When Harriet called, she found herself talking around it, not wanting to share the moment, keeping it close to her as she spoke about the classes, what she'd learnt, the boat, Liam's requests to get Marmite back.

The frustration welled and she let herself take it out on Liam. 'He called wanting Marmite back. It's like he wants to kick me when I'm down.'

'Bastard.'

'Bastard,' Eve agreed, biting on her lip as Harriet asked her what else was new. Harriet who never judged her, whose advice she listened to. She didn't want to hear it though, wasn't yet ready to share.

She ended the phone call feeling frustrated, the boat suddenly too small to contain her mood, her feet loud in the small space as she wandered from bench to table to kitchen and back, fidgety. Marmite watched her with a bemused look on his face, padding round behind her as if she were inventing a new game.

It had been two days without seeing him now. She didn't know what she expected but she still felt her insides tighten as she left the boat, walking into the village to the shops. She looked over her shoulder at the check-out, scanned the faces in the street, stared down the road at the dot that she knew was the sign to the vet practice.

She couldn't seem to shake her irritable mood, crying out when she dropped a jar of strawberry jam, as if something truly terrible had happened (which, frankly, it looked like it had). The weekend dragged by and even the thrill of taking the boat on another journey out, trying to expel the last, couldn't seem to rally her. She stomped to her pottery class on Monday morning in wellies. The sunshine was long gone, the sky filled with whitish, grey clouds that seemed to hang obstinately over the tops of the fields, dulling the water of the river.

She found her seat in the class and allowed herself to focus solely on the task. She was glazing her bowl, squeezing colours into a palette and dipping the paintbrush into the various pools, taking time over each detail, watching as the picture grew before her.

'You're really good at that,' Raj said, his teeth a neat line of white as he looked at her.

'Thanks,' she mumbled, blushing as Minnie then came over, eyes wide as she exclaimed at the small collection Eve was adding to. 'They're gorgeous, they're just getting better and better.'

Eve had also made a plate, realising as she made more, painted more, that she was going to give them to her family for Christmas. She was making a bowl and plate set for her dad, the same river scene. She was going to dress her dad's goose in mismatched clothing, squinting as she carefully painted in a lilac scarf and plum trousers. She felt a flush of pride as she continued, for the first time in days starting to relax again, revel in the peace of the class, the gentle strain of something classical wafting through the door from the living room, the put-put of the wheels as they turned, the quiet chatter of her classmates.

'That's really good,' Danny said, laughing as he peered over her shoulder.

He settled at his wheel, slapping water over the bowl that he was making, pushing down into the middle of the clay as it rotated.

Eve had looked up when he spoke, something about his voice making her stare at him. She found herself watching him work. He looked up, noticing her watching him. 'You, er, you all right there, Eve?'

'Fine, yes, just... resting.' There was something about him that made her want to share, to turn towards him and let it all spill out: the reason she had come here, the satisfaction she was getting from the lessons. But she simply nodded, embarrassed to be caught looking at him.

'Are you sure, you look a bit hot,' he said, frowning, pushing his blond hair away with the back of his hand. Clay was smeared over his palms and wrists.

'I'm really fine, just worrying about this glaze. It's hard to tell how it will come out, isn't it?'

'Well, by the looks of things it will come out pretty well.' He indicated her first two pots with his head, sitting on the shelf above them, proudly displayed. 'You are really good, you know.' The tone of his voice comforted her and she found herself feeling buoyed up once more.

It was a great class and Eve felt the soothing power of focusing on something else a powerful remedy to the fuss and hum of her head. She was shrugging on her coat, putting a hat on her head as Danny wound a scarf around his neck.

'You should come out one night before you run back to London. My brother and I often go to the Crosskeys, do you know it?'

Eve nodded. 'I know where it is. I haven't been there yet.'

'Well you should, nice place.'

She wondered whether he was asking her on a date and froze at the thought. It really was the last thing she needed.

'My ex cheated on me,' she said quickly. 'I'm not really, well, he hurt me and...'

Danny was trying not to laugh at her, his cheeks puffed out like a hamster.

'What?' Eve lost her train of thought completely.

'I wasn't asking you on a date, Eve.' He laughed, holding up both hands in surrender. 'Just thought you could meet my friends, my brother. I think they'd like you.'

'Oh, oh well, that is...' Eve could feel her limbs itch with embarrassment, her palms grow sweaty. 'That's really kind, I'm sorry, I...'

'Not to worry, Eve, no pressure,' Danny said, pushing his fringe out of his eyes.

'I won't... worry that is, oh God, I'm an embarrassment.'

'No, you're not.' Danny laughed. 'I get it, really, and your ex, by the way, sounds like a proper penis.'

'He is.' Eve nodded miserably.

'Well I'll let you know next time, maybe?' His smile was simple and easy and Eve found herself returning it. 'That would be good.'

'See you tomorrow, Eve. Bye, Minnie. Bye, Raj.' He waved and was gone through the living room and out the front door.

Eve couldn't help but bring her hands to both cheeks, cringing as she thought back to the conversation. She jumped as Aisha appeared beside her. 'Are you heading into the village?' she asked. Her small diamond nose stud winked as she spoke.

Eve nodded and Aisha joined her, light on her feet as if she was a child.

They started walking past the apple tree stripped of any fruit, the garden waiting for spring, and pushed through the gate and out on the path next to the river. Patches of water appeared through the treeline, the flap of a bird disturbed by the noise they were making, as they stepped over the mud frozen in its churned-up state.

'Are you excited, gearing up to everything?' Eve asked, determined not to blight her wedding happiness.

Aisha smiled slowly. 'So excited. And also terrified.'

Eve laughed. 'I imagine that's pretty standard. I think it is very sweet, that the two of you are making things for your guests. I imagine they'll love it.'

'Oh good, that's what I keep saying to Mark.' She seemed pleased with this, practically skipping along the path.

'So where are you headed?' Eve asked as they walked across the iron bridge, looking down at two canoeists passing underneath them. The river was a muted sludge of brown and greens today, barely any light reflecting off its surface. She thought of the contrast, each day on the river different, the water always shifting, reflecting the sky above.

'I'm going to work. I'm doing the late shift,' she explained.

'Where's that then?'

'The estate agent on the corner. Do you know it?'

'Oh,' Eve said with a little start. 'Do you work with Martin then?'

Aisha paused briefly before a wary, 'Yes, is he, um, is he a friend of yours?'

Eve couldn't help herself, the sentence exploded out of her. 'God no, he's appalling. I just rent the boat from you and have been dealing with him.'

This announcement had clearly flustered Aisha. 'Actually,' she said, composing herself, 'Martin's leaving at the end of the year.' She looked over her shoulder when she said it as if worried she was being watched. Eve turned round. 'He um... he hasn't been a great success.'

Eve giggled at the understatement and Aisha looked at her sideways, a helpless smile on her face. 'Well,' she coughed, pulling herself together, 'I better get going but it was lovely to talk to you, Eve.'

'You too,' Eve said, feeling the glow of sensing that she had made a new friend.

She watched Aisha leave, winding her way into the village, imagining her in the office desperately trying to make polite chit-chat with Martin as he spent time searching on the internet for another falcon for his collection, or whatever he did for fun. What a pairing.

She ambled to the boat, gratified to hear Marmite's excited bark as she approached, hauled him out as she opened the door, then watched him race around the common. In the distance she could see two angry geese waddling her way and she called Marmite back into the boat as their honking neared. *Don't be scared, Eve, they're only geese.*

'Marmite! Come on, Marmite! MARMITE.'

As she sat in the boat later that day, the woodburning stove crackling, one eye on her book, a novel she'd bought in the village that week – there were only so many unusual orchids she could take – the earlier peace was forgotten. Marmite was asleep on her lap, but even his steady breathing couldn't stop her getting restless. Her phone sat by her side but she had already called Daisy. She hadn't answered, but then to be fair, she had a job and so Eve had just left an absurd message part-song, part-chanting, to make her smile.

She stared out at the common and the few people dotted about. One man was sitting on a bench with a newspaper; a woman walked past holding two toddlers by both hands, bending down to their eye level as she spoke to them. She hadn't seen him in days. She had started to expect him, making sure she had bought biscuits and things for his sudden appearances, feeling excited if she spotted someone running in the distance. The Tupperware container he had brought the mince pies in was washed and sitting on the draining board ready to be returned. She stared at it as she walked past it, the box reminding her of that day.

Her eyes roved the boat and she felt that old sense of impatience. She hadn't felt fidgety like this since she had first arrived, used now to the pace of the boat and the sounds of the river, the movement of the boat, the leaves that floated past on the current. She gently lifted Marmite away from her and he opened one sleepy accusatory eye as she stood up.

Reaching for a recipe book, she moved across to the kitchen counter. Trawling its pages, not exactly sure what she was looking for, she stopped at a picture. She scanned the list of ingredients, remembering Greg telling her not to over-complicate things. It seemed straightforward enough and she realised as she trailed a finger down the list that she had the ingredients she needed.

Feeling a flicker of excitement, she set to work, reaching for the plastic scales and starting to tip flour and sugar into heaped piles. Searching for an egg from the fridge, she laughed as Marmite appeared in the gap.

'Typical,' she smiled, switching on the oven and rootling for one of the treats he loved at the same time.

'Sit,' she said, watching in delight as he obediently followed her order. 'Good boy,' she cooed, feeding him the treat and feeling another swell of pride as he returned to a spot in front of the stove.

Half an hour later and the whole boat smelt of golden syrup and sponge. She hopped up every two minutes to check on it through the glass screen of the oven and squeaked as she pulled out the loaf tin. It had risen; it was gorgeous. Biting her lip, she grabbed a tea towel and gently cut around the shape with a knife. This was the moment, she thought, as she turned it over and tapped the bottom. She felt weight in the tea towel and carefully flipped it back over onto a waiting plate. It had survived in one piece, the gingerbread soft in the middle and perfectly browned on top.

She sliced it and loaded all the pieces into the Tupperware container. As she covered the layers in pieces of kitchen roll, she grinned over at Marmite who had appeared again, thinking that whatever was in the container was his.

'Aren't I clever?' she said, untying her hair and rushing through to fetch her coat, pausing at the bathroom mirror to put on some pale lipstick, circling her eyes with brown shadow in smudged lines. She cleaned her teeth quickly, re-applying lipstick and looking at herself in the mirror. She briefly recalled her words to Danny earlier but blocked out the thought with a huff. She wasn't over her ex; this was just an innocent trip into the village. *Stop staring at me, smirking face in the mirror.* She poked a tongue out at herself. The smell as she walked back into the kitchen made her grin. She had done it all on her own, the scent of hot sponge coming off it in hot waves, the root ginger lingering in the boat as she went to lock up.

Putting Marmite on a lead and heading out over the common, she wondered whether he would mind her simply appearing at his workplace. She looked at Marmite and felt a stab of guilt for using him in this way.

Walking under the railway bridge, a train rattled above them. Eve, already jumpy, yelped as they moved through the tunnel. There were more decorations up today, every shop on the high street now making some effort. The baker had put a Santa and a sledge on the tiled roof of his shop; the delicatessen had sprayed snow into the edges of its windows; the café had a miniature Christmas tree outside, next to a blackboard offering a free mince pie with every coffee. Eve moved down the row of houses towards the vet practice, enjoying the small glimpses inside the front rooms of houses on the high street, smiling at the pinecones in bowls on tables, the fairy lights draped across mantlepieces, presents already wrapped and placed under trees.

The bell rang out as she arrived in the practice, a poster of an enormous St Bernard announcing half-price vaccinations for new clients. She was fairly certain Marmite had been vaccinated recently, remembered Liam moaning about taking a morning off work to do it.

Eve approached the desk, pursing her lips as the receptionist, a middle-aged lady on the phone, her chest wobbling as she spoke, finished her call.

She looked up at Eve, smiling with startlingly pink lips, 'Can I help you?'

'I was wondering if you had a free appointment?' Eve asked in a quiet voice, aware of the other people waiting in a line on the plastic chairs behind her.

Before she could continue, a familiar voice was heard, a door opened and Greg stepped through, his face flushed, his hair sticking up, a stethoscope hanging round his neck.

'Karen, can you pop through a moment and help... Eve.'

He stopped short.

'Oh!' Eve giggled, feeling absurd as she did so. *What are you, twelve years old? Stop giggling at him, woman.*

She straightened. 'I needed an appointment,' she said quickly. *Because that is why you come to a busy vet's practice during the day.*

Greg stepped forward, a look of concern on his face, bending down to take a look at Marmite. 'Has anything happened?' He was checking him over and she felt her stomach lurch. He seemed to be really worried.

'Oh... he, it was his...' *Agh, she had not thought this through, oh God.* And now, looking at him, she was reminded again of the kiss. His face was like one big pair of giant lips as he looked up at her.

'He was whining about something maybe in his... foot, leg, near his, on his...' *Wow, Eve, seriously, pick one.*

'Which leg?' Greg asked. Eve's eyes darted to one of the women on the plastic chairs, who seemed to be checking her watch as she witnessed this impromptu consultation.

'The right one, front one, that one,' Eve said, pointing at the nearest leg to her.

Greg was extending and feeling along the leg, waiting for Marmite's reaction. Marmite could not have looked more relaxed if he had whipped open some doggy cigarettes and stood there puffing.

Karen looked at Eve. 'Doesn't look like he's in pain,' she said, eyes narrowed as if she were about to pull a torch from her drawer and shine a light in Eve's eyes.

Greg's frown disappeared and he scooped Marmite into his arms. 'Karen, I am just going to examine this dog very briefly. I won't be long,' he said, turning to the other clients who, so bowled over by his smile, started nodding and chorusing 'no problem'.

'Eve, why don't you go ahead?' he said, indicating the door with his head and following her inside.

The consulting room was a plain square, a silver table in the middle, a stool on either side. Greg popped Marmite onto the middle of it and Marmite decided to walk up and down along it as if he were on a mini Dog Fashion catwalk.

Greg's mouth was twitching. 'So the leg, um... seems to be coping pretty well.' He raised an eyebrow at Eve, who felt her whole face was burning.

'Hmm,' she said, pulling herself back as if she had been underwater. 'I really thought he might have damaged—'

Greg had started chuckling softly. 'There's not really anything wrong with his leg is there, Eve?'

'I'm so sorry,' she said through gaps in her fingers. 'Oh God, I am never going to be able to face your receptionist again. She is terrifying. It's like getting an appointment with the prime minister.'

Greg laughed, his face splitting open and his eyes brightening. The strip lights overhead showed up the bags under his eyes and she wondered whether he was getting ill, he looked tired beneath the grin.

'I actually made you something and I just didn't want to leave things as we left them and, well, here,' she said, thrusting the container in front of him, not wanting to make him feel any worse, so relieved to see him again and feel that maybe nothing had changed, she hadn't ruined anything.

'Oh. Well, that's kind,' he said, staring at the container he was holding in two hands.

Eve was now feeling suddenly silly. She had come to his place of work, clients with sick animals were waiting in the chairs outside and she was showing him a cake she had made.

He peeled off the lid and lifted it up. 'They smell amazing,' he said, his face impressed, so Eve felt a rush of gratitude.

'Gingerbread,' she said. 'I kept it simple.' Then felt her palms slippery as she wondered whether he would remember his advice.

'Well, thank you so much,' he said, clicking the lid of the container back on and placing it on the table.

'Would you like to come for dinner or something?' she asked.

'Why don't I take you to dinner somewhere?'

Their questions had clashed and Eve continued babbling.

'Oh no, I didn't want to force you to—'

'I'd love to,' Greg cut her off. 'I've got hockey tonight but I can do Thursday? I could come to the boat just before eight? Does that suit?'

'Yes, brilliant, lovely, that would be great.'

'Right, I probably do need to see my clients now.' He indicated outside with his head.

'Oh yes, of course, yes,' Eve said, seizing Marmite from the table and nodding. 'Good, good.'

'Yes, it is good,' Greg said, his mouth twitching again.

He opened the door of the consulting room and she walked out, straight past the receptionist, trying not to meet anyone's eye as she headed for the door.

'Oh and, Eve,' Greg's voice stopped her in her tracks.

'Be sure to come back at any time if Marmite's leg plays up again.'

Eve didn't trust herself to reply, just mumbled something as Greg smiled and she pushed open the door, the bell signalling her exit.

Chapter 33

EVE TRIED to play it down, focusing on her classes, chatting with Aisha, Mark and Danny, phoning Daisy and Harriet, but it was always in the back of her mind. She found herself smiling as she recalled their day out on the boat, the trip to the Christmas market. She realised with a start that she was really excited about seeing him again, that she tingled in anticipation as she thought back to that kiss. She spent far too long wondering what to wear. Thursday came around and she stood in her pants in the bedroom, staring blankly at the small collection of clothes she had brought with her.

'What do you think, Marmite?'

Marmite got up, grabbed one of her favourite dresses and trailed it through the boat as a response.

'MARMITE!' she shouted, standing in the living room in her bra and pants pointing at him. 'DROP.'

He did so but only because a large eye appeared in the porthole at the same time as she said it. A loud honk made both of them jump.

'Leave us alone,' Eve called, covering her boobs as if the goose was perving on her in her underwear.

It had been ages since Eve had really made an effort on her appearance, so she was relieved to see that she had thrown in her favourite brown suede miniskirt, coupling it with her soft cream cashmere jumper with the short sleeves. Slipping on her knee boots and bending to zip them, she felt her hair, clean and blow-dried, falling over her face. She spent a while making up her face with bronzer, mascara and lipgloss. She hoped she wasn't over-dressed as she sat spritzing on perfume on the bench in the boat.

Had she made the boat smell too much of perfume? Would he want to come in for a drink first? She felt jittery, her stomach rolling. She was biting away the lipgloss as she told Marmite off for scrambling up her boots. She hadn't felt like this since the early days of dating Liam, when he had called at her flat to take her out. She blinked, refusing to let thoughts of him in. She fixed her mind on Greg, his gentle smile when he'd suggested they go out, his face when he'd seen the gingerbread she'd made. It was as if the awkwardness of the last few days had deserted them. For a second she pictured his face right next to hers.

She turned the television on, glancing for the fifteenth time at the clock on the wall, trying to look out for signs of him, but the common was too dark now. It was too cold to wait for him on the deck, she could hear the wind whistling around, the river slapping against the sides of the boat. She was glad for the warmth of the boat, hoped they would be going to a restaurant with an open fire, sipping red wine as their feet and hands warmed up.

There was a knock then and her insides leapt once more. Smoothing her hair, she stood up, surprised by her strength of feeling. Plastering a smile on her face, she opened the door, letting the wind whip inside, lifting her hair as Greg pushed through.

'You ma—'

'I'm so sorry to do this.' He was gabbling quickly, his hair sticking up from the wind, looking at her with urgent blue eyes so that her stomach did another flip. 'I can't stay. I didn't have your number or I'd have called. I've got to go, I'm afraid, it's an emergency.' He had already turned back. He was wearing the camel-coloured coat, his hair styled. Why was he leaving? He was smartly dressed; they were heading out to a restaurant.

'Right, I—'

He didn't give her time to react or respond, had already left her, slipping in his shoes back over the common into the darkness. He had barely registered her, hadn't looked properly at her at all. Now he was gone, a speck in the car park, diving into his car, the lights fired up and a screech as he reversed and turned left into the high street. Where was he going? What emergency could possibly happen at 8 p.m. on a Thursday night?

She had obviously misread things earlier, her sudden appearance at his practice must have forced him into things and he'd had time to reflect and change his mind. Then she thought back to the other times he had run off, checked his watch, seemed to be in that strange, distracted mood. She couldn't trust him; she barely knew him really. It wasn't enough that she felt this incredible spark between them; it was all in her mind. It was just like Liam and her all over again.

God knows what Greg was up to and she had been stupid enough to fall for it all again. They'd only just met really, but she felt so comfortable around him, relaxed and herself. No doubt he was seeing other girls. Maybe he always preyed on people new to the village. Either way, she felt stupid and silly to be making the same mistakes all over again. *Do you never learn, Eve?* You came here to reinvent yourself, start to live your own life again, learn a new skill, make new friends. You weren't meant to fall for a guy the moment you stepped off the train.

Eve stood on the deck, drops of rain clinging to her newly dried hair, making her mascara run. The wind howled round her as she stood there staring dumbly out into the darkness. Her arms broke out into goosebumps; her skirt dotted with raindrops. Somewhere behind her an animal called, a pitying sound, sharp, causing her to turn with a start. She felt like joining in.

Chapter 34

'**Y**OU DON'T need to keep dropping everything,' she said, taking her time over the words, her breathing heavy in the gaps.

Greg flicked his eyes across to Danny, who was standing by the window, his big arms folded so that he looked more like a bouncer than ever. 'We're not dropping everything, we want to come.' Greg took her hand and held it, trying not to react to the weight of it, the veins that seemed to protrude now on paper-thin skin. When had his tough old mum become this old lady?

Danny stayed at the window, his face grimly battling whatever thoughts were going on inside. This illness had made the brothers talk a little more but they weren't great at it. Up till six months ago they'd only ever talked about sport, women, Danny's cars, Greg's work. They tentatively spoke about treatments and outcomes, but it wasn't often and now, seeing Danny struggling, Greg knew he probably needed to ask more.

She had been on the waiting list for a few months and they'd been told others had been waiting for years. He knew he shouldn't hope, but the doctor had been clear; the damage to both kidneys was severe and dialysis was in no way a cure. She had an overnight bag packed and when the call came she

221

called one of them to get her to the hospital. This time they'd put her through the tests again but had refused to operate. The kidney wasn't viable; they weren't able to explain more.

Greg knew his mum was disappointed and scared but she looked at him with her steady gaze, half her mouth lifting at the corner, a mysterious smile, her eyes playful. 'There'll be another one,' she said, in a way that he knew was meant to reassure them.

Danny looked away, out over the grounds of the hospital car park, away from the words, the bleep-bleep-bleep of the bloody machine next to her, the drip puncturing her arm, the smell of disinfectant.

'I've written a list,' Mum said, indicating a piece of paper tucked between her book. Greg reached across and opened it, remembering the page number so he could return it.

'You can fold the page,' his mum said, the teasing tone in her voice, the bookworm berating her for taking books in the bath, folding the corners.

Greg looked at her, mock-appalled, relieved to cling onto this piece of normality.

She gave a soft laugh and it made Danny turn back towards them.

'Take a look,' she said. 'Both of you.' She turned her head to Danny. Her voice was raspy and cracked. It made Greg want to weep tears of frustration, remembering his mum singing embarrassingly at Midnight Mass, her voice soaring into the rafters, off-key but totally joyful, her voice screeching at them on the side of the hockey pitch, hollering at them to come in from the garden for tea, her voice filled with life and energy. He bit his tongue, terrified that he might break down and where would that leave them all?

He turned to the list.

Bank Password
Granny's figurines
White goods
Funeral
Rings

'The first one is simple. If it happens I want one of you to use my card and withdraw all the money from the account, the PIN number is 1981. There's not much but I want you to pay any funeral expenses out of it and then share the rest between you...'

The year 1981 when Greg had been born. He swallowed, unable to find a reply to her. His mind was slow to catch up with her as she continued.

'Granny's figurines. I know you don't like them and I won't be around to see where they end up, but the glass-fronted cabinet is an antique so don't just give it away. There's one figure I love though, the blue ballerina, and I thought it might be nice to keep for...' she paused, staring up at the ceiling, and then continued as if nothing had happened, 'any grandchildren you might have. They'd like it, I think...'

Greg could feel his throat blocking, his chest starting to hurt.

'The white goods in the house are old and probably about to go kaput, but I only bought the dishwasher last year and it's still under warranty with John Lewis so please don't just sell it on, one of you have it.'

'I don't want to listen any more,' Danny said, his voice gruff, as if he had just been winded on the hockey pitch.

'Mum,' Greg said, his hand resting over hers, 'this isn't necessary.'

'It is,' she said in a quiet voice. 'It might be. I just wanted to write it down. I wanted you both to know,' she said, turning her head, aiming the words at Danny's back, 'I've thought of these things.'

Greg felt as if someone had taken a knife and sunk it between his ribs; his whole chest ached as he said, 'We do know, Mum.'

She did well up now, her eyes misting over, one tear escaping down the corner of her cheek. Her colour had drained away, her skin had sunk. 'If it's not to be though, I don't want just to leave you with it all. I want to help.'

Greg felt the words blocked in his throat. Danny's shoulders were shaking as he looked back out over the car park. 'It's not going to happen though, they'll find a match.'

Greg thought of last night, the beating of his heart as he had raced through the streets of Oxford in his car, no doubt setting off speed cameras as he made his way to the hospital.

She'd been called at home, asked to go in straightaway. She'd been with her neighbour Peggy at the time, who had insisted on driving her there. She'd called both boys from the car. 'This might be it,' she said, determined to sound calm, not get their hopes up.

Greg hadn't been able to stay calm, had been preparing for dinner with Eve. He didn't have her number, knew he needed to go but didn't want to just leave her wondering. He knew he didn't have long, didn't want to miss it. There had been an accident, a kidney had become available. He didn't want to think about why, that someone else's world had just imploded. He didn't want to hope but he couldn't help it, his heart busting out of his chest when his mum had phoned and confirmed, agreeing to pick up Danny on his way.

Eve had looked wonderful and, as he arrived, he suddenly

wanted to throw himself into her arms, feel the softness of her jumper, stay with her and Marmite in front of the woodburning stove rather than face the rain-soaked drive to the hospital to see his mum, this new, thinner mum who struggled to talk for a long time, who needed visits three times a week for dialysis. He hadn't stayed a second though, afraid of missing it all, hoping he could see his mum before the operation. Eve had stood on the deck of the boat in the rain, Marmite silhouetted next to her, as he had turned back into the village, mind filled then with his mum.

And now they were here and there would be no operation. Mum would be returning home and Danny and him would have another few weeks, months, years waiting to see. A childish part of him wanted to scream through the corridors of the hospital, stamp and shout until someone helped them. Instead, though, he helped his mum into a wheelchair, pushing her slowly and carefully through to the car, hugging Danny silently just before they got in to take her home.

Chapter 35

SHE WAS walking to class along the edges of the river. The water had risen in the last few days, the weekend a miserable wash-out and she was surprised by the level. The path was littered with rotting leaves, some floating on the top of large puddles. Eve's boots were covered in mud, dots splashed up her legs and onto the back of her black leggings. The air smelt of wet earth and Eve imagined insects crawling over the landscape. She had her phone clamped to her ear and was partway through telling Harriet about Greg's disappearing act the night before.

'Well, he must have had a good reason,' Harriet insisted. 'Hold on, Gavin's here, I'm putting you on speaker phone...'

'Oh no... don't...'

'Gavin, it's Eve.'

'Hi, Eve.'

'Hey, Gavin.' Eve gave up fighting it, not sure she wanted to share everything with her brother-in-law.

'Eve's new bloke ran off last night before their date.'

'What new bloke?' Gavin asked.

'He's not my new bloke,' Eve insisted.

'The new bloke, he's a vet apparently, he's run off.'

'I'm so confused,' Gavin said. 'And don't they usually run off after the date?'

226

'The weird thing,' Harriet filled him in using Eve's exact words from moments before, 'was that he seemed dressed for a date and then, bang, he was off, diving into his ca... Gavin, are you listening?'

'Oh, I'm sorry, Poppy was pointing and saying "Phone".'

'Focus, Gavin, focus,' Harriet chided.

'Sorry.'

Eve giggled, feeling cheered already by talking to them both. 'So what do you think is up with him? Do you think he's seeing someone else?' She had spent an absurd amount of time wondering; running through different scenarios, new answers entering her mind, each more unlikely than the next.

'Maybe,' Harriet said quietly, probably not wanting Eve to get her hopes up.

'Yeah, but if he does I'm sure she won't hold a candle to you,' Gavin said, trying to steer them back from moping.

'Thanks, Gavin,' Eve said.

'Yeah thanks, creepy brother-in-law,' Harriet said.

'I wasn't being creepy.'

'I know, I know. Look, Eve, tread carefully, but you know,' Harriet mused, 'maybe he really did have an emergency to get to?'

'Or maybe he is a spy,' Gavin offered.

'Don't be ridiculous, Gavin.' Harriet sighed. 'Maybe he was seeing an animal,' she suggested. 'Don't vets have to do that?'

Eve considered this option. 'Maybe, but he was a bit smartly dressed for it.'

'Maybe he's a smartly dressed kinda guy. We are a dying breed, ladies.'

'Gavin, really. And, Eve, it definitely could have been a work emergency. I watched a programme about vets who always had to go out and rescue cats in trees and things.'

227

'Pretty sure that's firemen, Harriet.'

'Oh. Oh yes, it might have been.'

'So what should I do?' Eve asked, walking up the path to the side of the house, waving at Aisha who was standing smiling at her from the conservatory.

'You could turn up to his work again?' Harriet suggested.

'Er... bit extreme, isn't it? Why doesn't she just phone him?' Gavin asked.

'Um, hello, she doesn't have his phone number.'

'What?' said Gavin, clearly flummoxed. 'How is this possible? Eve, you are aware it is the twenty-first century and that basically the first things you do are (a) Introduce yourself, (b) Get their phone number and email, and (c) Instantly Facebook Friend Request them.'

'Not helpful, Gavin. Again.'

Eve stood outside the conservatory, the pottery class about to begin. 'Guys, I have a class—'

'I didn't know about the phone thing...'

'Well now you do, we need a new plan.'

'Yes, and maybe you should just wait for him, I mean, you know, in case he is a two-timing shitbag like your last boyf—'

'GUYS!' Eve called over them. 'I have to go, I have a class.'

'Oh right, okay, well, I'm sure you'll work something out, Eve,' Gavin said.

'I say wait for him to get in touch, but live your life, so don't WAIT for him, but just leave it because you are a strong, independent woman who any guy would be LUCKY to have—'

'Harriet, I really have to go, I get the gist.'

'Okay, well, be strong.'

'I will. I'll be strong.'

Eve hung up, jumping as Minnie's head appeared from the double glass doors. 'Why are you loitering out there? Come in, it's freezing.' She chivvied her inside, closing the double doors behind her, a theatrical shiver as she did so. 'Were you on the phone to a certain local vet?' Minnie asked, waggling her eyebrows as Eve felt her face go as red as the coat she was removing.

'No, nope, no,' she said quickly, not keen to fill Minnie in on what was happening; she would no doubt be unable to keep it to herself.

'Don't worry, Danny isn't here,' Minnie said and went to sit down.

'Why would that... I don't understand.' Had Minnie imagined that Eve liked Danny?

'They're brothers,' she said, laughing at Eve's expression. 'Didn't you know? Well,' she paused, 'I suppose they don't really look very similar. Although same noses perhaps?'

'They're brothers,' Eve repeated, wracking her brains now for any mention of Greg. Oh my goodness. She thought back to the conversation with Danny about the pub. She'd basically accused him of hitting on her. She felt her toes curl in embarrassment. That had been Greg's brother.

Aisha looked up from her wheel, a question on her face, and Eve headed straight to her seat, eyes on the floor, determined to be ignored. At least Danny wasn't here; he would have found it hilarious and she wasn't in the mood to be wound up by him.

Minnie, however, was clearly in the mood for gossip and was opening her mouth ready to continue. Raj, fortunately, chose that moment to intervene and Eve looked up at him with large, thankful eyes. As Minnie gave up, Eve was sure he gave her the tiniest wink.

'Eve, before we start, I was wondering... I wanted to start running some pottery classes for kids, you see, and I thought you might be able to design me something for a business card?'

Eve had been looking at his eyes, the dark lashes, the neat eyebrows, as she followed what he was saying. 'Design you...' She was confused now, her own eyebrows meeting in the middle.

'I thought one of your cartoons could be perfect. I'm great with pots but I'm no illustrator.'

'But I'm not an illustrator,' Eve said quickly.

'But your cartoons are perfect, they are really comic. I was hoping you might have an idea.'

And, already, as he said it, Eve was imagining what she could design for Raj. A duck on a potter's wheel, a cartoon dog trying to make something out of clay. A slow smile spread across her face as the images cascaded through her mind. 'I could have a go,' she heard herself saying and was rewarded with a flash of Raj's incredibly white teeth.

'Excellent, thank you.'

The class began and Eve continued to work on a large fruit bowl that she had started the lesson before. Her hands were caked in clay, slippery with water, as she gradually coaxed the edges up, the bowl taking shape, the satisfaction in her chest as she watched it transform. Grateful too that the spotlight had ceased to be on her, she listened in detail as Minnie grilled Aisha and Mark about their wedding. Eve was lapping up the details as if she had been out in a desert as they discussed the theme, their wedding band, Aisha's worries about the cost of bridesmaids' dresses, finding suitable readings.

'It's hard to find something people haven't heard before.'

'You could try Christina Rossetti, I read lots of hers and they have lovely words, the sentiments are perfect for a wedding. And have you looked at the website "Preloved"?

There are some great bargains on there.' Eve couldn't believe she had piped up, it had been weeks since she put away her own wedding scrapbook, with pictures of dresses and print-outs from the internet. Still, seeing Aisha's face light up as she scribbled the suggestions down, Eve felt happiness spread through her.

The week swept by, Danny failed to appear to lessons at all and Eve briefly wondered whether he was ill, too embarrassed to ask Minnie in case she teased her again. She became absorbed in her bowl, adding details to it every day. She spent the evenings sketching ideas for Raj's business cards, determined to come up with something he might like. She cooked recipes too, carefully following the recipe books and enjoying the quiet peace of waiting for things to boil now that life seemed less frantic. She knew she would be returning to her old life, racing around London, commuting to work, heading out, crammed into the Tube, walking quickly, feeling flustered. For now though, she could enjoy the slower pace, immerse herself in drawing and painting and pottery. She toyed with the idea of appearing at Greg's practice again but, as another day passed and he hadn't appeared, her confidence wavered. He would come if he cared, surely?

Chapter 36

DAISY AND Eve were perched in the bathroom, taking turns in the circular mirror. It was Ro-Ro's wedding in a few short hours and they were getting ready together as if they were back in London about to embark on a night out.

Daisy had appeared that morning, clothes bag draped over one arm, leather holdall in the other, stepping off the train at Pangbourne. Music was reverberating around the tiny space, pumped out of Daisy's iPhone, and they were taking turns choosing songs from the playlist. Eve was determined not to be a wedding drag, to look fabulous and show her friends she was moving on. It was bound to be a spectacular wedding, Ro-Ro's parents lived in an insanely posh house just outside Didcot, and the invitations in italic scroll on stiff cardboard had arrived with delicate layers of tissue paper separating the pages so you just knew money had been spent.

Eve had bought a ruby-red dress online and was wiggling into it now, holding her hair up so that Daisy could zip up the back.

'That's gorgeous,' Daisy said admiringly as Eve smoothed down the front.

It fitted perfectly, a thin belt nipping in the waist, the fabric clinging without showing every lump and bump. The low neckline edged with lace was pretty low but Eve reasoned that she would be wearing her cream woollen coat in church, which would keep her respectable. She had straightened her hair and clipped it back, outlined her eyes in liner, brushed on blusher and was now filling out her lips in a deep red. She felt glamorous as she burst into a snatch of the chorus, throwing an arm round Daisy as she sang.

Sitting on the bench and bending over to put on her heels before they headed out to the taxi that would be waiting in the car park, she thought she heard her name being called. Frowning as she repinned the front of her hair from her face, she jumped back with a start as a man appeared in one of the porthole windows.

It was Greg.

She sucked in her breath. Daisy was calling to her from the bathroom and Pharrell Williams was telling her to be 'Happy' very, very loudly. She had wondered whether she would see him all week and he was here. She clattered through the living room, not sure what she'd say or do. It had been eight days since his emergency. What kind of 'emergency' takes that long? She had convinced herself that there was nothing there, no spark between them, but looking at him through the porthole she felt her stomach ache. Then she remembered the days in between. He could have come by any time; what the hell was he playing at? She felt her fists curl into themselves, sick of men presuming they could mess her around all the time. Well, not this time.

She stepped out onto the deck, peering down over the side of the boat, almost a foot taller in her heels. He stood on the bank below, looking up at her. He looked good, relaxed, wrapped in his camel-coloured coat. She'd felt skittish all week, wondering if she'd see him every time she went into the village, roaming from anger to bewilderment back to feigning indifference. She'd wanted Danny to reappear in class so she could ask him, and was then relieved when he failed to appear.

'You look... gosh,' Greg said, pulling a hand through his hair. 'Look, Eve, I wanted to apologise for the other night. You must have thought it was very rude and—'

'Not really,' Eve said, feigning nonchalance, thrown by his sudden appearance. She was about to get in a taxi, go to a wedding, mingle, dance and forget the last couple of months.

'Well, it was rude and I'm sorry.'

'Not at all,' Eve said. 'An emergency is an emergency,' she continued, her voice brittle.

'Have you got a moment? No, it doesn't look like you have,' he said, almost talking to himself, indicating the red dress with a hand.

'Look, Greg, I don't know what is going on with you but I don't need to know. You've obviously taken long enough to think up some brilliant story.'

Greg looked up. 'Well, I wanted to explain.'

'Please don't bother. I don't need to hear lies.' Eve felt herself growing taller as she spoke.

'They won't be lies,' Greg said, taking a step forward.

'That's what they always say,' Eve said, Liam's face replacing Greg's in her mind as she spat out the next sentence, all the things she should have said to him. 'I've been messed around before so it's really not a big surprise.'

Greg didn't reply for a moment. 'I'm not "they",' he said in a quiet voice.

'We barely know each other anyway,' Eve said, satisfied to see him flinch.

'I know that but I thought, well, I felt...' He pulled a hand through his hair, his face hardening. 'Well, I obviously read it wrong and you obviously know me oh so well, so God forbid I dare to contradict you.' His voice was rising now, his fists curling.

'What's that supposed to mean?'

'You tell me, Eve, you seem to be able to know exactly what is going on with me.' He had lowered his voice again, his anger controlled and devastating.

She felt backed into a corner, not able to think things through before reacting. 'Oh, I am so sorry that your mysterious double life has been totally busted.' Her voice was laced with sarcasm. 'But I don't need to hear it, you are free to be with who you want to be. I don't have any claim on you.'

'You don't,' he said, his mouth in a thin line, his blue eyes glittering.

'Well, that's settled then,' Eve said, feeling as confused as her thoughts.

The taxi was pulling up in the car park beyond and Eve's eyes flicked over towards it. She wished it had come ten minutes before and she would never have needed to get into all this; she would have been on her way to a wedding.

She could hear Daisy moving through the boat in her floral dress and heels.

'The taxi's here, Daisy,' she called over her shoulder.

'Coming!' the call came back and then Daisy appeared, her ginger hair curled and smooth. 'I keep getting my stilettos caught in the... Hi, sorry,' she said, straightening as she spotted Greg on the bank.

'Hi,' he said, his hand half-raised in a wave, his face creased, brows drawn together. 'I'll get out of your way,' he said quickly, his face turned up towards Eve.

Eve had caught Daisy's appraising gaze. What did Daisy see, she wondered? A good-looking man with messy brown hair, a straight nose, purple shadows under his eyes? He sounded terribly weary all of a sudden.

'Fine,' Eve whispered, feeling tears spring to the back of her eyes and not wanting to give him the satisfaction of seeing he'd upset her. 'That's probably best,' she added.

'I... I actually thought...' He didn't carry on, went to step forward one more time, a hand up, and then it fell away. 'I was wrong.'

Eve imagined a terrible flicker of sadness on his face before he turned away from her. She watched him walk back over the common, shoulders down, as if she'd broken him. For a brief second she wanted to run after him and take it all back. What was he wrong about? What had he thought? But then she hardened herself to it. She had gone out with someone for four years and had never worked it out; she didn't want to get into it now. *You don't know him, Eve, and you don't need more lies.*

'Who was that?' Daisy asked as Eve turned to look at her.

Eve paused momentarily before replying. Her eyes had lost their earlier sparkle, her painted red mouth turning down. 'Greg,' she said, not meeting Daisy's eye.

There was obviously something about Eve's look that stopped Daisy asking anything more.

Chapter 37

HE REALISED he was looking forward to seeing her. The hospital had drained him and Danny had stayed that night, both of them gloomily moving around the flat, not even bothering to summon the energy to make a proper breakfast the next day. The milk had soured so they stood in the kitchen spooning dry cereal into their mouths.

He knew he probably needed to explain why he'd raced off. He had been meaning to tell her but the week had been jam-packed, Katie unable to do any extra days for him, visiting Mum who seemed to have deflated since the false alarm, struggling to conceal her disappointment. He hadn't wanted to tell Eve everything. She didn't need that; it was too much and she was only in the village for a while. But he knew that wasn't the only reason. He'd been avoiding people for weeks, everyone well-meaning but all asking the same questions in the same pitying tone, and when he was with Eve and she didn't know he could be himself, not waiting for the tilt of the head, the kind eyes.

He could hear music coming from the boat the moment he stepped onto the common, smiling as he imagined her dancing round the living room. It seemed to be pounding as if it were a party boat on Ibiza. He forgot sometimes she was from London, going out to bars and clubs. He'd have to take her into Reading. There was a brilliant cocktail bar overlooking the river in the centre that she'd probably really like. She didn't hear him knock and he didn't want to just burst in so he skirted the edges of the boat, feeling slightly ridiculous as he popped up staring into a porthole.

She was perched on the bench, her hair falling around her face as she bent to do up a shoe, her mouth falling open as she saw him a couple of metres away. He felt jolted by her, aware he had startled her but also taking in this impossibly glamorous Eve. When she stepped out onto the deck he couldn't think of any words to say. She looked beautiful. Her dress was stunning, the colour vivid against the backdrop of the steely sky, and her brown hair as glossy as any model in an advert. He could hear himself starting to speak and then got a hold of himself.

'Look, Eve, I wanted to apologise for the other night. You must have thought it was very rude and—'

She didn't let him carry on, cutting him short with a curt, 'Not really.' There was something different in her voice, her expression shut off so that he couldn't guess what she was thinking. She looked over his shoulder, not holding his gaze.

He wanted to get back on track. He didn't want to explain everything here and now, didn't need to load her up with all his baggage, but this wasn't going as he had planned. And where was she headed dressed up like that? It suddenly occurred to him that she was probably waiting for someone else. He found himself flailing. 'Have you got a moment? No, it doesn't look like you have.'

She looked at him then, seeming like the Eve that had appeared in his practice with gingerbread, the one who had hidden her head in her hands and laughed helplessly through her fingers. Then that look was gone and he knew this wasn't the right time for him to appear like this.

'Look, Greg, I don't know what is going on with you but I don't need to know. You've obviously taken long enough to think up some brilliant story.'

She sounded hard, her voice flat, her eyes cold.

'Well, I wanted to explain,' he said, his mouth trying to lift but feeling utterly despondent, his earlier hopes disappearing, the music jarring with his thoughts.

'Please don't bother. I don't need to hear lies.'

He felt his body react, a step towards her, his brain two steps behind. He was tired, the emotion of the past few days had floored him, leaving him with images of his mum in the hospital, his brother's face, new lines round his mouth.

'They won't be lies.'

'That's what they always say. I've been messed around before so it's really not a big surprise.'

Messed around? Is that what he had done? He didn't want to be lumped in with these anonymous men. 'I'm not "they",' he said, anger swelling in his chest.

'We barely know each other anyway.'

He didn't hear her then, replaying that sentence, the sting of it, over and over. He thought back to the times they'd spent together; their closeness hadn't simply been in his head. She wasn't even letting him tell her what was going on and suddenly he felt as if he was twelve years old again and the world wasn't fair and he wasn't being heard. The words were tumbling out of him now, all the pent-up rage he'd felt staring at his mum surrounded by beeping machines and equipment, anger at not telling Eve about it all in the first place that had got him to this point. *What an idiot.*

'... God forbid I dare to contradict you.'

She thought he was with someone else. The thought was

almost laughable; he'd been avoiding people for months, dreading their repetitive questions, the same looks. With her he hadn't felt the need to pretend; he'd found himself relaxing with her, dropping his guard. It had been an enormous relief.

'... I don't have any claim on you.'

'You don't.'

Stop this, Greg, apologise, she has every right to be angry, you have just disappeared with no explanation. He was about to say it, to step forward; he wanted to cup her face in his hands, take it all back. She looked amazing in that dress.

Her friend emerged from the boat as he took a breath.

'Hi, sorry.'

He lifted a hand, feeling absurd now with this audience. 'Hi.' He looked up at Eve, her mouth set, her eyes darting away from him. *What was she thinking?*

'I'll get out of your way,' he said, feeling the fight drain out of him.

'Fine, that's probably best.' She said the sentence in a small voice and he wanted to be back on the boat, on another day, alone, the sun behind them, sitting on the top of it playing backgammon and drinking coffee.

He was gabbling something at her, realising her face had closed off and she wasn't listening to him. Her mouth was in a line; she was looking out over the common to the car park. He needed to get out of here.

'I... I actually thought... I was wrong.'

He turned before he could carry on making a tit of himself, feeling his chest hammering, Eve's eyes on him as he walked back the way he came, knowing he'd blown it, knowing he had screwed it up.

Chapter 38

DAISY AND Eve were bundled next to a stone pillar, the whole church heaving with enormous bunches of pale-pink roses, pine cones and privet berries. The scent was intoxicating, mixing with beeswax polish and tickling the back of Eve's throat. She pulled on her skirt, the shift underneath riding up every time she sat down. She had shrugged off her wool coat, the radiators must have been blazing overnight, it was boiling. Daisy was fanning herself with her programme.

'I'm melting, I'm melting,' Eve whispered in her best Wicked Witch of the West voice to make her laugh. Daisy looked like she'd caught the laugh in her mouth, her cheeks suddenly blooming, which nearly set Eve off. She was pleased to feel more herself, had been quiet on the journey, regretting her abrupt dismissal of Greg. She didn't want Daisy to think she was going to be a downer; she'd been miserable enough these last few months.

'How many minutes late do you think she'll be?' Eve asked. 'I bet you ten pounds it'll be more than half an hour.'

Daisy looked down at her lap and didn't respond as Eve noticed a woman in a very large hat had turned to stare at them.

She knew she should be better behaved, but this was the first wedding she had been to since she knew she wouldn't be having one any time soon, and she hadn't seen Daisy for days and she was bored and…

'What the hell is he doing here?' Eve asked, looking in horror as Liam walked down the aisle in a petrol-blue suit, his sandy hair gelled down, his face newly shaven. She ducked behind Daisy so she was shielded from view. The woman in the hat glared at her again.

Daisy, turning to see who she meant, spun round, pale under her make-up, licking her lips. 'He must have been invited.'

Eve rolled her eyes. 'I know that but by who? Ro-Ro wouldn't do that. Is he gate-crashing?'

'Maybe Hugo invited him.'

'They barely know each other.'

Eve hardly took in the service. Ro-Ro arrived to a line of trombones. She looked spectacular. Tiny in a full ivory skirt and tight-fitting bodice, small breasts impossibly high, hair pinned back tightly into a low chignon, a cathedral veil falling over her shoulders. She sashayed down the aisle as if she were on a catwalk. She was made more prominent by Hugo's sisters, two sweating bridesmaids dressed in peach puffball skirts so that they resembled rather hot pumpkins.

Eve didn't have the energy to care, unable to shake her nerves at coming face to face with Liam. Even the verses of Jerusalem couldn't rouse her, only made her despair as she remembered it was Liam's favourite hymn. She was pathetic; she felt that she had been transported back to the early days when they had just broken up, her mind on a continual loop, wondering where he was, what he was doing. She found herself craning and twisting to catch sight of him in a pew ahead. At least he looked like he had come alone. She watched the back of his head as he dipped it for the prayers.

'Please God let me get over him,' she thought, suddenly angry at herself for caring, and clamping her eyes closed. Daisy sneaked a hand over hers and held it, giving it a squeeze.

'Don't think about the bastard.'

This made Eve stifle a giggle. Daisy rarely swore and they were in church. She squeezed her hand back. The woman in the hat turned and tutted at them. Eve kept her head down.

She managed to escape the church without bumping into him. Grabbing Daisy, they made their way along the road past polished cars, muddy 4x4s perched on the verge, to Ro-Ro's parents' house where the reception was being held. Moving through the gateway, flanked by two stone pillars with ball-post finials, they crunched up the driveway, their heels making for a wobbly route. Large iron poles were stuck in the ground, jam jars with tea lights hanging from hooks, a thin rope in between them covered in holly lining the pathway to an enormous marquee on the front lawn.

The marquee was wonderfully warm and smelt of spices from scented candles littered on occasional tables. Patterned rugs in rich colours lined the floors and through an enormous curtained entrance Eve could see the tables laid out ready for the meal, cutlery gleaming, light reflecting off wine glasses, enormous centrepieces bursting with roses and winter berries spilling over the pots they were in. A small group of red-robed carollers started singing in soft voices, their voices warming too.

'Back soon, need the loo,' Daisy said, tottering out again, following hand-painted signs. Eve accepted a glass of champagne from the silver tray of a waiter with oiled-back hair.

'Thanks,' she said, taking a gulp and wondering whether it would be possible to avoid Liam for the entire night. There were certainly enough guests. The marquee was filling up, people mingling, kissing, talk and laughter filling the air. Eve weaved her way through the crowd and then almost tripped over the cathedral veil.

'Ro-Ro,' she said, leaning forward.

'Not the face.'

She kissed the air next to her cheek, marvelling at her eye make-up, the pristine flick of liner, the tiny eyelashes individually glued on. 'You look very elegant,' Eve said, having to look up at Ro-Ro, who was around four inches taller than usual. 'How are you walking around?' Eve asked in amazement, momentarily distracted from her questions.

'They're Jimmy Choo and barely hurt.'

'So,' Eve said, knowing she had to ask and trying not to squeeze her champagne glass too tightly, 'how come Liam is here?'

Ro-Ro looked up to the sky. 'I invited him, remember.'

'Well, yes,' Eve said slowly. 'But then we found out he was sleeping with someone else and I assumed he would be dis-invited.'

'That didn't seem fair.'

Eve swallowed down the stamping-foot tantrum she wanted to produce. *Hmm fair, fair, fair, I know what isn't fair.*

'I didn't want you to be a Drama Queen about it,' Ro-Ro said, as if she had heard Eve's thoughts. 'Can you straighten it?' she said, spinning round to snap at one of her bridesmaids and indicating her veil. 'And, Eve, honey.' She turned back round. 'It's been four months.'

Eve wanted to step forward and slap her. She felt heartened that the bridesmaid made a hashed job of the veil, too busy chatting to a gaunt bloke in sunglasses as she also tried to put a salmon canapé in her mouth whole.

'We were going to get married,' Eve said through gritted teeth, a photographer choosing that moment to appear in front of the two of them.

As if on cue, Ro-Ro linked arms with her, turning her grey eyes to the lens and speaking out of the side of her mouth. 'Think of it as a good thing,' she said, releasing Eve as the photographer wandered off. 'It had to happen some time. You can move on now.'

'I am moving on,' Eve said, more loudly than she intended.

'Well then.'

'You could have warned me,' she grumbled, feeling that Ro-Ro might actually be right, and it didn't seem nice to bitch to someone on their wedding day anyway. She would have to save it for another day; she couldn't be the girl that made the bride cry. She stood there, biting on her tongue, trying to quell the anger that was bubbling.

'He was my friend too, you know,' Ro-Ro continued, smoothing her hair down and looking over Eve's shoulder. 'Oh, Piers,' she called out as a man in a grey top hat walked past, and she was off, tottering on her designer heels.

Eve stood, dejected, nodding numbly at the waiter with the slicked-back hair who topped up her glass. The carollers had stopped and the marquee seemed strangely cold all of a sudden, voices clashing, laughter braying, while every man seemed to look like Liam. Why did Ro-Ro still have to invite Liam? Had she done it simply because she hadn't been thinking?

Eve tried to push the thoughts out of her mind. She didn't want him to ruin the night. She vowed to avoid him; there were enough people to mask him. As she found her seat, she was gratified that he wasn't in her eyeline for dinner. Ro-Ro had seated her on a table of people she hadn't met before, perhaps an attempt to ensure all her friends mingled. She looked over at Daisy who was nodding at something the man next to her was saying.

Eve introduced herself to the two married men on either side, who spent most of the meal drinking red wine and talking over her about the stock market. Their wives could be peeked through the centrepiece on the other side of the table, deep into a chat about breastfeeding. Eve found herself knocking back a large amount of Pinot Noir, the speeches after the main course melting into one as she struggled to stand up to toast the bridesmaids.

Hours later, it seemed the meal was finished and, getting up, wobbling uncertainly in the direction of Daisy's table, Eve careered into a loose chair and landed in the lap of Liam, his petrol suit jacket off, tie loose.

'Eve!' he said.

'Gah!' Eve said, springing up from his lap as if he was on fire. 'Liam.'

She looked at him, his hair mussed up, his eyes not quite meeting hers. They were a bit wonky; how had she never noticed? Then again, maybe it was just the wine.

Liam's eyes narrowed. 'You look nice.'

'Thanks,' Eve said, pulling on her dress.

'I knew you'd be here,' he said.

'Of course I'd bloody be here,' Eve said, snapping, gratified to see Liam's shock as she swore at him. She never swore at him. 'Didn't know YOU'D be here,' she said, her earlier anger rising to the surface again.

'I wanted to see you.'

The words stopped Eve short, her mouth half-open, her mind a fuzzy mess, the wedding singer calling for the newlyweds in the background, the other guests clinking, chattering, laughing. *He wanted to see her*. She shook her head in an effort to untangle her thoughts.

'I'm glad you've come over,' Liam continued.

God, why did he have to confuse her like this. She felt her heart softening, then forced herself to stand taller. 'I didn't come over,' Eve bristled. 'I was going to dance.' She went to point to the dance floor and poked a man with a moustache in the chest. 'I'm so sorry,' she gushed.

The man glared at her and moved on.

'Well, I'm glad you did come over,' Liam said.

Eve couldn't help it; she felt a spark of pleasure as he repeated it. Was he about to erase the last few months, tell her he missed her, beg her to return? She prepared herself to be frosty. *You must be cool with him, Eve, you can't melt if he professes to miss you, think about what he did...*

'Christmas is round the corner...' Liam said slowly.

Was it the early nights, the log fires, the carols in the shops, the tinsel and the candles? Were they reminding him of last year? Was he back there in their family home asking her to marry him? Had he planned this speech, knowing she would be at the wedding, the whole day reminding him they had wanted the same thing? She felt her brain grow fuzzy with questions, mouth dry, palms damp.

'And I want my dog back,' he slurred, clutching a wine glass to his chest.

Eve blinked. Her thoughts came to a screeching standstill, a lump forming in her throat as she realised he hadn't been thinking any of these things. He hadn't been thinking about their last Christmas together, the selfies in matching Christmas jumpers, the excitement as they'd clinked glasses, the hugs round the Christmas tree, the air smelling of pine needles as she'd torn open his present, not caring what it was as her eyes caught sight of the new diamond ring on her finger.

'Well, you can't,' she said slowly, hoping her voice wasn't giving her away as the words choked out. 'Anyway,' she tried to compose herself, swallowed, 'I don't want to get into all that here.' Eve heard her voice, laced with self-importance, not caring.

'Where are you hiding him?' Liam asked, and Eve felt a flush of relief that she hadn't told him where she was now; her hideaway in Pangbourne was hers.

'I'm not telling you.'

'I'll find out,' he said, stumbling to the side.

'Liam, mate,' Hugo said, pumping his hand and barrelling straight into their conversation. 'Oops,' he said in a pantomime way when he realised who they both were. It allowed Eve to make her excuses, knowing they were watching her as she moved away.

She suddenly really wanted to be back on the boat; Marmite on her lap, dressed in her pyjamas, the woodburning stove on, baking something with cinnamon and gossiping on the phone to her sister who would be calling Liam names. For a second, another face flashed in her mind but she swatted it away. She didn't need another man to confuse things. She couldn't keep falling for untrustworthy people. Liam had made so many promises and now here he was, this stranger, in a suit she didn't recognise and an unfamiliar expression on his face, as if they really had only just met.

Ro-Ro and Hugo cut the cake and danced their first dance, Hugo staring straight at her breasts as she towered over him in heels, her model friends like swaying Twiglets all around them.

*

Hours later, Eve had come off the floor, her feet aching from dancing rather too energetically with a man in a kilt. She had avoided Liam for the rest of the night, despite noticing him brooding, slumped in a chair on the side of the dance floor at one point. He was nowhere to be seen now and she looked around for Daisy, realising she had barely seen her all night. She thought she saw her in a corner, whispering urgently to a man who seemed mostly hidden in shadow. Eve started walking her way, skirting round a couple snogging just off the dance floor and a five-year-old being swung in a circle.

She was still some way off when she realised Daisy had turned, her floral dress lifting as she spun round and marched away from the corner. Stepping back into the room, her eyes glittered darkly, her mouth in a thin line, Eve went to call to her, briefly set off course by a small girl in plaits racing past her in a netted skirt. When she looked up again, she saw Liam just behind Daisy, ruffling the back of his hair and looking about him. Eve frowned, the image not quite adding up.

Daisy stepped across to her, brightening. 'Shall we escape?'

'Was that...?' Eve couldn't finish the sentence as the five-year-old from the dance floor was sent flying into her legs and she doubled over.

'I'm so sorry,' said a man with such rosy cheeks that he looked to be on the verge of a cardiac arrest.

'Just an accident,' Eve said, feeling tears springing into her eyes. 'Let's go,' she said to Daisy, hobbling away, wanting to get out, wrap herself up in the winter night and head home.

'Definitely,' Daisy said in a steely voice.

Chapter 39

Grandma's Christmas Pudding

500g vegetarian suet
250g plain flour
250g white fresh
  breadcrumbs
500g dark brown sugar
25g ground almonds
1 tsp each of nutmeg,
  ginger, mixed spice
½ tsp of salt

500g each of currants,
  sultanas and raisins
250g mixed peel
rind and juice of one
  lemon and one orange
2 tbsp black treacle
10 eggs, beaten
200ml brandy

Method:

- In a large bowl, combine suet and all dry ingredients thoroughly (by hand easiest). Add all fruits and zest. Warm treacle and add with eggs and brandy. Stir until combined. Leave covered for 24 hours. Next day, if mixture stiff, add a bottle of Guinness. Fill pudding basins with lids. (Will make 4 to 5 larger puddings.) Do not fill higher than 4/5 cm from top. Simmer for 7/8 hours. Be careful to top up regularly with boiling water. On Christmas Day reheat in same way for 2 hours. These puddings, stored in a cool place, will last for 2 years!

RETURNING TO the boat after the wedding, Eve felt utterly desolate. She had planned to stay with Daisy in her B&B but she made her excuses, not wanting to be around anyone, catching the last train back from Didcot to Pangbourne, wanting to see Marmite, return to the safety and comfort of the boat.

The weather was dreadful, water bashing the boat at every angle, the river churned up and running furiously along, reeds flattened on the surface almost pulled from the silt, the trees stripped of leaves, the branches creaking all around her at night. The temperature seemed to have plunged by ten degrees and no amount of jumpers or coats could stop Eve's teeth chattering, her toes like little ice cubes, numb with it through socks and boot slippers. She spent the rest of the weekend feeding the woodstove, cuddling Marmite to her as they watched a string of dreadful films.

She appeared at class on Monday, sitting quietly at the wheel, wishing Danny was there to grin at her. Aisha came over at the start of the lesson, wearing a new blue nose stud that caught the light.

'I was wondering whether you were staying on in the village into the New Year?' Aisha asked.

'I, well, I came for the course,' Eve said, realising with a huge sadness that it would be finished in just over a week, and she would have to leave.

'Well, it was just, we're looking for a new agent in the office to replace Martin in the New Year – if you were looking for work.'

'Oh,' Eve said, thrown by the idea. 'Oh, that's kind, but I

have a job,' Eve said, picturing the office in London, Daisy at the desk next door, the warm atmosphere, even Ed with his obsession with obscure stationary items. She'd been so grateful to Daisy for getting her an interview all those years ago.

She walked all the way back to the boat that day wondering about the conversation. She did love the village and was amazed how easy it had been to let her London life go. She thought of the pace of life, the time she had spent on her drawings, the business card she had designed for Raj, the small stack of pottery pieces she'd now made, the ones she had painted that stood proudly on the shelf in the house ready for her to take away. She thought of the people she'd met: Aisha, Danny, Minnie, and then one face that seemed to be on a loop at the moment. She wrapped her coat tighter around her, determined not to replay what she'd said to him for another time, relieved when her mobile rang.

'How was Rachel's wedding?' her mother asked the moment Eve had answered the call.

'Yes, great, good. It went well,' Eve said, not keen to go into particulars, still wearing her hat and scarf as she opened the door of the boat.

'A wedding and at Christmas time – how lovely,' her mum said, trampling over any sensitivity around the issue.

'Yes, Mum, I know.' Eve sighed, clicking the kettle on and leaning against the kitchen counter, phone cradled to her ear. 'It was very fancy,' she summarised. 'Good food, they had those roast beef canapés Dad always bangs on about...'

She bit back the news that Liam had been there, that she suspected her best friend was guilty of something she couldn't quite put her finger on. Mum always wanted to know about the food anyway, 'Salmon for starter.'

'Ooh fish, can be risky,' her mum cut in.

'Hmm, very daring. Lamb for main and Christmas pudding for dessert.'

'Not everyone loves it, can be a heavy option,' Mum said, as if she were a judge on *Masterchef* and was delivering her verdict. 'How was the lamb done?'

Eve frowned. 'Er... very well? In a sort of gravy thing?'

Her mum sighed down the phone. 'You really are hopeless.'

'Thanks, Mum.'

'Eve?' Her dad's voice was a welcome intrusion. 'I'm on the upstairs line. Hi, Brenda.' He chuckled. 'I can see youooooo.' Eve pictured him leaning over the banisters and looking at the top of Mum's head.

'Your father had a beer at lunch. David, you really shouldn't have a beer at lunch.'

'It was a pale ale. So, Eve, how is life at sea?'

'She's not at sea,' Mum pointed out. 'She's on a houseboat on the river.'

'It's a turn of phrase,' Eve chorused with her dad, continuing to answer. 'Good, thanks, I'm learning how to make a teapot tomorrow in class. And I've been cooking,' she tacked on, this news blurted out of her before she could put it back in.

'Cooking?' her mum said, sounding suspicious. 'You don't like cooking.'

'Well, I'm getting to grips with it a bit, I've had some help...'

'David, will you stop dropping things on my head.'

Eve could hear Dad chuckling.

'What are you doing, Dad?'

A sheepish,'Nothing,' before her mum explained, 'He's throwing balls of paper at me.'

'I was sending you notes,' Dad said, a rumble of laughter down the phone.

Dad must be drunk. Fortunately the note-throwing had distracted her parents from asking any more.

'How's Scarlet?' Eve asked, realising she hadn't heard from her little sister in weeks.

'She has got herself a new job,' Dad said in a cheerful voice.

'Oh, the shame.' Mum was clearly not as thrilled.

Eve frowned, wondering for a moment what she could possibly be working as. Scarlet had had some pretty interesting jobs in the past so the mind boggled.

'She's working in a shopping mall in Newcastle,' Dad said.

'Well, that's not too bad, Mum,' Eve comforted her, imagining her sister on the shop floor, helping customers to buy clothes or cosmetics.

'As one of Santa's elves.'

There was a pause as Eve conjured this image. 'Ah, oh, well...'

'She's twenty-five,' her mum said. Eve could picture her shaking her head. 'Her friends are on graduate schemes. And she is working for Father Christmas.'

'Probably a great boss,' Dad said, chuckling, 'He has a reputation as a very jolly fellow.'

'David, I didn't laugh yesterday and I won't be laughing today. Ouch! STOP throwing things at my head.'

'But that one said "Sorry".'

'Er, Mum, Dad, I better go, I've got um... stuff to do...' Eve didn't want to get tangled up in their next row.

'Oh bye, love,' called Dad, the sound of a receiver being replaced, never one for a drawn-out goodbye.

'Well, you'll call again soon, and you will think about coming home for Christmas, won't you?'

'Mum.' Eve's shoulders sagged. 'We've talked about this, I don't—'

'Well, just say you'll think about it, just a little think.'

It wasn't like her mum to beg so Eve found herself saying, 'I'll think about it. Okay, I really do have to go now.'

She lay on her bed, feeling drained from the phone call. It was too cold to do anything but get under the duvet, Marmite snuggled next to her.

Chapter 40

'**Y**OU SEEM distracted again, Eve.'

'Hmm.'

'Distracted,' Minnie said, her eyes peering at her over turquoise glasses.

'Oh, I suppose I am. I was just wondering how big to make my teapot.' She held up a ball of clay as if to prove her point.

Minnie looked over at Danny's wheel, his bowl untouched, left under a tea towel as if it were a cake out of the oven. She sighed as she shook her head. 'I hope he's all right,' she said, her face drooping.

'Why wouldn't he be?' Eve asked, worrying now that something had happened; Minnie's eyes had dulled. 'Have you heard from him?' Eve missed having him working next door to her, chattering on as he worked at his wheel. Now that she knew he was Greg's brother she wanted to see him even more, wanted to find out if Greg had said anything about her. He had been away a while.

'He won't be coming in for a few more days. His mum, you see, she was rushed into hospital in the summer with – GERALD!' she called suddenly.

Gerald's face appeared in the doorway.

'What was Linda rushed into hospital with?'

'Linda?'

'Linda Burrows, used to work in the delicatessen.'

Gerald appeared in the doorway. 'She had diabetes, I think. Collapsed in the high street.'

'That was it. She'd always managed it well, apparently, but it was obviously bad, completely ruined her kidneys apparently. She was put on a transplant list, been on it ever since. Dreadful. Danny's been helping her.'

Eve felt her skin grow cold. Greg's mum was ill. She felt terrible, her hands clammy as she listened to Minnie talking. She had to visit the hospital several times a week; she had to have a tube fitted into her abdomen; she carried around an enormous handbag that rattled with pills; they thought she was getting a transplant; the operation couldn't go ahead apparently. Awful. Minnie's voice faded in and out, each revelation making Eve feel even worse.

She hadn't let him explain, she'd just cut him off, tied up in the drama of being her. How often had Harriet gently warned her she could react too quickly, how many times had Daisy quietly suggested she take some time to think about things before flying in? She felt guilt weigh her down into her chair, the wheel in front of her swimming, unable to focus on the clay, on the tools, on Raj's patient face explaining how to make a spout. She thought back to the last time she had seen him, how incredibly off-hand she'd been. She hadn't even pretended to listen or care or think about what might have happened to him.

She was frozen to her wheel for the rest of the lesson, unseeing, making little progress, not able to concentrate or enjoy the atmosphere. Her teapot wobbled and sank, her foot slipping from the pedal, Raj there, frowning with his neat eyebrows, talking to her, Eve answering him a split-second late each time.

She left the class, oblivious to others around her, picturing Greg's face, trying to recall what she'd said, what he had said. Had he been trying to explain? How had she never thought to ask?

She sat on the boat that night wondering what she could do, walking around, Marmite staring at her as she looked at him blankly. After a couple of restless hours she got up, knowing what might make her feel a little better. She made gingerbread as the sky grew dark outside, and the whole boat filled up with its smell.

Chapter 41

Christmas Cookies (Lebkuchen)

50g butter
150g caster sugar
Vanilla essence
1 egg plus 1 yolk,
  beaten
100g honey
½ ground aniseed

1 level tsp of ground
  cloves
1 level tsp ground
  cinnamon
1½ lbs self-raising
  flour
3 tbsp milk
Egg white for glaze

Method:

• Cream the butter, sugar and a few drops of vanilla
  essence. Add egg and yolk, honey and spices. Mix
  in the flour and milk. Knead until smooth and firm.
  Roll out to ¼-inch thickness. Cut into different
  shapes. Brush with egg white. Bake at 180°C until
  golden brown.

• To ice: Can be eaten without but, if you wish, can
  decorate with icing made from egg white, icing
  sugar, lemon juice and colouring.

SHE WOKE up with the same questions running through
her head. How had she not asked about his family? Why
hadn't he mentioned it? She bit her lip as she recalled the

moments before Ro-Ro's wedding, looking down at him from the deck. They came to her in slow motion now, exaggerated, weighted with a significance they hadn't had then. He had seemed less energetic, less quick to smile, but she had imagined that was because he had felt guilty about dumping her before their date. Why hadn't she given him more time to explain? How absurdly arrogant of her to imagine that was why he had behaved like that.

If her mum was ill, she'd be bursting with the news, needing to tell everyone. She couldn't keep her emotions in check at times; she wondered how Greg hadn't taken her by the shoulders and screamed it at her. She knew that wasn't him, though, remembering the occasional moments his eyes would lose their brightness, his voice growing dull as if he were wading back to the conversation through his murky thoughts. She quickened her pace.

She wanted to see him, to fix things. There was something wonderfully easy and warm about him; when he was with her she felt herself relax. She clutched the bag to her. She had made them on the third attempt, appeared like a flour-coated mad woman in the Co-op to buy another batch of ingredients, looking down as the shop assistant sniggered to see she was still wearing her apron. Cooking seemed a good way to apologise and she remembered the day she had handed him the gingerbread, simple really, and yet when she'd seen his expression she'd felt she had handed him the keys to a Ferrari.

She hoped the icing would have set, the sprinkles stayed in place. Christmas cookies seemed appropriate, but they'd been seriously tricky to make. She had risen to the challenge, believing somehow that if she could make them beautifully that her efforts would be rewarded. As she glazed the third batch with egg white, she had sent up a little prayer that he would forgive her.

The high street now was awash with lights and colour, the shop windows glittering with coloured paper chains, lights and bows. Windows edged with fake snow, carols spilling onto the street from inside the shops. There were deals on Baileys, packs of mince pies, tubs of Quality Street. The weather was slushy and bitter. She realised with a jolt that it was Christmas Eve in two more days.

The ground was dotted with rain, ominous clouds hanging over the village, forcing everyone to put umbrellas or hoods up, dress children in anoraks and wellies. She kept her head down, stepping round puddles in her knee boots, not wanting mud to mark her knee-length woollen coat. She had made a big effort today, had spent a while in the circular mirror pressing her lips together, thin lines flicking upwards on her eyelids, scrubbing it all off again and starting again.

She felt a leap in her chest as she saw the sign for the vet practice up ahead. It swung slightly in the breeze outside and she slowed down her pace, fixed her expression, tried not to run through what she planned to say. *Be natural, Eve. Natural.* She tried to convince herself that she didn't really mind if he didn't hear her out but the last couple of days had been lonely in the village; she had grown used to expecting him to pass by, she knew it would hurt if he rejected her. For a second she realised she hadn't thought of Liam for days. That thought made her stop still on the pavement so that a mother with her pram just behind almost ran her down.

'I'm sorry,' she said, as the mother manoeuvred past her with a disgruntled sigh.

She pushed open the door and the bell rang out in the small space. She noticed the empty line of plastic chairs on her right and was relieved not to have an audience. The busty receptionist was up ahead and Eve felt herself blushing furiously as she approached her, flashbacks of the last time rolling in a loop across her memory. The receptionist, Karen, looked up as she stood at the desk, her expression blank before recognition made her mouth curl upwards.

'Hello, how can I help?'

Eve had sensibly left Marmite behind on the boat so that she wasn't forced to conjure up a new set of lies, give Marmite a dreadful recurring leg condition.

'Hello, good morning.' Her voice was the smartest version of her voice. 'I was wondering, please, if I could see Greg.'

Karen looked at the computer screen in front of her as if checking for appointments. 'He's free,' she said, lifting a pair of round glasses onto her nose from a chain around her neck to peer through. 'Friday at 11.40 a.m.? Is it for your dog? If I take his name, we tend to book the appointments in the animal's name here.'

Eve stuttered over her reply, forcing herself to lick her lips and slow up. 'Oh sorry, no, I meant, um... now. Is he free now?' Eve tried to peer through the glass square in the door behind her to see if she could spot him, but all she could make out were shelves of jars and medical equipment and an advent calendar, most of the boxes now open.

'He's not in today, I'm afraid. There's a locum in – Katie Langham – would you like to see her? I suppose I could squeeze you in just after lunch; she has a small gap there if you'd like to come back then.'

Eve didn't catch much of what Karen said but she had heard the first part. 'Oh.' She wanted to ask where he was but forced herself to stay quiet. It wasn't her business. Then, after a couple more seconds, when clearly no more information was forthcoming, it burst out of her. 'I hope everything is all right?' she said.

Karen pursed her lips; she was wearing a startlingly bright shade of pink. 'He's away for two days on CPD.'

'CPD?' Eve repeated. That sounded serious. What had happened? Was that something to do with transplants? She hadn't heard the term.

'Training,' Karen confirmed. 'A training course. So I'm afraid it will have to be Katie. Now what is the name of your animal?'

Eve came out of her reverie and stared at Karen's patiently waiting face. 'My animal? Oh, Marmite. But, well, it's not about my animal.' *Oh, Eve, you don't need to share this.* 'I mean, what I mean is, I just wanted to quickly grab Greg for a chat, I mean not grab, just, well, it wouldn't take long.' *Stop talking, Eve, you sound slightly scary. He isn't even here, she doesn't need to know this. Great, now she is giving you a funny look. Stop. Talking.*

Eve stopped talking and Karen opened her mouth, then shut it again, perhaps recognising there was no good reply.

Eve had a stroke of inspiration then. 'Do you have his mobile number? Perhaps if I could have it—'

She was cut off by the bell over the shop door and a woman wearing a knotted scarf on her head pushed in backwards holding a cage. She turned, tutting at the weather, the wind furious and loud before the door closed again and all was calm. Inside a hamster rustled about, tiny flecks of sawdust escaping the cages of the bar as the woman stepped towards the desk.

'Karen,' she said warmly.

Eve was still waiting for Karen to produce the mobile number, not wanting to repeat the request in front of this woman.

Karen cleared her throat. 'The thing is, I can't really do that, you see, because of the Data Protection Act.'

The hamster woman's eyes widened and she was unashamedly staring at Eve.

'Oh right, of course, that Act,' Eve gabbled, laughing out loud and trying to sound like she didn't care in the least.

The hamster woman started laughing too, which was slightly odd, and more sawdust fell to the floor.

'Right, I'd better go then,' Eve said, feeling completely ridiculous as Karen waited to serve the hamster woman.

'Our out-of-hours number is on the poster by the door,' Karen called after her, 'if Marmite needs anything.'

Eve didn't hear her as, red-faced, she pushed the door and stepped back out onto the high street, strands of hair whisking across her face in the wind.

As she walked back to the boat she forgot to watch where she was going and stepped right into the middle of a deep puddle, the water seeping straight into her boots, soaking her socks and making her toes feel squelchy and disgusting. A car swept past, spraying her with rainwater. She felt all her energy seep away. The hours preparing the cookies, picturing his face as she handed them over, what she was going to say. And now there was no hope of seeing him; she couldn't face returning to the practice now. She thought back to Gavin's comment then; he was right, who didn't swap mobile numbers? She couldn't believe it. As she walked under the railway bridge and out of the rain, she realised she was still clutching the bag of Christmas cookies.

She felt hopeless as she let herself into the boat. Perhaps if she hadn't been, she might have noticed the figure standing on the bank opposite the boat, eyes trained on her as she approached, watching her enter, listening to the distant sound of her dog greeting her with a run of barking. As it was, she failed to see anything as she beckoned Marmite to her and fed him a run of Christmas cookies.

Chapter 42

HE WAS barely able to keep his eyes open, the room too warm, all the radiators blazing and him in his suit jacket. The lecturer was showing them a PowerPoint of the operation he was walking them through, and normally Greg liked to take notes. He was a real geek on these courses, desperate to learn something that justified him spending two days away from the practice. He had been pleased when he saw this course was available; he was keen to expand the operations he could offer without referring them and this would be the first step to doing that. The woman in front of him, short blonde bob and enormous dangling earrings, turned and grinned at him as he jerked awake again. Had he been snoring? He wondered, trying to smile back, but feeling woozy and disorientated.

He'd arrived late last night after staying with Mum for too long. She'd looked even more frail, the skin along her collarbone paper-thin, the veins in her hands protruding in angry blue lines, her hair wispy now, as if all the energy required to make it glossy and full was needed elsewhere. They'd watched a movie together, eaten a Chinese takeaway – well, Greg had eaten, his mum had picked at the noodles, swirling them around her plate. Greg had felt a churning worry in his stomach as he got up to put the plates in the dishwasher.

He hadn't spoken about the day in the hospital, hated the false hope, the race to see if they could perform the operation, knowing she would have been praying for it and then loathing herself. His mum had never been one to put herself first and Danny and he were always hoping they could repay her for all the things she had done for them. Would the call come? Would she get the operation?

She had been to the hospital that day for another round of dialysis. Danny was going to drive her there, stay and play rummy by her bed, read to her from the crap magazines that she loved, eat the grapes and chocolate they stocked up that she never had an appetite for. He was glad Danny was able to get there; one of them always tried. It was a bit easier for Danny; he already had the mornings off and the lads at the garage had been brilliant, sometimes covering for him into the afternoon. Greg had used Katie for locum work but he found it harder to drop everything, was forced to rely on Danny when a call came from Mum and he was with a client or doing an operation. He hated not being able to get there.

His eyes flicked now to his mobile that he'd left on the desk next to him on Silent, just in case that call came. He felt terrible for wishing for it, knowing it normally meant bad news for another family, but then a far larger part of him roared around his head, desperate for the news to come, deafening all other thoughts. He just wanted her to get better.

The next slide jolted him, a photo of a dog that reminded Greg of Marmite. It was a Morkie but this one had no light patch above the eye, less of a cheeky sparkle in his eyes that were a lighter shade of brown. He wondered whether Eve would still be on the boat when he got back to the village, realised as he looked down at his notepad that he had written her name. What was he? Twelve years old? He hastily scrawled it out, coughing and sitting up straight. *Listen to the lecture, Greg, you have paid money to come today, you need to learn how to do this.* The blonde bob turned and smiled again, but Greg was too busy staring at the lecturer as the next slide showed the insides of the same dog.

He was standing at the tea urn, a stack of digestive biscuits on a paper plate next to it. He had taken one, remembering the first time he had been on Eve's boat, the sad, bare cupboards that were now often stocked full. He bit into the digestive biscuit, his mouth turned up as he chewed. Did everything come back to her? There was something there, a tangible spark that made him bite his lip in public. He felt protective, absurdly so, wanting to wrap his arms round her, make her laugh.

'Bit sad, isn't it?' The woman with the blonde bob indicated the biscuit, opening her handbag to him. 'I bring my own. Do you want one?'

He laughed quickly as he peered inside, a pack of Jammy Dodgers open.

'Go on then,' he said, taking a bite, transported back to his childhood in an instant. Danny had always loved Jammy Dodgers.

The woman stood with him for a bit, sipping on her tea and eating biscuits. She was asking him questions but Greg found he couldn't focus on her, kept asking her to repeat things. The questions got shorter until she gave up and turned her back on him, taking the biscuits with her. *God, Greg, seriously, you really need to look at your life.* Maybe he should ask for her number? Meeting Eve had reminded him that there was a whole world out there. He needed to get back out into it. Then he pictured Eve's face, her cheek dotted with flour, her earnest expression as she helped him cook. He wasn't interested in getting anyone else's number but he wasn't sure how to fix the things he'd said, knew he should have explained earlier.

He walked back to the lecture hall, the corridor lined with posters and announcements, the smell of dust and disinfectant clashing as he paused outside the double doors. He had a few minutes before the last lecture of the day and reached for his mobile.

'Everything okay, Karen?' he said, peering through the square of glass. There was no lecturer there as yet; other vets ambled about the room, talking and laughing. Normally he'd enjoy the social side of these courses but he felt strangely detached today, happy to move through it anonymously. He imagined Danny standing next to him, head in hands, calling him a loser.

'I haven't burnt the place down,' she bristled.

'Of course you haven't. Has it been busy? Katie happy?' he asked. Katie was a reliable locum based in Reading. She had two small kids and had left her full-time job to look after them. She was an excellent surgeon though, and good with people. He never had any complaints. She also brought Karen home-made baked goods, so had hit it off from day one with those underhand tactics.

'Very, I think. Pretty steady, although a few booking to see you when you get back, so you'll have a hectic Friday.'

'No dramas then? No big news?'

'Well, the big news is that Katie brought in these heavenly triple chocolate muffins this morning, and they are so good I have almost persuaded her to turn professional.'

'Please don't, Karen.' Greg laughed, enjoying listening to the familiar voice. 'We need her.'

269

'There was a visit,' Karen said suddenly. 'But it can wait. I gave her the out-of-hours number, she wanted your mobile.'

'Sounds about right,' Greg said, picturing a client that wouldn't take no for an answer. He was used to being on call, it was part of the job, but when it wasn't possible there was an out-of-hours service to take in animals that got sick overnight.

He noticed a woman with tight brown curls walk to the front of the hall, shrug off her suit jacket and open up her briefcase. 'I'd better go, Karen, last lecture's about to start, but I'm glad it's gone well. I'll speak to you again tomorrow. You know where I am, though,' he said, pushing open the double doors.

'Yes, yes, you have fun, let your hair down,' she told him.

'Will do. Wild times,' he said, smiling as he pressed the button to end the call.

It was typical that as he sat in his seat, as the whole hall settled down, as the blonde woman moved down the row to sit next door to him, his phone lit up again. He recognised the number immediately, answering it, already out of his seat, apologising, holding it up to his ear, one hand on his things, moving down the hall, around people, back out into the hallway as he told his mum he was on his way. He'd look up the hospital when he was back in the car. They couldn't be this unlucky again? Could they?

Chapter 43

Christmas Fruit Loaf

Makes 1kg loaf

Ingredients:

310ml water	1 tsp salt
500g white bread flour	2 tsp dried yeast
25g caster sugar	40g butter (melted)
1 tsp mixed spice	50g sultanas
	50g dried apricots

Method

- Put the flour, yeast, water, sugar, salt, spices into a large mixing bowl. Make a well in the centre and pour in the melted butter. Mix everything together to form a dough. Add fruit. Knead again. If too dry add warm water. When smooth transfer the dough to a greased bowl, cover with a tea towel and leave until doubled in size (approx. 1 hr).

- Pre-heat oven to 180°C. Separate the dough into two loaves and place in oven for 20 minutes. Allow to cool in the tins.

SHE FROWNED as she pushed the door open, immediately struck by a strange sense that something wasn't quite right. Dropping the shopping bags at her feet, she realised that Marmite wasn't scurrying up to greet her, his tiny legs slipping and sliding over the parquet kitchen floor, his bark joyful as he leapt to climb up her legs, scramble into her arms and lick her face in a satisfied way. In fact, the boat was silent, strangely quiet, as if Marmite had always made a lot more noise.

'Marmite.'

Eve moved through the living room, searching about her as if Marmite were about to appear to say, 'Aha! I have learnt a new game!' but he didn't come running and Eve wondered if he had fallen asleep on her bed. Moving through the bathroom, past her line of underwear hanging over the bath, she frowned. Marmite had often decided to remove her pants and socks from their hanging space, bringing them to her as if to show off his powerful finding skills, and she would sigh and return them to their pegs, before he would leap and bound and bring them back again. Today, however, they were as she had left them.

The double bed that she had hastily made that morning was crisp and clean, not even a recent compression in the duvet cover to suggest that Marmite had been anywhere near it. Eve started opening the wardrobe doors, worrying that he had managed to get stuck somewhere.

'Marmite, come out, there's a good boy,' she said, her voice taking on a tinge of panic as she speeded up her search, moving through the bedroom, the drawers, to the small square of space at the back that kept the mop and the hoover. The cleaning products were all there; she always put them out of reach but maybe something had happened, what if he had swallowed bleach? She felt her breathing thicken as she looked under the sink, in every drawer, back through the bedroom, in the bathroom and living room, peering inside the bench, than in the kitchen cupboards before moving out onto the deck to skirt the boat.

She stared at the water, skittering clouds reflected on the surface, a bite in the air. If he was outside he'd be freezing by now. Eve wrapped her arms around herself, her skin already breaking out into goosebumps, her nose red, her eyes stinging as she looked out at the river, into the piles of reeds, along the line of drooping willows, terrified of seeing a small body. There was nothing. How had he got out? She should have taken him to the shop; she nearly did. She pictured his trusting face, the patch of lighter fur above his left eye, the way he would open his mouth before she deposited a treat. She felt tears threaten, calling his name louder now so that a couple walking along the iron bridge stopped and looked over at her.

'Eve, darling, Eve.'

Eve whipped round, her eyes wide, hope filling her chest as she heard her name being called. Someone had found him! Someone was bringing him back. It was Minnie waving at her with one gloved hand, the other holding onto a large fur hat, Sandy on a lead looped round her wrist.

Eve stepped across the boat towards her. 'Have you seen him?'

'Have I seen who?' Minnie asked, dropping her hand and taking a step nearer.

'Marmite,' Eve said. 'He's gone!' Her voice became increasingly higher in pitch.

'Oh no, I haven't.' Minnie looked about her, patting her pockets, as if Marmite could appear from underneath her quilted Barbour. She moved across and stepped up onto the deck, removing her hat so that strands of hair stuck up. She moved inside, Sandy following, talking all the while. 'Where was he last? Could he really have got out? Maybe you should phone the local police, they're very good...'

Someone else taking charge seemed to calm Eve down enough to think more clearly. It was obvious that Marmite was definitely not here and she didn't dare believe he had fallen in the river. It seemed so unlikely, but then at the same time it all seemed impossible. He wasn't Dog Houdini, how the hell did he get out of the boat?

'I'll put the kettle on and you have a think about what to do. Tea often helps, I think, in most situations tea often...'

Eve was sure she had seen a phone book on the shelves somewhere.

'Darling?'

She remembered now; she had used it as a makeshift table for her tea in the bathroom.

'Darling...' Minnie's voice entered her consciousness.

'Hmm...'

'Who's Liam?'

Eve turned, a frown forming on her face, a hand wiping at her eyes. 'Liam?' She stopped in her tracks, phone book forgotten, staring at Minnie's face, one neatly pencilled eyebrow raised. 'Why do you ask?'

Then she saw the note in her hand.

'I don't *care* what he told you, how could you give him the keys?' Eve's voice was bouncing back at her from the thin walls of the boat as Martin's nasally voice calmly replied, 'He told us he was your fiancé and that he had left his briefcase in there and he was due in court.'

'He's not even a bloody lawyer. He works in PR.'

'Well obviously we realise that now,' he said, not a note of apology in his voice. 'But he seemed legitimate.'

'Oh, legitimate, really. God, do you always go around handing your keys out like sweets? He's stolen my bloody dog.'

'Well, I am terribly sorry,' Martin said, not sounding at all sorry. 'And we can look into changing the locks now. We will have to inform the landlord.'

'It's all a bit late now, isn't it?' Eve felt her fists curling around the phone, her knuckles whitening. She knew she was getting angry at the wrong person; she knew how persuasive Liam could be. She might have made the same mistake herself, but she would at least have had the humility to apologise.

Minnie tiptoed towards her, holding a steaming mug. 'Tea,' she mouthed as she placed it down and then mimed Eve drinking it before tiptoeing back again.

'Well—'

'I will phone you back, I need to call him now.'

'Happy to help,' he said, his voice tinged with sarcasm.

Eve switched off the call before she said anything else.

'What a tit,' Minnie commented.

'SUCH a tit,' Eve said, picking up her tea and almost scalding her tongue with the first sip. Sandy padded over to stand next to her, his solid presence a comfort.

'Well, I'd better go now, leave you to it,' Minnie said, her bracelets jangling as she swept a piece of hair behind her ear. 'I'll see you in class soon, though, Eve. You take care,' she said, giving her a quick hug.

Eve watched her go, over the iron bridge and down the path the other side. She'd only been gone a few seconds when Eve yelped as a nearby bush started rustling and swearing. A figure emerged, leaves in his hair, hat askew.

'Gerald,' Eve exclaimed with a start.

'Is there anyone else on the boat with you now?' he asked her, stepping over and trying to peer inside.

'Sorry?'

'Anyone else, I saw Minnie go in – who was she meeting?'

'Meeting?'

'There's no need to cover for her,' he said.

'I'm not covering for her. There's no one here, you can check,' Eve said, baffled as to what Gerald was looking for.

'Well, if he's not here,' he said, muttering and walking off. Eve watched him wander away, worried that he was losing the plot. She would have to say something to Minnie. For now, though, she had her own drama to deal with, stabbing at Liam's name on her phone as she thought back to his note on the side.

He didn't answer. Of course he didn't. She was sent straight to voicemail and left an absurdly angry, rambling message that essentially said, 'Dog, kidnap, fuck, bollocks, revenge, mine, dog' on a loop.

How dare he come here and steal her dog? Who had told him where she was? She pictured Daisy at the wedding. She had been talking with him in the corner, Eve was sure of it now – had she said something?

Later, she wasn't angry, she was just horribly lonely. Marmite had been a brilliant companion. He adored the boat, often clambering on the bench to peek out of the porthole, racing around on the deck, clinging to the side, diving into the river after sticks and shaking himself off in surprise when he dragged himself to the bank, only to be bundled into two towels by Eve, gratefully licking her face as she rubbed at him and warmed him up. She wondered where he was now; would he simply forget her? She stared at the spot on the bed where he'd seemed to permanently reside, lying flat over her feet in the night like a reassuring hot-water bottle, with her feeling his heartbeat despite the thickness of the duvet cover.

She wandered around the boat that evening at a loss as to what to do. She couldn't face walking along the common without Marmite striding next to her, tail high, tripping along and then racing ahead once he'd spotted something in the long grass. She sat mindlessly watching television, unable to rouse any energy, the wind howling outside, rain falling in slanted sheets.

She wished that Greg was here to sit with her or to play backgammon, and felt guilty as she realised he was probably with his mum or at work doing something sensible and she was being self-pitying and pathetic. He had a calming presence and she knew why so many of his clients must love him, feeling utterly reassured as he patiently explained what he needed to do to their animals. She wished she hadn't been so quick to jump to silly conclusions; she hadn't made a new friend in years who she felt so at ease with. She wondered where he was now and if he was all right.

She stood up, heading to the kitchen and reaching for the line of recipe books. He had mentioned that he sometimes made bread in winter, something comforting about filling the house with its smell. She searched the index of each book and then felt a faint flicker as she read the words. Grabbing her purse from the side, she headed out, book under her arm, to buy the ingredients.

Four hours later, she was eating a plain white bloomer and she felt the warmth spread down to her toes. The outside was crispy and the inside was still warm from the oven. Marmite would have loved it and she stared sadly at the crumbs on the floor which would have been hoovered up immediately. She went to bed, the boat feeling impossibly quiet without his gentle presence.

Chapter 44

Grandma's Pink Cheese

1 beef tomato
250g tub of full-fat
  soft cream cheese
1 level teaspoon tomato
  ketchup

½ tsp mixed herbs
1 to 2 finely chopped
  spring onions or
  chives
1 clove garlic (crushed)

Method:
- Sieve peeled tomato into the cheese. Add all other ingredients, stir and put in fridge till needed. Good as a dip or as a canapé topping.

SHE WAS grateful to wake the next day and have somewhere to go. The boat was impossibly cold, her feet numb as she moved through to the kitchen to put the kettle on, shivering as she pulled her dressing gown tighter around her. Twisting the rest of the loaf into a carrier bag, she headed off to class.

'Danny!' He was sitting at his wheel, his bowl uncovered, his hands covered in clay, an oily mark on his cheek. She felt her whole face split open.

'How have you been?' she said, noting her head had automatically tipped to the right, her voice dropping.

'You heard about my mum?' Danny said, nodding as he continued. 'She's had the operation, she's recovering. They say she'll be out for Christmas.'

'Oh, that is good news,' Eve said, sitting at her wheel and smiling at him. 'We missed you,' she said, looping the apron over her head.

'I missed it. I've also got a whole load of things to catch up on. Teapot, eh? How fancy are you!'

'I am now an expert potter.' Eve nodded, so pleased to see Danny back and in good spirits. They had similar noses, she saw that now. Perhaps the same grey flecks in their blue eyes. She couldn't keep it in any more, couldn't help ask. 'And how is your brother?' She stared at the spout of her teapot as she spoke, determined not to give anything away.

'My brother, eh? I had no idea,' he said, both eyebrows raised.

'No idea...'

'That you knew him,' he finished, with a chuckle. 'I'll say you said hello.'

'Oh God no, please don't tell him anything, I—'

'Calm down.' He laughed, hands held up, streaks of murky water dripping down his wrists.

As he spoke, she realised they had the same teasing tone in their voices, the same roll of laughter when something caught them unawares.

'Oh, it's just I doubt I'm his favourite person right now. I said some really stupid things to him.'

'To be honest,' Danny said, serious all of a sudden, 'he needs people around him. It's been sort of worse for him; he's been acting the older brother, must be tiring.'

'Are you okay?' Eve asked, noting the purple shadows under his eyes.

'We've had some late nights but it looks like it went well, it's good. But yeah, thanks for asking.'

'I hope so...'

'Eve, this bread is gorgeous, I had no idea you were a chef.' Minnie was passing plates round, the bread still soft, now slathered with butter.

Eve turned, protesting immediately. 'Oh, I'm not, I just felt like bread. It seemed... comforting.'

Danny looked at her quickly, one eyebrow raised. Eve frowned at the clay in front of her, desperately hoping he would stop his scrutiny.

'Eve.'

She half-turned, her foot hovering over the side of the boat, a frown already forming. It had been a long class and she had almost finished her teapot. She had been thinking about how to paint it.

'Eve.'

It was her name. Eve scanned the common, realising a figure was grinning at her from the car park in the distance. Harriet, one hand on a pram and the other holding a large wicker suitcase.

Eve's face broke into a huge smile, her heart lifting at the sight. 'Hey.' She waved back, going to meet her.

Harriet rolled the pram towards her, bumping it over the common, the ground hard as concrete underneath, bald patches now churned-up divots of mud. She looked as if she had just come from the office; high heels, pencil skirt and a jumper with a pussybow collar beneath a matching suit jacket.

Eve walked quickly across to her, throwing an arm round her sister, who seemed to glow. 'What are you doing here? And you brought my gorgeous niece.' Poppy was awake, and she reached into the pram and removed her niece, holding her high in the air so that she gurgled before bringing her down and pulling her soft little body into her. Poppy was smiling, touching Eve's face with two pudgy hands, pushing her cheeks together so that her voice came out in a strange gargled mess, 'Tchis ish such a nicesh shurprise.'

'I had to come, you sounded dreadful. Poor Marmite.'

Tucking Poppy back in her pram under her blanket with her favourite toy, Eve took the basket from Harriet's hand. 'What's in it?' she asked, surprised how heavy it was.

'Our Christmas lunch,' Harriet said, grinning and pushing the pram onto the boat, 'Now show me your boat and let's have a drink.'

It was too cold to stay outside for long and they ended up spreading a rug on the floor of the living room and laying out all the things Harriet had brought down. Opening the basket, Eve unfastened straps of leather that held plates, cutlery and wine glasses in place, and laid them out. Poppy immediately picked up a spoon and started bashing everyone and everything with it.

'She's in a destructive phase,' Harriet explained as Poppy smashed her toy Lamby in the head with her spoon.

'Er... I can see that,' Eve said, quick to scoot the two wine glasses out of the way.

'Hey, what's this?' Harriet asked, picking up some of the sketches for Raj's business cards.

'Oh,' Eve said, almost launching herself across the boat to

remove them, 'just something silly, well, for a friend, they're nothing.'

'Eve, they're really good,' Harriet said, her face completely serious.

She picked up a couple more, laughing at some of the designs and Eve felt her hands unfurl, her shoulders drop; silly really to hide her love of cartoons from her sister.

'You could do this,' Harriet told her, keeping one of an angry goose chasing a woman in her hand.

'I'm not sure,' Eve said. 'That was just a one-off, a friend who wanted business cards.'

'You're really talented,' Harriet said, setting the picture to one side and looking thoughtful for a moment.

'I'm talented.' Eve laughed, looking at the picnic basket. 'Check out you, the domestic goddess.'

Harriet had made turkey sandwiches, bought crisps and salad, and then revealed a small Tupperware container from between two icepacks.

'Is that...?' Eve took it and held it up.

'Yes, the dip you love that we always have on Boxing Day. Didn't want you missing out,' Harriet teased.

'You're amazing,' Eve said humbly, marvelling at how thoughtful her sister could be and how she always seemed to make it look easy. Eve knew how much she was doing and felt her stomach bubble with warmth. 'Thank you.'

'Pff!' Harriet dismissed her with a hand. 'So,' she said, her face serious now, 'Marmite. I've been thinking on the train down and I've come up with a plan to get him back.'

Eve smiled slowly at her sister, the steely glint in her eye, 'Go on,' she said, wondering what Eve would come up with.

'Well, we could do one of two things. One – we could send round some heavies and force Liam to return him...'

'I don't know any heavies,' Eve said, letting out a sigh.

'Gavin and I don't either. Which is why I have thought of option two,' Harriet assured her quickly.

'Which is...?'

'We threaten him with legal action. Send him a letter accusing him of kidnap, unlawful imprisonment, breaking and entering,' Harriet was counting the charges off on her fingers.

'That sounds, extreme,' Eve said slowly, realising her sister was only half-joking. 'And Marmite is his dog too,' she added begrudgingly, her chest aching at the thought of another night without him.

'Well, we can think of something better,' Harriet said, clearly wanting to distract Eve from further gloomy thoughts. 'For now, let's eat.'

'I'll get us drinks,' Eve said, getting up and patting Poppy's head as she passed, earning herself a smack with the spoon. 'I made mulled wine with Greg,' Eve remembered, rummaging in the freezer, 'and he told me to freeze some. It's amazing, actually, you can put it back in the microwave and it's ready in thirty seconds. Ping!' Eve explained, wondering why her sister had slanted her eyes at her.

'Ping? What is going on?' she said slowly.

'What?' Eve said, one hand up to her face as if she had a mark on her.

'You *made* mulled wine and also *woooooooo* Greg?' Harriet said, smirking at her.

Eve's eyes slid away from Harriet's face and she turned quickly to put the mulled wine in the microwave. 'No, I totally ruined it with him.'

'You can't have.'

'I did,' Eve said miserably.

283

'All right, all right, don't have a panic attack, just come and tell me all about it.'

'I can't, I ruin—'

'Here!' Harriet demanded, pointing at the stool.

She was so forceful, Eve forgot the drinks and went and sat on the stool.

'So what happened?'

And Eve told her, the ridiculous conclusions she'd jumped to, the way she'd accused him of being a liar and then, the worst of it, the fact that his mum had been desperately ill in hospital.

'Wow,' Harriet said, her face cringing as Eve finished.

'I know,' Eve agreed, hiding her head in her hands.

'Well,' Harriet said, 'you can fix this. You're down here for another week, you can see him.'

Eve swallowed slowly, biting her lip as she stood. 'I really hope so,' she said, moving back over to the microwave.

She poured them two mulled wines: the smell instantly reminding her of him. She found she was doing that a lot, perhaps hoping he'd appear and she'd be prepared. She was cooking more, taking care over recipes, trying to impress the invisible presence. She wanted him to know that she had taken his advice and she was enjoying it.

She handed Harriet one of the glasses.

'I can't, actually,' Harriet said, putting a hand up.

'You're driving,' Eve said, realising too late.

'Yes, and also the baby,' Harriet said slowly, raising an eyebrow at Eve who, instead of working it out, stared at Poppy who was now spinning on her bottom in a circle.

'I wasn't going to offer her any. I'm not mental. She's a baby.'

'No, not that baby,' Harriet said, placing one hand on her stomach. '*This* baby.'

284

Then Eve understood and her face broke into an enormous grin. 'Wow, really, another baby, two babies, oh that's, wow, two babies.'

'Yes, please stop reminding me now,' Harriet said, laughing. 'Do you want to see the scan?'

'Yes, of course,' said Eve, moving over to her, kneeling on the floor, despite the fact that she couldn't recognise scan photos. Harriet knew this after the last time, though, and thought it was hilarious that Eve looked at the wrong part, cooing over a cloud shape just above the actual baby, believing it to be very bouffant hair.

She frowned at the photograph for a while, locating the head, and then tilting her head to try and make sense of the rest. 'Ooh,' Eve said, nudging Harriet, 'it's a boy.' She was pointing in the middle of the picture.

'That's an arm.'

'Ah!' Eve said, then pulled the photo towards her and tilted her head again. 'Very cute,' she announced, sounding baffled, and handed it back to Harriet.

She had drained her mulled wine. Her sister was having her second baby. They had discussed names and Greg and plans for work, and Harriet had left her with a tight hug and a whispered Happy Christmas, wheeling away Poppy, who had called 'Theve, Theve,' as she curled her fist into an attempted wave.

She watched them go, the car disappearing into the high street. She adored her niece, who seemed endlessly fascinating now that she was able to interact, to move, to chatter, even if Eve and Harriet couldn't always understand the gibberish that she spoke. She loved her constant wonder at things, the ducks on the river, pointing at them with a surprised yelp, pointing at the tree, Eve, a spoon. She adored the way her hair stuck up in all directions and her skin smelt of soap and goodness. Now she would be joined by another baby, a brother or a sister, and Eve would be able to watch them grow up too.

It was only a momentary flicker, but Eve knew it was there, tugging in her subconscious. A little bit of her felt sad. Harriet had known it when she had broken the news; it was probably why she came down to tell her. She was thoughtful and generous and would have known that for Eve the moment would be bittersweet. Harriet and she had always discussed having babies together. They imagined having them together, swapping tips and raising their children at the same time. They would play together and be like siblings rather than cousins. When she was engaged to Liam she had been excited about the idea of starting a family, and when Harriet had announced her first pregnancy it had seemed like perfect timing. She knew she still had time, didn't want to be selfish about it, but sometimes she was gripped with a sudden fear that she wouldn't have anyone to raise a family with, would have to choose whether to go it alone. And Harriet's kids would be older; they wouldn't want to hang out with their younger cousins.

Eve blinked, knowing she was being self-obsessed and ridiculous. She couldn't change what had happened and she knew she couldn't have stayed with Liam and had his children after the lies. She stepped back onto the boat, clearing up the glasses, circling the cloth around them in soapy water.

She pulled her laptop towards her, wanting to check something, something that had been niggling at her since Marmite had gone. As she caught sight of the date in the bottom right of the screen, she started. Christmas Eve was only two days away. She knew she was unsettled from seeing Harriet too, the talk about babies, but she found herself clicking on his Facebook photo. The picture still made her stomach lurch. Liam hadn't changed it since he'd first joined. Him grinning in a striped top, clutching a football to his chest. Hair mussed up, amber eyes glinting, white teeth flashing.

She didn't need to click on his photo albums to know what was in them, she knew them off by heart by now: their holiday to Corfu, their trip to Guernsey, the last Christmas at her parents' house. She'd studied them obsessively in the week he had left her, touching the screen like a woman possessed. All these pictures, still online now, as if they were still together, still smiling warmly for the camera. It was strange; she wished she could delete them all in one swipe. Instead, though, she found herself carrying on, something in the back of her mind; an image she had seen but couldn't place.

There was a new album, photos from the last few months. She knew it would hurt, it was always a bad idea, but, too late, her finger had moved and she was staring now at Liam, his hair shorter, standing with his football mates. They were in a sports centre somewhere, some five-a-side tournament; he was grinning into the camera without a care. The next one he was in a bar, cheeks flushed pink, holding a bottle of beer, one arm looped over the shoulder of Paul, his mate from university. She'd liked Paul.

She couldn't stop herself now, trawling through the other albums as if she was a junkie looking for a fix, forgetting her original reason for looking, just wanting to see them all again, remember them together. There he was in the flat, paintbrush aloft, laughing into the camera. There they were at a dinner party, candles burnt down, faces gleaming. Harriet, Gavin, a cluster of old schoolfriends crammed into their flat for a house-warming.

Then one of Marmite. She leant forward, drinking in his little face. His tiny nose, his doleful eyes, the patch of fur above his eyes. Marmite curled up next to someone's leg, staring into the camera. Eve thought for a second that he looked sad, as if he were staring straight through the computer screen and through to her. She touched the screen, tracing his face, and then felt ridiculous, about to close the laptop and stop all this. That was when she noticed the leg, a skirt rucked up so the thigh was visible, jolting her back to that day. The smooth thigh: it was familiar. As Eve's eyes travelled along it, she noticed the distinctive feature; two moles. She knew where she had seen them before. On a small screen but there was no doubting it. It was the Immaculate Vagina.

'Oh my God, Daisy. I know her.' Eve launched straight into it, pacing up and down the boat as she gabbled down the phone at Daisy, her laptop still frozen on the same photo.

'What? Eve, slow down, what are you talking about?'

'It was Marmite, with the vagina, Liam, I know her.'

Eve waited for a response, wondering for a second if the connection had been lost. 'Daisy?'

'I don't understand,' Daisy said, but she sounded different now. Her voice was strangely slow, as if she were struggling to get the words out.

'The vagina, the girl, the girl who slept with Liam, I know her.' Another pause. Eve pulled the phone away from her ear and frowned at it. 'Daisy?'

'I heard,' Daisy whispered, and it was the sad tone of her voice that made Eve frown. *It couldn't be? Could it?*

'Oh my God,' Eve whispered, coming to a grinding halt in the middle of the boat. 'Was it you?'

She thought back to the last few weeks. The strange diversionary tactics, the troubled looks, the whispered conversation in the corner at Ro-Ro's wedding.

The ensuing silence seemed to confirm it.

'Oh my God,' Eve said, sucking in her breath, dots in her eyes, the inside of her brain screeching. She felt the boat was suddenly too small, she needed air, space. She turned in a circle as Daisy's voice came down the phone at her.

'It wasn't me, Eve, it wasn't me,' Daisy said. 'But...'

Eve couldn't believe what she was hearing: Daisy, her best friend, her quiet, loyal friend who she had known since school. They had done everything together; shared secrets, giggled into the night, wailed and cried on each other after break-ups.

'What do you mean "But"?'

'I... well... I wasn't sure...'

Eve felt her body turn to stone as she waited for Daisy to carry on, but there was nothing on the end of the line apart from her stuttering. 'Oh my God. What, Daisy?' Eve knew she was shouting. She felt out of control all of a sudden, desperate for this to be an enormous joke. 'Do you know something?'

'I'm not sure. I didn't want to just...' Daisy sounded terrible now, pausing, jittery.

Eve felt her voice, hard and direct, no teasing, no jokes. 'What aren't you sure about?' Her knuckles were gripping the phone as she waited for Daisy to speak.

'I wondered, I thought maybe I saw something and then—'

'God, what, Daisy, spit it out for fucks' sake,' Eve said, all the emotion of the day bursting out of her.

'I think.' Daisy swallowed. 'I think, maybe, it was Rachel, Ro-Ro.'

'What?'

'I think...' Daisy was crying now, soft tears between the words. Normally Eve would have melted, Daisy was her best friend, her gentle best friend who baked and kept her flat clean and who loved her. 'She said something once, it just didn't make any sense, but then when you told me what you'd seen...'

Eve felt cold. Her best friend had been carrying around this knowledge and hadn't told her. She had known.

'I asked him at the wedding, asked him to tell you, but he denied it. So I didn't want to say anything in case I wasn't right. I should have asked her but I couldn't do it. I know that's pathetic but...'

Eve listened dumbly as Daisy carried on, knowing she was right. Thinking back to the times when Ro-Ro had been at their flat, her brash laughter, her eyes following him around the room.

'I've got to go,' Eve whispered.

'No, don't, Eve, don't. I'm sorry, I should have had the balls to ask her, to force her to tell you...'

'Yes, yes, you should have done something,' Eve said, her words blurring into each other, tears streaking down her cheeks. It felt good to let some of the anger out and she didn't wait to listen to Daisy's responses, just let her have it. 'You should have told me because we are meant to be best friends.'

'I know, I know...'

'I don't think you do,' Eve said, hanging up on her.

The quiet on the boat was unnerving and, as Eve wiped at her face, she moved out onto the deck. She wanted the sting of the wind and the cold. It whipped around her, her hair blowing across her face as she stared out at the river, the water moving past silent, black.

She couldn't believe it. Daisy had been carrying this knowledge around with her. Eve thought back to all those times Daisy could have said something. Why didn't she? Why hadn't she told her? Eve felt queasy, hands gripping the bar at the back of the boat, the steel cold.

She thought of Ro-Ro, all the times they'd forgiven her for putting them down or saying mean things. She was an old friend and somehow that had made it all right, something to be shrugged off, laughed at. Eve swallowed, knowing she needed to confront her now. She stepped back inside the boat, the mobile sitting on the table where she'd left it, approaching it as if it were a bomb that might go off. Snatching it up quickly she pressed on her name in the contacts list.

'Rachel.'

'Eve, I've told you. I really hate it when you call me that.'

'Hmm,' Eve said, feeling anger coursing through her, every vein distended, her hand gripping the phone to her ear. 'Do you know what I really hate?'

Ro-Ro sighed in a bored sort of way and Eve was suddenly there with her in her flat, watching her tip her head to one side, inspect her manicured nails. She replied, 'People who claim to be from Oxford University but actually went to Brookes, toys that are marketed for boys that girls could play with, the man with the bear from that insurance advert...'

All these were true, and suddenly the fact that this girl knew her so well diffused the anger. The rage left her, her shoulders sagged and in a small voice Eve simply said, 'No, Rachel, I just hate it when a supposed good friend sleeps with my fiancé.'

Ro-Ro didn't wait long enough, the response high-pitched and too fast. 'Don't be absurd.' Then she laughed, a quick, high laugh, dismissive, as if she was at a cocktail party and Eve had accused her of having Botox.

It was the laugh that made Eve continue, knowing it was absolutely true, that it was her, the woman in the photo. 'Was it the once? Twice? Had it been going on for years?' She felt bile rise in her throat as the words came, not knowing whether she was ready yet for any answer.

She could hear rustling, sentences in the background, the sound of a TV.

'Is that Hugo? Oh, I bet he'd love to hear this...'

The noises continued and then the sound of a door closing, quiet, quick breaths, and then Ro-Ro hissing in whispered undertones, 'Once, all right, well, a couple of times. Oh, for fuck's sake, I'll kill him for fucking telling you.'

The voice was so ugly, warped in a way Eve had never heard before. The hurt, the idea that she and Liam would be colluding together over when to tell Eve or not, made Eve feel more nauseous. She'd forgiven Ro-Ro for her snappy comments, her scathing remarks, but this was new. She made her feel as if they had no history together at all, as if there was no affection.

'Liam didn't tell me anything.'

That pulled Ro-Ro up short. She fell silent again before saying one word in a quiet voice, 'Daisy.'

'It wasn't bloody Daisy,' Eve screeched, her voice loud in the small space, surprised to see her own snarling mouth in the dark porthole in front of her. 'She suspected but she was too bloody loyal to you to drop you in it, wanted to be sure.'

Eve felt a wash of guilt, realising she had shouted at the wrong friend earlier. Now that the truth was out, it seemed more horrible and disgusting than the not knowing; maybe she'd been trying to protect her.

'Look,' Ro-Ro said, her whispers pleading, clearly still hiding in her kitchen. 'Look, it's COMPLETELY over now. It was all over before I got married, I wasn't thinking... Are you going to tell Hugo?' She sounded scared; for the first time, she sounded afraid.

Hugo. Eve felt so sorry for the beaming, red-faced groom she'd seen a few days before, standing at the front of the church making promises to this glossy liar.

'I... it's over. Please, Eve, it would just hurt him...'

Eve bristled at the question, her speech, no apology, just hoping that her perfect world didn't come falling down around her ears.

'I'm not. You should, though,' Eve said.

Once she'd heard it, Ro-Ro was all for reconciliation. 'I am so, so sorry, Eve, I don't know how it happened. I wasn't thinking, I was getting married,' she said. 'It all seemed so daunting. You don't understand... the pressure.'

'You see I do understand, though, don't I? I was meant to be getting married too.'

Ro-Ro at least had the decency to shut up.

For the first time since the break-up, Eve felt a flood of relief that she hadn't married Liam, that she wasn't trotting down the aisle to stand and make vows to someone who would lie and cheat on her with a friend of hers. She was finally glad she had booted him out; there would have been no coming back from it.

'I suppose you told him where I was living in one of your cosy tête-à-têtes?' Eve said, realising now why Ro-Ro had invited Liam to her wedding. He had been like a trophy to her.

'He asked. I didn't know it was a secret.'

'Well, he's taken Marmite,' Eve said. 'Not that you'd care about my dog when you don't give a shit about me.'

'That's not true,' Ro-Ro said and her voice was different, lower, filled with an emotion Eve hadn't heard from her before. Then there was a voice in the background and Ro-Ro suddenly piped up, 'Excellent, well, I am glad we talked.'

'That's Hugo, isn't it?'

'Yes, yes, absolutely. Well, speak soon, okay?'

'No, Ro-Ro, we won't be doing that.'

'Oh, Eve—'

And she was gone as Eve jabbed at her phone and cut her off. She wouldn't be talking to Ro-Ro ever again.

Missing Marmite, unable to stand the boat without the pad of his paws, his excited bark, she picked up a blanket and returned to the decking, thinking over all the times she had spent with Rachel at school, the times she had visited the flat with Liam and Eve. She thought briefly of Hugo and wondered whether he would ever find out, whether Ro-Ro would do it again with someone else. Eve hoped not; she knew what it felt like to be involved in the fall-out.

She wasn't sure how long she stood out on the deck, the strange empty silence making her feel as if she were the only person on the river that night. She knew she should have been feeling happy for Harriet, but it seemed like for ever ago and only managed to highlight how alone she was. She shivered. Her jumper not enough to keep out the cold: she felt as bleak as the landscape around her. Her teeth were chattering as she looked up at the sky, a bank of cloud obscuring any stars. Without Marmite to nestle in her lap, his wet nose to find her hand, his chocolate eyes to follow her around, the boat felt all wrong. Maybe it was seeing Harriet too, knowing that she'd tried to run away from her family, hating that she had hurt them in doing so. They truly cared about her and she had selfishly decided to abandon them.

She looked around her, the river curling round the bend, the sound of the weir distant in the darkness, its relentless task. She knew she had to let Liam go, she knew she needed to move on with her own life, but somehow she couldn't seem to find the strength. She'd shouted at Daisy, hurt her, and her family too by shunning them at Christmas. She'd lost Marmite, shouted at Greg, and accused him of things that he hadn't done. Now she was here, completely alone, and Christmas was round the corner.

Well, Eve, you wanted to be alone for Christmas. She'd certainly got her wish.

Eve shut her eyes, a pathetic figure, one slow tear making an unsteady path down her face and dropping into the still water below her.

Chapter 45

MRS MCLAUGHLIN was due to appear at any moment. They had kept Pepper in overnight but her condition was no better. She lay, lacklustre, staring out with desolate eyes from between the bars of the kennel, the newspaper soiled around her, no energy to get herself up, the water and food untouched beside her in bowls. Greg knew with a sinking heart that it wasn't good.

He heard the bell go and turned as Mrs McLaughlin stepped inside. She seemed to have aged ten years since their last appointment, her head down, her hands shaking as she moved across to reception. He felt his whole body lurch as he thought back to the woman who had first bustled into the practice, chirruping at her husband, smoothing out the crossword, fetching them pens, carrying Pepper in a basket, lifting her onto the table. Her determined steely eyes as she took in what Greg was saying, humorous, quick. He didn't recognise her as she stepped across to him, holding up a tissue to her mouth, already preparing herself.

The cheery tinsel seemed to emphasise her grey face as she raised a weak smile. 'Happy Christmas.'

He swallowed, hating that it was Christmas Eve and this was how she was spending it. 'You too, Mrs McLaughlin.' He was so tired from the long nights, fretting about Mum, worrying whether she'd respond well to the transplant, holding it together for her and Danny. He had barely registered it was Christmas, could hardly focus on anything. He was grateful to Karen for her cheery smile, her offer to work later on Christmas Eve.

'Mrs McLaughlin, do come in,' he said, guiding her with one hand on her back. She followed like a dutiful child.

She didn't cry as she placed a hand on Pepper, still lying on the table in the consulting room. Pepper lay there as Mrs McLaughlin stroked her ever so lightly, her gold wedding band flashing in the strip lights over their heads.

'Would you like a chair, Mrs McLaughlin?' Greg knew that he should keep clients standing. It was the better way to break news, he had been told that on a course once; better still if they were walking because their body doesn't let them go into shock. He didn't care about that course now or what he should or shouldn't do; he just couldn't bear to see her so hopeless.

She looked up at him, her old self for a moment. 'No, Mr Burrows,' she said, smiling a watery smile.

He nodded briskly, trying to retain a grip on the situation, worried for a brief moment that his voice would crack. He looked somewhere just above her eyes, not able to focus yet on her, as he said in a slow, careful voice, 'I'm afraid, as we feared, the cancer is back. I'm afraid that's why she's struggling to breathe. The best thing,' he said, pausing to clear his throat, 'the best thing, Mrs McLaughlin is—'

'To put her to sleep,' Mrs McLaughlin finished for him, her gaze steady, and he held it for a few seconds before silently nodding a response.

The decision seemed to galvanise her and she straightened, stroking Pepper's fur once more. 'Can I stay? I'd like to be there.'

'Of course,' Greg said.

'And what do you do... after?' she asked, swallowing slowly, the only outward sign she was struggling.

'Whatever you feel is right. You could take Pepper home and bury her or, if you like, we could organise a cremation for Pepper.'

'I scattered Harold's ashes,' she said in a quiet voice. 'He wanted that, never wanted to be put under ground, was claustrophobic, the old softie,' she said, a ghost of a smile on her face. 'I'll do the same.' Her voice cracked as she said, 'They'd like that. I imagine they'd want to be together.' A tear formed in the corner of her eye and made a slow path down her face, trailing through the powder on her cheeks, marking a wobbly line. Greg had never wished so much that he could have done more in all the years he had been a vet.

Not trusting himself to speak, he went to fetch the folder where they kept photographs of different urns. He watched her select one, taking care over her choice. He spoke to Karen, who followed him back into the room, putting a hand on Mrs McLaughlin's shoulder.

They stood in the consulting room and Karen moved round the table to hold Pepper, smiling kindly at Mrs McLaughlin. Greg fetched the syringe, training his eyes on Mrs McLaughlin. 'This will take effect very quickly but you may notice that Pepper gasps or twitches.' Mrs McLaughlin brought the tissue up to her mouth again. 'If this happens she won't be aware of anything. It is just her body's reflexes, but it can look quite distressing.'

Mrs McLaughlin took a breath and nodded at him.

Greg gave her time to prepare herself and then gently slid the injection into Pepper's front leg, finding the vein. It didn't take long and Pepper lay there. Mrs McLaughlin made a small noise and Greg felt his own chest heavy and constricted.

'I'll get the cremation organised and she will be back with us in about two weeks' time, and I'll call when her ashes are here.'

'Thank you, Mr Burrows,' she said, swallowing. Greg wanted to put his arm round her and was so glad when Karen did just that, moving her to the door, chivvying her along. Just before they left, Greg started to speak, not wanting to leave things like that.

'What was your best memory of Pepper?' he asked, making both Mrs McLaughlin and Karen turn back round.

She looked at him unseeing, her eyes moving left to right as she thought. Then her mouth slowly turned upwards and the softest chuckle shook her body. 'I'd make a cake every week for Harold. Victoria Sponge was his favourite. We got back into the kitchen to find Pepper licking her paws. She'd eaten her way through the cling film and had polished half of it off. Harold and I laughed so hard we had to sit on the kitchen flagstones until we'd recovered.'

Greg watched the animation on her face, her pale-brown eyes clearer, her back straighter.

'You're a lovely man,' she said, nodding to herself. 'Harold always said you were a gent.'

Greg felt warmth settle over him. 'Thank you, that means a lot.'

Mrs McLaughlin nodded, turning to put her hand on the handle of the door. He watched her back for a second as she took a breath, and then stepped out into reception.

Chapter 46

SHE WAS heading home for Christmas. She had packed a bag that morning, feeling more certain with every item she threw inside. She wanted to see Harriet, her parents, Scarlet, and she wanted them clucking about her, reminding her that life went on and that people loved her whatever happened.

She had phoned Daisy, stopping her before she had even begun. 'I'm sorry, Dais'. I am so sorry.'

'I'm so sorry.'

'No, really, truly, Daisy, I should never have shouted at you like that.'

'I deserved it,' Daisy said, her voice small and sad, so that Eve wanted to reach through the phone and give her the most enormous hug.

'You didn't, you didn't do anything wrong.'

'Did you speak to Ro-Ro?'

Eve sighed. 'I did. It happened a couple of times apparently. Do you know what? I didn't need the details. The whole thing just left me more sure I've made the right decision.'

'You really have,' Daisy said. 'I'm proud of you.'

'Sherrup.'

'Okay, Happy Christmas.'

'Happy Christmas, Dais'.'

She had felt instantly better, talking to her best friend again, knowing that Daisy would never do anything to deliberately hurt her. She walked to class the next day feeling like one of the stones weighing her down had been lifted away.

It was the last class before Christmas; they were collecting up their pots and bowls. The conservatory had been decorated beautifully. Large wrought-iron candlesticks with twisted stems held scented candles, the flames dancing and letting off a mix of orange and cinnamon scents. Christmas cards were crammed on every available surface and gold and silver cut-outs in the shapes of bells and snowflakes were stuck to the walls. Gerald was looking twitchy every time Raj stepped near one of the many bunches of mistletoe that Minnie had hung around the place.

Eve carefully wrapped her items in newspaper and loaded them into a large bag. She couldn't wait to give the teapot to Harriet. She'd painted it with large poppies as an ode to her niece and she knew Harriet would love it. She had bowls and plates for her parents and a pot that could be used to hold candles for Scarlet, pens for Gavin. She had made one extra piece, staring at it for a few seconds, a lump in her throat, before checking over her shoulder and bundling it into the bag.

Kissing Minnie on the cheek, ruffling Sandy's fur, she felt an ache as she was reminded of Marmite. He'd always loved to see Sandy, hopping around his legs, his tiny playmate, following around the older, bigger dog with excitable brown eyes.

'You have a wonderful Christmas,' Minnie said, dressed in an extraordinary red velvet ensemble complete with grey fur trim. She looked like Mrs Santa Claus. Eve made a mental note to never introduce her to her dad.

Gerald was there, dressed in a Christmas jumper that Eve

congratulated him on, realising too late it was not worn in irony. She scuttled away just before she heard him strike up a reluctant conversation with Raj. It was only when Raj announced he was leaving in the New Year to teach pottery classes to children in Spain that Gerald really perked up.

Danny was there too, chatting to Aisha and Mark, and Eve wandered over to wish them all a Happy Christmas.

Aisha turned as she approached, her hair even glossier in the light from a nearby candle. 'Eve, I saw all your pots, they're brilliant. You are such a talented artist.'

Eve felt her cheeks warm as Aisha continued to compliment her.

'No one does deranged geese better than you.' Danny smiled, winking at her.

'Thanks. Quite a niche market, though,' Eve replied, hoping she might be able to draw Danny to one side and talk to him. She didn't want to embarrass herself, hoping they might get a chance to speak before she had to leave.

'Eve, we were actually wondering,' Aisha said, turning to hold Mark's hand, 'whether you would mind doing some sketches for our wedding invitations? Would you be interested?'

'Oh, I...'

'We wanted something hand-drawn and we were hoping you might be able to design us something.'

'Wow!' Eve said, temporarily at a loss for words, the request blindsiding her. 'Yes, of course, I'd love to,' she gushed, feeling a warmth spread through her.

'I saw Raj's business cards, they were fantastic,' Mark commented, an arm round Aisha's shoulders.

'Thanks,' said Eve, feeling absurdly happy. 'And, Aisha, I'm, um, I was hoping I could get you to put a word in for me, at the agency.' She was gratified to see Aisha clap her hands together. She could start to see herself in the village, had friends here now. Maybe it was time to do something completely new with her life. She wanted options, an opportunity to start afresh.

She was running out of time to speak to Danny. He was talking to Mark about the football matches over Christmas and Eve didn't want to drag him away or ask him anything too private in front of other people. It worried her, though, that he seemed to have bags under his eyes. He gave her a quick grin when he noticed her looking over at him and she mouthed 'Happy Christmas' as she left, knowing she didn't have all day. She almost told him where she was headed but couldn't bring herself to in front of other people. He would probably only have laughed.

She was going to see Greg. She wanted to see him before she left, felt this desperate urge to tell him that she was sorry about his mum and everything that had happened. Seeing Danny taut and worried, hiding his fears behind smiles, only made her want to see Greg more. She didn't give herself time to change her mind, but headed back to the boat to drop off her bag of pottery, removing one piece from it. Throwing a moth-eaten bottle-green jumper over her dungarees and pulling her plimsolls on, she locked up hastily, almost slipping on the icy deck in her rush to get out before she changed her mind.

The common was crisp under her feet, crunching as she slipped and trod over to the gate of the car park, the wind turning her bare ankles blue. She wished she had brought a coat, marching along the high street with arms pumping to try to keep warm, the temperature making her nose run and her ears ache. She wouldn't be deterred, hearing her footsteps slapping in the echoey space under the railway bridge, the cold winter sunlight temporarily blinding her as she emerged from beneath it. She jumped as a high-speed train whistled past, the carriages bumping and squealing just above her head, so that her thoughts were temporarily drowned out. She imagined people wrapped up in layers, carrying bags of presents home with them, looking out as the countryside whizzed by and they headed home for Christmas.

She could see Karen trussed up in a red polo neck tapping at the desk as, tilting her chin up and feigning more confidence than she felt, she pushed the door open. The bell rang out and then a stuffed Santa started singing noisily as she crossed the surgery. Karen rolled her eyes, clearly weary as the tune faded out. This obviously wasn't the first time she'd heard it. The reception was decorated with poinsettias and tinsel was hung all along her desk. Eve darted her eyes to the right and realised with relief that she was the only customer.

'Is Greg here?' she asked, stepping forward, her voice laced with excitement.

Karen looked her up and down, clearly growing more familiar with her barging into the practice without booking an appointment. 'He's left for the day; we're closing early because it's Christmas Eve. The last appointment just finished.'

Eve wondered why Karen's mascara had run. 'Are you okay?' she asked her, stepping forward.

'I'm fine thank you, just, well,' she said with a sigh, 'it was a tougher day than some.'

Eve nodded. 'I'm sorry,' she said, at a loss now as to what to do, utterly deflated that she'd missed him. 'Oh,' she said, the piece of pottery wrapped in a paper bag clutched to her chest. 'Could you make sure he gets this, please?'

'Of course,' Karen said, taking it from her.

Eve walked back across the surgery, her shoes squeaking on the linoleum floor, setting off stuffed Santa into another round of song.

Peppermint Creams

2 egg whites
500g icing sugar, sieved
Peppermint essence or oil

Method:
- Whip egg whites to soft peaks.
- Gradually add icing sugar.
- Add a few drops of peppermint oil.
- Can add colouring if wished.
- Mix to stiff paste.
- Roll out to ¼-inch thick. Cut into small rounds.
- Leave for several hours to harden.

Taking care over the thin layer of snow that had peppered the ground, turning the tarmac of the car park into a dotted carpet, she pushed open the gate to the common and looked up at the boat. She couldn't believe it at first; from this distance it was possible it could have been any dog but, as she heard a familiar bark and he saw her and started racing towards her, she was in no doubt at all. His ears were perked up, his bark resounding around the empty space, and she bent to pet him, stroking him over and over, bundling him into her arms so that he wriggled and squirmed in delight, his rough tongue on her chin.

'Okay, okay.' She laughed, putting him back down on the floor.

It was only then that she realised there was someone else in the park with them. He was standing awkwardly, hands in his pockets, then out again, shifting from one leg to another as she neared the boat. The snow had started falling and it drifted down into his hair, resting there, tiny flakes that she wanted to reach up and brush away. His nose and cheeks were pink with the cold and he gave her a small smile. She felt her body react, a flip in her stomach at the familiarity of his face.

'Hey, Liam,' she said, her voice soft as she approached, Marmite forgotten as he yapped and spun about them.

She wanted to rage, to shout and to scream, haughtily demand him to go away. She pictured Ro-Ro then, pointing at him and shouting, 'Be gone,' but she couldn't summon up the energy. She realised with a start that she didn't feel as strongly any more. His face was already starting to fade into her past, nestled with faces of other men that she had loved and broken up with. A little more vivid, perhaps, but still firmly in that line-up now.

'Eve,' he said, the snow falling more heavily now.

'You'd better come in,' she said and, scooping up Marmite, she walked over to the door of the boat and stood back, watching him duck his head and step inside. She kissed the top of Marmite's fur and then followed him in.

It was so strange seeing him sitting on the bench of the little boat. He had picked up the orchid book and was now trawling its pages, not focusing, stopping, looking up and trawling again. She waited for the kettle to boil, unable to resist watching him. His sandy hair was cut differently, spikier at the front and shorter at the back, and under his coat he was wearing a shirt with a narrow tie. He looked like a trendy hipster, different from the Liam she held in her memory.

'Have you?' She indicated his hair, suddenly recognising another change. 'Have you dyed your hair?'

His neck went red as he blustered a reply. 'Just some tints,' he admitted, patting the top self-consciously.

Eve felt her eyes widen, her eyebrows lift; Liam had always been pretty scathing of men who did too much to their appearance. She swallowed down a catty response, not feeling she had the energy to tease him for it. In fact, as she handed him his tea, milk, two sugars, she felt detached, as if they had just met and were having to make polite conversation.

'Peppermint cream?'

'Sorry?'

'I made some,' Eve said, opening the fridge and pulling out a baking sheet with rows of circular white fondants. 'This batch is the best,' she said, her voice laced with pride as she popped four onto a plate, a fifth straight into her mouth.

Liam took the plate, his face still a startled mix as he bit into one. She could tell he was impressed as he returned for a second one. 'When did you get into making these?'

Eve shrugged, picturing Greg and her eating them at the market, icing sugar on his nose. She'd wanted to make something, she realised, that reminded her of him. She wanted to cook with him again; cooking with Greg just felt right. They complemented each other, moving around the kitchen without clashing, her tidying and tasting, veering away from the making. Him forcing her to take notice, then stepping back to allow her to take over, quietly instructing her if she started to panic. She felt happy to tackle different recipes, had started to enjoy coming up with ideas.

'I have done a bit of cooking while I've been down here,'

she said, sitting down on the stool and lifting Marmite to her.

They ate in between stilted conversation. He was heading home for Christmas.

'Alone?' Eve couldn't help asking.

'Alone.' Liam nodded. 'I'm not seeing anyone else, Eve. The girl. It's over. It was—'

'Ro-Ro,' Eve finished for him, a glimmer of triumph as he almost choked on his peppermint cream.

'Did she tell you?'

'No.' Eve sighed, her shoulders sagging. 'But it doesn't matter any more.' As the words left her mouth, she knew it was true. 'So why are you here, Liam?'

He swallowed slowly, a hand up to self-consciously pat at his hair. 'It wasn't the same,' he said, indicating Marmite. 'He was pining for you and, well, he was our dog, it just didn't feel right, taking him like that.'

'So...' Eve held her breath.

'I thought I should bring him back. To you.'

'Are you saying I can keep him?' Eve asked, slowly, her whole body gripped as she waited for him to reply. Looking at Marmite now, she was desperate to keep him; she missed everything about him. His cowardice in the face of angry geese, him tripping her up by weaving in between her legs, his excited bark when they were racing around the common.

'I'm going away, for work, and I thought it would be best if he stayed with you, he clearly likes you,' he said, motioning to Marmite, who she had scooped up without thinking, her comfort blanket.

'Thank you,' Eve said, realising that this wasn't easy for Liam. He had never been the best at climbing down after an argument. 'I'll look after him.'

'I know you will.'

'Wait here,' Eve said, depositing Marmite back on the floor and heading to her bedroom, knowing exactly what she was looking for.

She returned, her chest a little tighter as she held out her hand, the engagement ring clutched in her closed fist.

'Here,' she said, dropping it into his. 'I think it's also about time I gave this back.'

He started to protest but she stopped him. 'Please take it. It was lovely of you to give it to me in the first place but I want you to have it back now.'

He stopped short, his face suddenly hopeless, skin sagging as he nodded at her. 'I'm sorry about it all, how it turned out,' he said. He unzipped his pocket and put the ring inside, swallowing slowly as he looked back at her.

Eve stepped forward and kissed him on the cheek. 'Me too,' she said, her eyes filling with tears, knowing this was the goodbye that they should have had.

'Well,' she said, a small smile on her face.

'Well.' He wound his scarf around his neck. Turning to go, he ducked his head through the door and stepped back out onto the bank. She followed him out.

'Hey,' he said, turning back to her. 'Are you headed home for Christmas?' he asked as if it were the most obvious thing in the world and, as Eve looked up at him, she heard her voice change as she smiled from the deck of the boat, the breeze lifting her hair.

'Of course.'

Chapter 47

The Perfect Turkey Roast

Ingredients:

1 turkey   Bag of potatoes
                                   (King Edwards)

Method:

Turkey:

- Put turkey in large tin. Cover breast with salt. Cover with foil.

- Add tsp of French mustard, salt and pepper and dissolve in cup of boiling water. Then add 1 litre boiling water.

- Roast 170°C. (Approx. 15 minutes per 500g and then sit for 15-20 mins before carving).

- If stuffing the turkey cook for longer (up to 30 mins approx.).

- To check when turkey is cooked put a knife in where meat is thickest. If juices run clear then turkey is cooked.

- Slowly pour off excess fat and use juices for gravy.

Potatoes:

- Peel and chop up potatoes. Parboil them for 10 minutes on the hob.

- Place them on baking tray and cover them in oil or goose fat. Put them in oven for 20 minutes at 220°C then turn down to 170°C for 1 hour.

- Turn them every 20 minutes or so.

- Select vegetables you wish to add and follow instructions.

Stuffing:

Ingredients:

1 medium onion	Packet of sage and onion stuffing mix
2 rashers of streaky bacon	6-8 large open mushrooms
200g pork stuffing	Tsp of mixed herbs
	Salt and pepper

Method:

- Prepare sage and onion stuffing mix as per packet instructions.

- Finely chop the onion and bacon.

- Put in saucepan in oil on low heat until softened.

- Take off heat, add pork stuffing with a little cold water so it doesn't stick.

- Put back on heat, keep stirring. Add finely chopped mushrooms (or mince them).

- Add herbs and seasoning.

- Cook slowly on low heat for 10-15 mins, keep stirring.

- Then add sage and onion stuffing mix. Mix well.

- Either serve or put in bowl ready to stuff turkey with it.

Bread Sauce:

Ingredients:

1 small onion
600ml of milk
200g of white sliced
   bread (put in blender)

Generous sprinkle
   of ground cloves
Salt and pepper

Method:

- Finely slice onion and fry in generous knob of butter on low heat.
- In a separate bowl add fresh breadcrumbs mixed with milk, salt and pepper.
- Add cloves to onion and butter.
- Then add rest of mixture. Cook 2-3 minutes until mixture boiling.
- If set aside to have later, add milk if consistency too stiff, reheat before serving.

Gravy:

- Pour the juices from the turkey, add a tsp of cornflour, a small glass of red wine, the leftover vegetable water if needed.

IT WAS worth the journey home just to see Harriet's face after opening the door. She had obviously been mid-sentence, mouth half-open, turning away from the door as she pulled it towards her. And then she stopped, dropped Poppy's stuffed toy lamb on the floor, grinned, and launched herself at Eve, enveloping her in the tightest hug.

'Yay!' she said, muffled by Eve's hair.

Eve moved inside, brushing snow from her coat and laughing at Marmite who was licking at it, unsure what was on his fur. Mum appeared with a puzzled expression in the kitchen doorway, holding a wooden spoon. Then, as Eve looked up at her, a slow smile spread across her face and Eve walked over and hugged her too.

Mum patted her briskly. 'Good, good,' she said, wiggling away and turning back to the oven, one hand up to wipe at her face. 'Gosh, something in my eye,' she said, her voice cracking. Harriet grinned over at her.

They ate dinner, Gavin, Dad, Scarlet, Mum, Harriet and Eve all crammed round the circular table in the kitchen swapping news and jokes, the windows steamed up in the corners, Christmas cards littering the dresser, tinsel framing the pictures, party-popper threads dangling from the lampshade. Scarlet was still single, her latest man had decided to spend Christmas on a shaking retreat in Bali to 'loosen his energy' so they'd parted ways. Scarlet didn't seem that fussed by the break-up, although she did later confide to Eve and Harriet that she regretted the tattoo on her ankle of a ram, his star sign, that Mum had yet to see.

They loved their presents, Dad instantly deciding to eat his Christmas cake from his plate, Harriet's eyes bright as she turned the teapot over in her hands.

'It's amazing, honestly, Eve, it's really good.'

'Excellent, really excellent,' Mum said and Eve beamed at her.

As the laughter and the games continued over bottles of red wine, Eve relaxed into her chair, Marmite snoozing at her feet, feeling full of contented love for her crazy family. She felt a brief flicker as she wondered where Greg was and how his mum was getting on. She hoped she was at home for Christmas, Greg and Danny able to be with her. As she kissed her dad goodnight, standing there in his bottle-green corduroys and pea-green shirt ('extraordinary, he looks like a broad bean,' said Mum), she hugged him close, feeling enormously lucky and stupid for ever wanting to miss being at home for this.

Christmas Day morning was bittersweet. Woken by Harriet, a bleary-eyed Scarlet behind her, Eve wasn't given time to think about the year before, just swept down to breakfast and out to church, seeing Gavin and Harriet linking arms as Eve carried Poppy, pointing and gurgling in a red wool dress, in her arms. Scarlet had stayed back to keep an eye on lunch so that Mum could go to church. Dad was walking by her side, resplendent in a tweed cloak. When she did think of Liam, she prodded the feeling, realising it didn't have quite the same sting. As she sang the carols and looked round at her family, she felt her voice rising higher and higher, wanting to celebrate, wanting to sing.

Lunch was the usual feast, crackers were pulled, jokes were told and they all stuffed themselves full of turkey. The roast potatoes were perfection: soft on the inside and crispy on the outside, the turkey was stuffed with delicious meats and the gravy was thick and warm. As Eve dabbed at her mouth, laughing as Harriet tried to force-feed Gavin a Quality Street chocolate, 'I can't, H, I'll actually burst', she grinned over at her dad who gave her the smallest wink.

They watched movies in their pyjamas, Scarlet and Eve curled up on the living-room floor on a sea of cushions under a duvet, giggling as if they were twelve years old again. Dad kept falling asleep next to the reading lamp, Mum kept asking who everyone was in the movie, Harriet and Gavin patiently explaining. Before she went upstairs, Harriet drew Eve to one side, handing her an envelope. Eve frowned as she slid a finger along to open it.

'What is it?' she asked as she pulled out a slip of paper with a username and password written on it.

'It's for your new website,' Harriet said with a slow smile.

'Website?'

'Your illustrations. I stole a few from some of the notebooks in your flat; there were loads but I hope you don't mind. They're really good, Eve, I think you've got something. You've already had an email through asking about designing a card for someone's child's birthday.'

'Really?' said Eve, her stomach suddenly erupting into bubbles. 'That's...' She bit her lip, hugging Harriet tight, 'Thank you, Amazing Sister.'

'I'm the best,' Harriet said, kissing her on the cheek. 'It's been a good day, hasn't it?' she asked.

'It has,' said Eve, padding upstairs to her bed, her stomach aching with food and laughter, her mind already on the things she could do next year. Perhaps she could work part time, try to get some commissions from the website? She felt a bubble of excitement at the prospect. Marmite was already asleep in a basket in the corner of her room and she grinned at the shape of him in the dark. She felt an overwhelming sense of relief: coming home had been the right thing to do.

There were texts from Aisha, Minnie, Daisy, all wishing her Happy Christmas which she sent kisses to, a text from Ro-Ro that she ignored. Nothing from Greg, who still didn't have her number. She wondered for the twentieth time that day whether he had enjoyed Christmas. She didn't know what they were doing. It might not have been the best day; she shouldn't presume. She wondered whether she would see him when she got back to the boat, hoping she could still fix things with him, hoping that he didn't hate her. Wrapped up in her checked pyjamas, she fell asleep whispering him 'Happy Christmas' out loud.

Chapter 48

Christmas Soup

1 onion, chopped
3/4 large leeks, chopped
3 sticks of celery,
chopped
3 large potatoes (King
Edward or similar),
chopped

2 litres of stock (made
from turkey bones,
simmered for two
hours)
1 tsp mixed herbs
1 level tsp Bouillon
Salt and pepper,
to taste
100ml single cream

Method:

• Fry onion in oil in large saucepan.

• Add all chopped vegetables.

• Cover with stock and seasoning.

• Cook for 30 mins until all vegetables soft.

• Blitz in blender till totally smooth.

• Add the cream.

• Serve.

'So I saw Eve on Christmas Eve,' Danny said, swallowing his soup.

'Who's Eve?' Linda asked, looking up. It wasn't just in Greg's mind, she seemed healthier today; her cheeks fuller, pinker, her eyes glinting. 'Greg, this is delicious,' she said, spooning another mouthful.

'Thanks, Mum. Eve is a girl from Danny's pottery course.' He saw Danny grinning at him under his messy fringe. 'Oh, sod off, Danny.'

'You boys.' Linda chuckled. 'Is she nice, Greg?'

'She's great,' Danny said, shooting Greg a look.

'And you would know how?' Greg asked. For a brief moment he felt fully back; they were eating the usual Boxing Day lunch round their table together, with all the usual jokes and the teasing. He smiled before taking up his spoon.

'Sat next to her for the last month in class, didn't I. She's funny and good-looking, mate, and clearly blind because she likes you.'

'Daniel.'

'Yes, Daniel.' Greg laughed, covering his mum's hand. 'Thanks, Mum. And how about you, Danny? Any lucky lady?' Greg asked, enjoying watching his little brother squirm in return.

'I don't have time for women, mate. I'm playing the field.'

'So that's a no then,' their mum said, shaking her head.

'Harsh, Mum,' Danny said, pouting at her and getting up to remove the bowls.

Greg was grinning as he got up to help him wash up.

They spent most of the afternoon watching the end of some drama series Mum liked, but mostly eating all her chocolates and grapes that people had delivered. 'So many grapes, I will be all grape by the end of this year.'

It had been a great day and, as Greg shrugged on his coat in the hallway, he was pleased to glimpse his mum in the front room standing up to hug Danny, already moving more easily, seeming to have some of her strength back.

She came into the hallway. 'Be careful in the snow,' she said, offering him a cheek to kiss.

'Will do, see you tomorrow. Can I get you anything before I go?'

'No, don't be silly, I have everything I need and I'm feeling much better, love, truly,' she said, and for the first time, Greg dared to hope it was really true.

They left the house together. Danny was heading to Andy's to watch a match on Sky, but Greg wasn't in the mood. It had started to snow again, lightly but persistently, the car covered already.

As he turned to get into his car, Danny suddenly stuck an arm out to stop him. Greg frowned and looked round.

'I wanted to say...' Danny pulled a beanie down over his blond hair, snow already clinging to the wool. 'You can relax now, bro, she's going to be all right, and I'm all right.'

Greg looked at him, feeling his chest loosen a bit, the weight he'd been dragging around start to lessen.

'You don't have to keep looking after us, think about yourself, okay?'

Greg didn't know how to reply, unused to seeing his brother with this solemn expression on his face, his nose turning pink with the cold.

'And that Eve, she is a good one. I think she got cheated on by her last boyfriend, you know,' Danny said.

That made sense. Greg thought back to the row outside

the boat, how she had so quickly accused him of his double life. It had seemed so out of character, this strange outburst.

'I should have told her about Mum, kept running away, but I didn't want to bring her down, didn't want another person feeling sorry for me.'

'Yeah, I know what you mean. If the lads are any nicer to me at the garage I'll have to start buying them all rings.'

Greg laughed as Danny carried on. 'You can fix it, mate. You know, she'll be back in the village for our last few lessons of the year, if you wanted to see her.'

Greg looked at him, as if Danny had been able to see inside his head these last twenty-four hours. He'd been thinking about her a lot, had walked by the boat that morning, the portholes dark, the lights all off. She had obviously gone away somewhere for Christmas. She'd come into the practice on Christmas Eve, left something for him; Karen had texted him to let him know. He wished he had been there to see her and would stop by the practice and pick it up.

'Good to know,' he said, trying not to look too interested, not wanting his brother to keep taking the mickey.

'My present to you, bro. Happy Christmas,' Danny said, pushing his fringe out of the way.

'You going to get a haircut in the New Year?' Greg asked, not wanting the spotlight on him any more.

'Nah, chicks dig it,' Danny said, making Greg roll his eyes.

Danny stamped his feet, looking up at Greg quickly. 'Well, let's just have a man-hug and be done with it all right, my balls are about to freeze off.'

'Niiiiiceeee,' Greg said, pulling him in for a hug. 'Thanks, mate,' he said, his voice gruff, a quick cough into his hand.

'We're pathetic, aren't we?' Danny said with a laugh, going to walk away and then remembering something Aisha had said at the last class. He turned back round. 'You got any plans for tonight?'

Greg shook his head.

Danny grinned. 'You might have now.'

Chapter 49

HEADING BACK to the boat for the final few days of the year, Eve felt calmer than she had done for months. It had started to snow as the train pulled into the village; the fields coated, the sky swirling with snowflakes. The tops of the houses in Pangbourne were all hidden under a blanket of white.

She walked through the snow towards the common, a feeling of calm settling over her, glad to be back in the village. She missed the high street with its shops decorated with holly, the low-ceilinged pubs, the people smiling and nodding at each other, faces that she had started to recognise. The snow had been shovelled back and the pavement was coated with a layer of salt, the pieces crunching unevenly under her wellies as she walked. Underneath the railway bridge she marvelled at the difference, as if she were walking straight into a Christmas card as she stepped back out into the white world the other side, Marmitre trotting beside her.

Overhead, snow clung to the branches, tiny flakes drifting down when the wind blew. Snow lined the gutters and coated the rooftops, built up around the fence posts on the gate leading to the common. Then, stretching out, the fields and trees were covered in a thick layer, footprints barely able to make their mark, with the river, silver in this light, calmly moving through it all. It was a beautiful scene and she stopped, realising how familiar this felt, knowing then absolutely that she would apply for the job in the agency with Aisha. She wanted to continue to live here; she felt like she was coming home.

As she moved off, nearing the boat, she frowned, worried then that she had left the lights on. The circular portholes were glowing yellow, the boat lit up. She thought she made out movement inside. Her heart was beating a little louder in her chest as she approached one of the portholes. She saw the back of a head and her stomach dropped.

Pausing as she stood on the bank, her eyes wide, she felt her palms dampen, her mind racing.

Marmite didn't give her any time to think straight, barking and yapping as he streaked to the front of the boat. She followed him as if in slow motion, smiling as she took in the door that was framed with holly, mistletoe hanging in the porch inside. She picked Marmite up, took a deep breath and opened the door. As she stepped inside, her face broke into the most enormous smile as she gazed around.

'Oh my goodness,' she whispered.

It was a riot of colour and candles. Red and silver tinsel lined the walls, counters and picture frames. Tea lights in jam jars flickered inside wreaths of holly and ivy. Fairy lights were strung up too and the lights were dialled down so that the whole room glowed and twinkled. The smallest Christmas tree, dripping with baubles, sat on top of the stool in the corner, a couple of presents neatly wrapped and perched underneath. The smell of pine needles merged with the smell of cooking and the sizzle of something in the oven had her stomach rumbling.

Then there was Greg standing facing her in the kitchen, an enormous smile on his face and an expression that took her breath away.

'Thank you, this is... how did you?'

She was lost for words, embarrassed to feel a lump in her throat, unable to finish her sentence.

'Aisha told us you rented it from them and, well, Danny thought I might like to ask her for the key. Do you mind? I hope...'

He walked over to her, his head practically hitting the top of the boat, a navy jumper darkening his features and making her swallow slowly. 'I just wanted to wish you a Happy Christmas,' he said.

The words made her insides wobble and melt.

She reached up a hand to touch his face, laughing at the day-old stubble. 'Of course I don't mind. Thank you. Happy Christmas.' She stepped forward so that she was inches away from his face. She took a breath, breathing in the scent of him; the pine needles and woodsmoke making her head spin.

'And thank you for the mug you made me, I love it,' Greg said.

'I wanted to make you something,' Eve said, feeling her whole body glow with the compliment.

'I liked the picture of us on the boat.'

'Good,' Eve whispered, unable to really believe he was here, standing in front of her like this. Then something caught her eye just behind him. 'What is that?' she asked in amazement, the golden crispy body of a turkey on the side. It seemed smaller than the turkey they had at home.

It was his turn to laugh now, looking at the plate behind her. 'Oh, um... I made dinner. I thought we'd have goose,' he said, his eyes flashing.

Eve put a hand to her mouth. 'No way,' she said as realisation dawned.

'The fine is relatively small for killing a goose and...'

'But you're a vet,' she said in a shocked amusement.

'Anything for you,' he whispered, stepping closer to her and then laughing uproariously as, just outside the porthole on the bank of the river, came a loud, disgruntled honk.

Acknowledgements

Thank you to a number of people who have helped along the way: 'CatWoman' Fran for your extensive cat knowledge, Ben Major on the intricacies of being a vet, Jane Masoli, Tamara Gall, Lucy Brain and Jess White for medical questions, Sarah Jasmon on boats, Liz Robinson on pottery. Bronwyn Petrie and Keith McIver for inviting me onto their houseboat. Charlie at Urban Writers and the gang there for the brilliant week in Devon. Trish on a bus, Rachel Hawes and Aimee Horton for car advice. To Kirsty Greenwood for plentiful email cheering.

Darley Anderson is a brilliant literary agency and the whole team there are great. In particular thanks to my agent Clare Wallace for her straight-talking, excitement and support. To Mary Darby, Sheila David and Emma Winter for being so enthusiastic about my books in the rights department.

Corvus have welcomed me into the fold and I am so grateful for their enthusiastic support and belief in my writing. To Louise Cullen for her excellent editing tips and her calm under pressure. It is such fun working with you. To Alison Davies for being fabulous and energetic in her role. To Francesca Riccardi for her digital know-how and brilliant sense of humour. The whole sales and marketing team at Corvus who truly love books – I salute you.

My Twitter crew – yeah homies – chest-bump – you know who you are. Above all the brilliant bloggers who spend so much of their time reading and reviewing books for free – you guys rock, have a mince pie on me.

Finally thanks must go to my own family – my gorgeous niece Poppy for letting me steal her name and her 'nom, nom, nom' noises. To my siblings Naomi, Charis and Henry for reminding me family rocks. To Daddy – keep wearing the canary-yellow cords and Converse trainers. To Mama Christmas for the recipes and so much more. And lastly to my own hot vet Ben (I have no idea where I get the inspiration) – you are fabulous and make this whole writing lark a lot more fun.